Printed in the United Kingdom

Lulu Publishing

ISBN: 978-1-4710-9389-0

First Printing, March 2012

www.Caseykelleher.co.uk

Rotten to the Core

Casey Kelleher

"An eye for an eye only ends up making the whole world blind"

~ Mahatma Gandhi

Kate threw her mobile down onto the sideboard.

Why wasn't he picking up? It's gone two thirty, please God, answer your phone, she thought.

Kate went back to picking up the shards of glass from the grubby kitchen floor. There was always some domestic going on down this street, no matter what time of the morning it was. The neighbours were very good at pretending to be deaf when they needed to. Getting involved would be more than their lives were worth, and they were all very much aware of that. This morning's shenanigans had been a little more eventful than most, thanks to her brother and his infamous bad temper. Kate wrapped all the bits of broken glass up in newspaper before carefully putting it in the bin: wouldn't want anyone to get cut. She knew that there would be enough bloodshed to come. Billy would make sure of that. When he lost it, he really lost it, and tonight she feared would only be the beginning of her troubles. He had gone mental, worse than she had ever seen him. She had never had the misfortune of being on the receiving end of his temper until now, and she had watched horrified as he had smashed and thrown everything and anything he could get his hands on. She had even thought at one point that he was really going to hurt her. She had seen Billy kick off loads of times, but this was the first time that she had been the direct cause.

Billy O'Connell was a big bloke, six foot two and built like a brick shit-house as some would say. Intimidating was an understatement, he was one of the most feared men this side of London. Feared but also respected. He was only a year older than her but it may as well have been ten years the way he carried on, always thinking that he knew best and that it was his right to know all her business. Kate should have guessed that he was going to react like this, it was stupid of her to think otherwise, but surely he would see it through her eyes, surely one day he would accept how happy she was.

He had seemed in such a good mood when he had got home, and Kate had forced herself to tell him. She had been making herself physically sick all day by bottling it all up inside. It would only be a matter of time before somebody told him, knowing what this lot round here were like. It is better coming from me, she had thought. They had been sitting together at their little kitchen table and she had fetched him a whisky, thinking it would soften the blow a little. Boy, how wrong she had been!

Now she was once again alone in the house, Kate slumped down on one of the only chairs that had escaped being broken into pieces. She placed her head in her hands, and she prayed that Billy wouldn't be returning anytime soon.

She just couldn't understand how he could have been so angry, so disgusted with her. She grimaced as she went over the night's events in her head. There would have never been a good time to tell him, though, she thought, and it hadn't helped that he'd been out drinking with his pathetic cronies all evening. She hadn't seen him looking so chirpy in ages and it had seemed like the perfect time. He had been telling her all the funny things that he and his mates had been up to that evening in The Dog, the local pub that he and his friends 'invaded' most weekends. They had spent most of the evening winding up the pretty new barmaid on her first shift. Really laughing, he was, as he told Kate of the night's events. She reasoned with herself that he would eventually come round to it all, and that now was a good a time as any. Slowly plucking up a little more courage, she thought: it's now or never.

"Billy," she said quietly, feeling her nerve go as soon as her mouth opened but realising there was no going back now. "There's something you should know."

She watched him take another swig of his drink; whisky was his favourite, it always took the edge off. He was drinking more and more lately, not that anyone would have the balls to mention it to him: or not to his face anyway. As she sat across from him, she was aware, as always, of how much she reminded him of their mother, Kate had the same blonde hair and piercing blue eyes as she had, God bless her soul. Poor old mum, she thought, what a struggle her whole life had been, their old man had upped and left when they were just babies, leaving

3

their mum to struggle with not a penny to her name. Same story with most families nowadays, but back then it was a bit of a stigma, the nosey old neighbours, with nothing better to do but gossip and look down their noses at her. Their husbands may be useless pieces of shit drinking away most of the money, but at least they had husbands: what a joke. Her mum had never let any of that bother her, though: "Mindless people with meaningless lives" she'd say. She was what you would call 'old school', a real tough cookie. She had more important things to worry about, like keeping the debt collectors from the door and putting food on the table for the only two people that mattered in her life, Billy and Katie, her pride and joy. Kate's mum may have been a tough lady, but she had a heart of gold where her kids were concerned. There was nothing that she wouldn't give them, and she always had time for them. Even when she was up to her tired, lined eyes with worry, she always had time to sit and listen to them. Kate felt saddened at how Billy had acted back then, bringing aggravation to their door on an almost daily basis. He had been a nightmare as a teenager, and she cringed now just thinking about some of the things he had said and done. You don't realise the hurt and pain that you cause at that age, she guessed. All he seemed to think about back then was his main priorities, his mates and making a name for himself, which he certainly had now. He had definitely taken their mum for granted, Kate thought. Kate had always tried to be the peacemaker, always trying to smooth things over for Billy. Even though there had been times their mother had seemed genuinely upset and angry with Billy for all his getting up to no good, Kate knew deep down that their mother had always loved him very much. She just wished that he would realise it too, instead of always feeling guilty. There was no use feeling guilty, she thought sadly, Mum was at peace now. It was hard for Kate to believe that it had been almost a year since she died.

Knocking back the last of the whisky, Billy glanced up at his sister. When the time was right, Kate was going to make somebody a really great little wife, he thought; she would often have him a nice dinner on the table if and when he chose to come home, and she kept the place nice and tidy. She was a real homemaker. He never really returned the favour in that respect, but he was sure she knew that he appreciated it, deep down. He was paying the mortgage, after all, it's the least she could do really, he justified. Kate had been acting a bit shifty tonight though, Billy thought, and looking closer he could see that she looked really knackered. He could see bags under her eyes and that she was deathly white-looking, too. Something was definitely up.

"Billy, listen," Kate's voice was almost a whisper as she tried to get her words out. Something in her tone had him feeling wary now; the whole mood in the room had changed, and he could feel the tension in her voice – or was it fear?

"Go on," he pressed.

"Well, you see, it's... well... it's just that... I've met someone... I've got a fella... and he makes me really happy...." She was babbling; she could feel the words tumbling out without really thinking first.

Billy gave her his full attention.

"He treats me like a princess, Billy, I've never been so happy; I know it sounds really daft but it's like what happens in films, you know? I love him...."

"Who is it?" She could see Billy was getting really impatient now.

"Look... please, Billy, please don't be mad...."

"Get to the fucking point: who the fuck is it?" Billy bellowed; he slammed his glass down on the table, making Kate jump.

"Look, Billy, please don't be angry. It's Jay."

"Jay? Jay who? Tell me that you are not talking about Jay Shaw." He was rising to his feet now.

Slowly nodding, Kate could see the veins throbbing in Billy's forehead; his face was red with rage. He looked like a volcano on the verge of erupting.

"That major fucking waster, are you taking the piss or what?" He was staring at her intently. She'd heard the expression 'if looks could kill', now she completely understood it.

"Please Billy listen.... He is really good to me, he really is a nice bloke, and you have just got to give him a chance...." She was crying now, she knew there was worse to come, and that from the way he was reacting he would never see it from her point of view.

"A chance... give him a fucking chance? I'll tell you what I'll give him, Kate, a pair of broken fucking legs, that's what I'll fucking give him! You and Jay are over, do you hear me? I'm going to go and give that cheeky fucker the news myself!" Billy was fuming; if that lowlife scumbag thought he had any chance with his sister he had another thing coming.

It had all seemed to happen in slow motion after that. Kate remembered seeing him go towards the front door and chasing after him, begging him not to go, begging him to leave her poor Jay alone. He shoved her out of the way with such force that she screamed it at him, at the top of her lungs in a desperate bid to get him to see sense:

"Don't you dare lay a finger on him, Billy, I mean it!!!! You don't know everything." She was really sobbing now.

Through her sobs, he heard her say quietly: "I'm pregnant, Billy, I need him."

It was all a bit blurred after that, her brother had just gone completely loopy. She had sat huddled in the corner of the room, her knees bent instinctively to protect her stomach and her head buried under her hands as Billy had smashed up the whole place. She hadn't dared to speak in case he realised that she was still actually in the room.

"What a major fuck up, how could you have been so stupid?" he bellowed, as he emptied the cupboards onto the floor, smashing plates and cups. "You're no better than any other slag on this estate now." He was kicking the cupboard doors, as he paced the kitchen. "You've really gone and fucked your life up."

He must have burnt himself out; because the next time Kate looked up, he was heading out of the front door; that had been about two o'clock this morning: which thankfully, Kate thought, was the last time she had seen him.

She had called Jay straight away, to warn him that her lunatic brother was on the warpath. He wasn't answering his phone, so she had just left a teary answer phone message asking him to call her as soon as he got it.

So she was pregnant: big deal. Billy was probably more worried about his own life and his own reputation than he was about hers. The way Billy had reacted you would have thought she had just told him she was selling herself on the streets for a fiver a go.

She wasn't as stupid as Billy had often assumed: she and Jay had been together for just over a year. A whole year ago when Goldie's nightclub had first opened, from the moment Kate saw Jay, she just knew that he was for her. She had managed to keep it a secret from Billy up to now, which pleased her no end, especially given the way he had just reacted. Billy liked to think he knew everyone's business around here, she knew he would no doubt be even more enraged when he realised that he was the last one to find out about his little sister's fella.

She placed her hand on her stomach and felt a warm, fluttery feeling. She couldn't believe that she had a tiny baby growing inside her: Jay's baby. It was still early days in her pregnancy so she wasn't showing. She still had to remind herself, sometimes, that it was really happening.

Jay wasn't like most men where she lived. He didn't need to go around threatening people to gain respect; he kept his head down and worked hard for his money. She had known that he was special the moment she had met him. Why couldn't Billy just be happy for her and keep his bloody nose out of it?

2

Paul Goldie felt as if he had really arrived. Goldie's was going to be London's most happening nightclub.

With Paul, you always knew where you were. He was as straight up as they came; you give respect to get respect, he always said, and he lived by that. He was an excellent boss and he treated his workers fairly. He was always cool and calm where business was concerned, but if anyone was stupid enough to cross him they would pay dearly. He wouldn't take any shit from anyone. Everyone wanted a piece of Paul. Men wanted to befriend him, to have him on-side, he was that sort of bloke, the life and soul of the party: wherever he was, was generally the place to be, as he had a real vibe going on. As for the women, they threw themselves at him. He was a real looker, dark and rugged with twinkly eyes: the whole package. Most importantly, though, he had 'that spark'. One of Paul's main qualities on which he prided himself was his intuition; he lived by it and it had taken him far. He knew who the people were who always seemed to be after something. The ones who always seemed to be on the take, out for whatever they thought they might be able to get. They were easily spotted from the word go, and he never let them close. Sometimes he would use them to his advantage, play them at their own game, but he preferred to surround himself with people he could trust. To have a few real friends was always better than to have a room full of fake users was his creed.

Looking around the club he felt a surge of pride at what he had achieved in such a small space of time. The top floor of Goldie's was a private members club, a modern day gentlemen's club. The exclusive membership cost a lot, but money wasn't an issue with the members. Quite the opposite, in fact, the more money some had the more others tried to outdo them. If there was anything big or worth knowing about going down in London, you could bet your life someone in that room would be the brains or the brawn behind it. No women were allowed access, apart from the ones provided for the men's personal pleasure. Sexist it may be, but that's what his punters wanted and that was what they got, and what's more that's what worked.

The area was kitted out so tastefully it was hard to imagine the sordid goings-on that it would no doubt be used for. It was already a huge success and word had spread quickly among the men. It was just a chilled out place for like-minded men to have a few drinks, talk business or if the mood took them to indulge in a bit of pleasure. That pleasure came in the form of top London call girls who were paid to cater for the men's every whim. There were a few large booths so that the men could have some privacy with the girls should they choose to, which most of them regularly did. The men were happy because their wives would never find out, the girls were happy because they got tipped well for their services, and Paul was happy, because his little empire was raking him in an absolute fortune. There were drugs being handed around like Smarties up there, but Paul knew when to turn a blind eye. Drugs were a mug's game, he would never fall victim to depending on them to get his rocks off. But, of course, there was money to be made supplying them, and Paul had a couple of guys there to make sure that his members got what they wanted. His stuff wasn't cut with anything dodgy, so the men knew they were better off getting their gear here. It was not something that he personally got involved with, it just wasn't his thing, but he was more than wise to the whole supply and demand thing, and if there was a demand, he would be sure to be the one supplying, it would be stupid not to.

The specially fitted big plasma screens flashed up scenes in the main part of the club, and were very popular with the members. The screens allowed them to watch young girls grinding about on the dance floor below them and to keep a general eye on those coming in and out of the club. There were cameras fitted everywhere in the club and the security and bouncers were shit hot; if anyone even looked like they wanted to kick off they would be dealt with immediately. With the things he had going on here, Paul wanted minimal trouble.

With all this in mind and the right décor and music, the club had a vibe about it. It was the place to be, and Paul was like the cat that had got the cream. He smiled to himself as he looked around at the club; it had only opened last week and it was heaving, there were at least four hundred people in already and the night was young.

Emma handed Kate a shot glass and picked up her own from the bar.

"To us, babes: the hottest girls in here," she giggled, as she unsteadily lunged towards Kate.

Emma was pissed already, and it was only nine thirty in the evening. Kate wished they had slowed down on the shots now. She could more than handle her drink, but her friend was a bit of a light-weight. Kate had just wanted to have a good night; now she was worrying about her tipsy friend.

"Em, you're going to have to take it easy, babe; I'm not spending the night in the toilets again. This dress cost me the best part of my wages, and I'm not having you puking anywhere near it. Here, let me get you some water," Kate insisted.

"No, Kate!" slurred Emma. "I'm fine honest, I'm just enjoying myself. Chill out."

The music was booming, the DJ had worked in some of the best clubs in Ibiza and his tunes were going down really well; the dance floor was packed and as he played a new tune that had only just been released that month, everyone started cheering.

"Oh my God, it's our song," shrieked Emma, as she dragged Kate towards the dance floor.

Emma was singing along as she threw herself about on the dance floor, grinding sexily with any bloke who happened to be nearby. She wasn't naturally pretty like Kate, but she did have two huge attractive assets, both 34E to be exact, and most men spent more time looking at them than her face. Emma wore too much makeup and always made sure that if there was a party going on, she was the main attraction. She and Kate had been mates since school, and although she thought the world of Kate she was a bit jealous of her too. Kate could give any model a run for her money. She was naturally pretty, she didn't even need makeup. She was tall and skinny too, which always pissed Emma off as she couldn't even seem to so much as look at a cake without gaining five hundred calories.

Emma had to work that bit harder when she was out with Kate to let the men know where the real action was: it generally worked, she had slept with so many she had lost count. She'd even managed to get herself a bit of a reputation, but she didn't care. It was like a competition, which Emma was winning and in which Kate wasn't even aware she was participating.

The girls danced for what seemed like ages, then: "Em, babe, I need the loo, you coming?" Kate shouted over the banging music.

"Yeah, babe, I could do with a break, this guy behind me is getting right on my tits now, keeps groping my arse every five seconds."

They both looked round to see a nerdy-looking guy smiling at them whilst putting his arms out towards Emma's waist.

"Urgh, get off you fucking loser," Emma shrieked.

Kate led her friend by the hand off the dance floor.

"Ha, bet you thought you'd pulled some real fit bloke until you turned around," she laughed. "Come on."

The bathroom was done up to look like a posh boutique, with ornate mirrors and cosy expensively upholstered furniture; there were a couple of beauticians on hand to touch up the girls' makeup. Whoever had set this up had a bit of class, Kate thought, looking around.
The toilets were packed. "Why is it that the women's loos always have a really long queue even though we have more bogs than the men?" Emma moaned impatiently, as they waited for the cubicles to become free.

"Probably because we're all so busy standing around in here talking about the fellas and doing our make-up," laughed Kate.
She was right though you could hardly move in here for there were so many girls hogging the mirrors and gossiping about so-and-so being pregnant and so-and-so cheating, it was worse than a playground: girls can be so bitchy, Kate thought. Just then, right on cue, a big feisty girl wearing a dress at least two sizes too small for her came marching up behind them, shoving Emma so hard in the back that she went flying and landed in a heap on the floor.

"You cheap little slag, I hear that you think you have a chance with my Jake," the girl snarled.

Everyone was watching. Kate glared at her friend, unsure of what was going on. Emma seemed to be a magnet for trouble, what had she got herself involved in now?

Emma picked herself up from the floor, trying to look at least a little bit dignified. Jake, she thought, oops. She knew she had a chance with him, or had already had her chance, she thought, remembering the drunken shag they'd had last Friday. He had been well up for it, she had recalled. She had been out with the girls from work and had bumped into him in a bar in the high street. He invited her to join him and a few of his mates at their table and they had bought her drinks all night. Jake was quite a giggle, she had thought at the time, and flattery had got him literally everywhere. He had put his hands up her skirt and whispered in her ear, telling her how hot she was making him. He told her how much he wanted her as he had slid his hands higher up her thigh and she had felt his fingers probing inside her knickers; he had made her feel so horny that she hadn't cared if he had a girlfriend. They didn't even make it back to her place, she thought, remembering how hard he had taken her on the back seat of his car and how he had kept groping her breasts like they were his brand new toys. He was a good-looking fucker too, she remembered, but he didn't really do it for Emma, too busy getting his own pleasure she recalled, all four minutes of it. It had all been a bit disappointing, really, and not worth this amount of shit.

"Oh, so you're Jake's girlfriend," Emma smirked, as she smoothed down her skirt.

"Listen: I don't know what you've heard, but let me tell you – I wouldn't touch 'your' Jake with someone else's fanny, let alone my own." There were a few shocked giggles and a now-confident Emma took that to mean that she had the upper hand. She also had centre stage, which was just how she liked it. If this girl wanted a ruck, Emma wasn't going down quietly.

"Jake isn't picky, love, let's face it, I mean: look at the state of you! He'd probably shag his own nan if the room was dark enough," Emma continued.

"You nasty bitch," shrieked the girl, as she once more lunged for Emma, dragging her down on the floor again. The girl began raining blows on Emma with her fists. Kate tried desperately to pull the girl off of Emma, but the girl was too heavy and too angry, she was still walloping Emma.

Kate jumped on the girl's back, trying to do anything to make her leave Emma alone. She had the girl's greasy hair in clumps in her hands and got a slap herself in the process. Luckily at that moment two bouncers came in and dragged the girl off Emma, who now looked awful, her face red and puffy where the girl had repeatedly hit her. Her top was ripped and a whopper of a fat lip was just beginning to show. She managed to get off the floor, shouting to the girl who was being led away: "He was a crap shag anyway, love, don't know why you're so bothered."

The girls who had been standing around watching were now going off to do their own thing, the entertainment was over. Emma looked in horror at her battered face in the mirror. Then she grinned.

"Fuck it!" Emma grinned as she turned to Kate, as she wiped the dripping blood from her nose, "she's only gone and smudged my bloody makeup."

"You're not funny, Emma." Kate was fuming. "She was going to bloody batter you, you're lucky that those guys pulled her off you. I think we should leave, too; you look like shit and I've got a thumping head from that slap she gave me."

They got their coats. Kate was glad the night was over. Sometimes you just have crap ones, she thought, what a waste of a new dress. As they walked to the door, to leave, Kate noticed one of the bouncers that had come to her friend's aide earlier; he was definitely giving Kate the eye. She smiled at him, wishing that she wasn't so shy when it came to blokes. It was her brother's fault that she never had any confidence with men. No man wanted to know her once they found out who she was related to, and if anyone did let on they were interested, they were soon warned off when Billy found out about it.

She didn't really have any experience with men; not unless one sloppy kiss with a boy at a school disco four years ago counted. Back then, at sixteen, she was the only girl she knew that hadn't even slept with a boy, let alone had any sort of relationship with one. Oh well, she had thought then, I'm going to save myself for somebody special, and so she had. She wasn't short of offers, but they were all the same, little clones of her brother, wannabe thugs. She could see them coming a mile off and had no interest in that kind of life: she wanted more.

"You off then?" the bouncer asked. He was looking at Kate close up now and liking what he saw, appreciating the beauty before him.

"Yeah, I'm really sorry about all that trouble, thanks a million for helping us out," she said, feeling herself blush; this guy was gorgeous, and Kate couldn't help but notice how his eyes roamed her body as he spoke to her.

"You're welcome, sweetheart," he smiled. "I'm Jay."

"Hi... I'm Kate...." Her cheeks were burning, she felt like an embarrassed little kid.

"See you again Kate, I hope." Jay gave her a wink, as he turned back to the long queue of people waiting to get in.

"Oh... my... God!" exclaimed Emma, linking arms with her mate, as they tottered down the road towards the taxi rank. "You've only just gone and bloody pulled, Kate."

"Really, do you think so?" Kate asked.

"Duh: he was practically dribbling over you; he was well fit too, you jammy cow."

Maybe tonight hadn't been such a waste, after all, Kate thought, as she lent her head back onto the seat in the warmth of the taxi, daydreaming about the man that had made her heart beat louder than a drum.

3

Tanya couldn't sleep; she had been lying in bed for over an hour tossing and turning, unable to switch off. She was used to being on her own; she was an only child who had been left alone by her parents all the time when she was growing up. It was a pattern in her life, and she had grown to enjoy her own space.

She could stay in her house for days and see no-one and it wouldn't bother her. Although she had been feeling a bit lonely lately, she admitted to herself. She had wondered a lot over the last few weeks what it might be like to be part of a proper family. She wasn't particularly maternal, but she guessed that that would be something that would come to her naturally if and when she ever did get pregnant. She wondered what it would be like to have someone call her mummy, to wake up in the morning and have someone to tend to, other than herself, for once.

She could not imagine what it would feel like to be needed. She herself had stopped needing people a long time ago, her parents had seen to that. During her childhood she had been left with nanny after nanny. People who had been paid to spend time with her, as her parents had been far too busy. She had spent many a birthday and even a few Christmases feeling disappointed and unloved. It had become the norm for her, and she knew it was the reason why she often distanced herself from people.

Her thoughts were interrupted by a noise at the front door, and she worried for a second that somebody was trying to break in; she listened harder and she could definitely hear the sound of metal scraping against her front door, was it a screwdriver perhaps? She quickly reached for her mobile so that she could call someone if she needed to, when she heard the door slam and Billy's familiar footsteps stomping through the hallway. He must have been trying to use his keys, she thought, breathing a sigh of relief. She looked over at the clock, two thirty, and she smiled to herself. As he was unexpectedly turning up at this hour of the morning, he must have been missing her.

Billy had bought the house for Tanya. It was small, but she had done it up well and it was now very classy-looking. She knew that he had bought it as another of his investments; he owned properties all across London. He had invested well and even if the purchase of the flat was primarily to make a bit of money in the future, she wouldn't be complaining anytime soon, as it felt like it was hers.

When she had first moved in, she had put flowers in every room. Billy had said that it was hers to do as she pleased with, so she had been able to decorate it herself, which she had thrown herself into. Every room was different, all neutral colours and gorgeous textures. It was of course filled with designer furniture and accessorised with lots of funky lamps and vases. It was just like the pages of any good home interiors magazine, and she adored it. Her very own place all bought and paid for, who'd have thought?

Tanya had tried on many occasions to get Billy to move in to the house, but he kept putting it off, especially since his mum had died, last year, and he said he needed to look out for his sister, Kate. Tanya didn't have much time for Kate; she was a nice-enough girl, she supposed, but it pissed her off how Billy went on about her all the time. She knew it was silly, but sometimes she felt Kate was almost like 'the other woman' in her relationship. Kate was always Billy's first thought, and Tanya knew that on that score that she could never compete. She had to put on a front when Kate was around or even talked about, she was well aware that if Billy even suspected her dislike of the girl he would choose Kate over her in a heartbeat. Resentment bubbled inside her about it. The way Tanya saw it, Kate was the only thing stopping Billy making a proper commitment to her. She just wanted them to be a proper couple, to cook nice dinners for him and snuggle up on the sofa watching television in the evenings. He always said he liked to come and go as he pleased and didn't want to have to answer to anyone. She loved him, and would bide her time; in the meantime she would take whatever he was willing to offer her.

She threw on her gown over her tanned, naked body and went towards the lounge to see him.

Billy was sitting slumped in the armchair and the room was in total darkness. He didn't even bother to acknowledge her when she came into the room.

"Babe," Tanya said quietly, "are you okay?"

Billy was staring straight ahead with a real glare. Something had really rattled his cage, she thought, although she had seen him in worse states in the past.

"Do I fucking look okay, Tan?" he grunted.

Tanya could smell drink on him, knew that he had been out with the lads earlier because he had rung her from The Dog. Something must have pissed him off, because he had sounded fine then, quite cheerful for a change.

"Kate is up the duff," he said, turning to look at Tanya, trying to gauge her reaction.

Tanya was surprised to hear that Kate was pregnant. She knew immediately who the father was. Everyone knew about Kate and Jay, the pair of them behaving like love's young dream. They had been an item for almost a year and even though they both thought no-one knew, they had been seen about here and there and Tanya had known about them for a while.

How Billy hadn't got wind of it sooner was a miracle, as far as Tanya was concerned: he knew everybody and everything. She had been waiting for Billy to find out about Kate's little romance, hoping it would cause merry hell. It certainly wouldn't hurt the soft cow to know how it felt to have somebody interfering in her relationship, Tanya thought.

"Guess who the fucking daddy is?" he asked, still clearly fired up.

If he found out that Tanya had known about his precious sister's little relationship and not told him, he would go ballistic. She leant down to light the half-smoked joint she had left sitting in the ashtray from earlier that evening, hiding her face with her hair to mask her expression.

"Jay Shaw: the snide little fucker!" Billy's fist clenched as he spat Jay's name.

"Oh my God, Billy." She knew she was going to have to blag it now; she hoped that she sounded more convincing than she felt. "I didn't even know that they were seeing each other. How's Kate? What's she going to do?"

"Funnily enough, Tan, I didn't stick around long enough to sort out a fucking birthing plan with her," he said. "Shaw has really got it coming to him now." He took the joint and took a long drag, then blew a stream of smoke through his nose.

He couldn't believe the news that his sister was having a baby. He was going to have to think long and hard about how he would deal with Jay.

He looked up at Tanya, as if he had only just remembered that she was there. Although her hair was a mess and she had no makeup on, she was still stunning-looking. They'd been together for two years, and even though Billy tried to keep it as casual as he could Tanya had stuck it out for longer than any other bird he had been with. Okay, so Tanya was a bit high-maintenance, always demanding only the best for herself and the house, and could be demanding, but weren't most women? On the plus side, Tanya never questioned his whereabouts. She wasn't the clingy, possessive type, and she knew exactly how to please him in the bedroom. Tanya was naturally pretty, with long brown hair, green eyes, a toned body and immaculate nails. Most girls could only wish to look that good, thought Billy; she was the perfect woman in that respect. He loved having her on his arm for all to see: his bit of arm candy.

Billy grinned, his mood softening slightly; yeah, he was a lucky bloke. He could see her nipples pressing on the slinky material of her dressing gown and felt himself getting hard. He stood up and groped her breasts as he kissed her hard.

"Come on, Tan, let's go to bed. I'll deal with this shit tomorrow." Smiling, as Billy led her upstairs by the hand, Tanya couldn't wait to get into bed and snuggle up with her fella. She had fallen for Billy the second she had met him. He was as cocky as they came, and this, mixed with his confident boyish grin and the air of danger that surrounded him had been a heady combination for Tanya. The fact that he seemed to be doing well for himself and had an endless flow of cash had also played a part. Billy was hers, but it narked her the way he always kept her at arm's length and wouldn't let her get too close. She knew half his anger was because he bottled everything up inside. Tanya knew there was history between

Jay and Billy: it had been going on for years. She had started digging for information once, intrigued by how Jay rattled Billy's cage so much. She had more than learnt her lesson: he had gone mental at her. She had never mentioned Jay to him again.

Only Billy knew the real reason why he hated Jay with such a passion, Billy had never told a soul. There was no way on this earth Billy would be letting that piece of scum anywhere near his sister: that was for certain. Kate must never find out the truth.

4

It had just gone three in the morning and Jay had finished his shift at the club, which had once again been maniacally busy. His mobile had been ringing for almost an hour and he had been trying his hardest to ignore it, as it was Kate: again.

He switched it off and shoved it into his coat pocket. He wasn't in the mood for Kate and her clinginess. He had had a long old evening and what he was in the mood for now was a nice bit of light relief. Getting into his new Beamer, his pride and joy, he knew just where to get it from. Jay enjoyed working the door: Goldie's was the only place to be these days and he really felt part of it all. He got on well with the other men and despite a little bit of trouble here and there, the place certainly had its perks. In the year he'd been working there, he had taken advantage of as many of those perks as he could physically manage. It was like a meat market, and he could have his pickings, his phone was over-flowing with women's numbers.

Jay was a typical player; he had an attitude of treat them mean, keep them keen, and it worked a treat in his book. There were two types of woman as far as Jay could see. The cheap tarts who thought that they were something special: able to tame any man and stop any wandering eye. They were the ones who thought that their drunken one-night stand was the start of a beautiful relationship and that they could suddenly have a say in his life. The others were the more desperate type. The ones who were grateful for any attention you threw in their direction, always eager to please, and then counted themselves lucky that Jay had even so much as looked at them in the first place, when he decided it was time to walk away after he got what he wanted. Both types, as far as he was concerned, were more trouble than they were worth in the long run. Women, generally, were all grief.

Kate had blown both those theories out of the water; at first, anyway. When Jay first spotted Kate, he just couldn't resist, he had known that she was Billy O'Connell's sister, and because of that the thought of having sex with Kate had a lot more than the obvious appeal. He hated Billy with a passion, especially after everything that had happened with Jay's dad. The police may have come up with nothing when they investigated his father's murder, but Jay knew it had been Billy who killed him. He missed his old man every day. Saying that his dad hadn't been a popular bloke was an understatement, and Jay had been witness to why on many occasions. His old man would literally rob old grannies if he had to and Jay had often been made to play decoy for him. Driving along he remembered when his dad had actually made him fleece some old bird one night in town. He had only been a boy. His dad had made him sit down on the pavement and pretend to cry; it was getting dark so the chances of a passer-by not stopping were slim. The woman had bent down to comfort him and sounded quite concerned as she asked him if he was okay. Jay had stood up quickly, pushing her backwards with all his might onto the pavement, just like his dad had told him – "Catch her unawares, boy" – then grabbing her handbag from her wrinkly, frail grasp. He had then fled to where his dad had been lurking somewhere nearby. "Chip off the old block," he got called that time, and he was given a fiver for his "help". Jay had been ten, and even then he knew that he had done wrong, but he also knew that his old man would give him a hiding if he refused to help out and eventually the guilt wore off.

Jay had been pushed into more and more muggings and then burglaries, and as he got older and stronger he started acting as one of his dad's heavies, pulling in any outstanding debts that were owed. Jay got used to it as the norm. He accepted his dad for what he was and started to become like him.

He remembered sitting in the pub one night with his dad, he must have been twelve or so, both of them sitting there thick as thieves putting together their latest scam, when some guy stumbled over to them a little the worse for wear. He didn't say anything but glared at Den, Jay's dad, and then to Jay's horror the man had brought a glass bottle down on Den's head with a loud thump. Blood had poured out of a gaping cut, and Jay's dad had fallen to the floor. The pub went silent as the man spat in Den's face and said simply "scum" before calmly walking out.

Not one person in the pub that night had helped, in fact many of them looked in disgust at Den, and they had probably thought that he had deserved that and then some. Jay had seen everyone get back to their chatting and drinking and carrying on as if nothing had happened. That had been more shocking to Jay than the attack on his dad, the fact that no-one came to his aid. His dad had been treated like he was nothing. He remembered watching his dad trying to pick himself up off the dirty floor, with blood trickling down his forehead. That night, Jay had felt for the first time an overwhelming urge to protect Den, realising that he was all his father had.

Jay thought back to when the police had turned up at his house the morning that his dad had been found murdered. Jay knew, straight away, who was to blame. Although it could have been dozens of men who had done it, his dad had pissed many people off and had an awful lot of enemies, Jay knew exactly who it was. Billy may have had a lot of faces as back-up, but not all of them were as loyal as he would have liked to have thought. People talked. Of course the police couldn't prove it, but Jay knew. Oh yeah, he hated Billy with a passion alright, but he would bide his time. Billy's time would come.

In the beginning, Jay made Kate promise to keep their 'relationship' a secret from everyone, and Kate had been more than happy to do so, as it was in her favour too, she knew her brother would have put a stop to it otherwise. Jay was a looker, he knew that; he had a toned body and money in his pocket, so he wasn't used to having to chase women. Most girls would be gagging to have a bit of him, so Kate had proved a bit of a challenge, which was new to him. Being really shy, she had made him wait longer than any other bird he had ever been with to get inside her knickers. The four long months had driven him wild. She had told him that she was a virgin and by the time he finally got her into bed he was aching for her.

Jay had enjoyed the challenge, and for months knowing that he was her first had given him the horn each time he fucked her. But the novelty had soon worn off, and it wasn't long until he was back to his old self, wanting a less innocent and needy girl and craving easier, dirtier ones. He was bored with Kate, and he had been secretly disappointed too that Billy hadn't found out about their relationship. He had been waiting for the fireworks to start for months. The relationship had now run its course, and he had been happy to let it fizzle out before she had dropped the bombshell.

A baby... his baby: what a shock.

He had always fancied being a dad; he thought he would make a good one. He could see himself with a son; a little boy of his own. It was not an ideal situation, and he certainly didn't believe in settling down, but the more he thought about it the more the whole thing was growing on him. Kate would be a good mum to the kid, even he could see that. She was nothing like most of the lazy slappers around here, and she was completely oblivious to his goings on, really naive. Maybe he would stand by her after all; have his cake and eat it. He smiled to himself as he

31

parked the car. Maybe it would all work out. Oh, and he couldn't wait until Uncle Billy found out, he chuckled to himself.

He walked to the next street, making sure his car wasn't anywhere near the flat that he was going to. He didn't want to be seen. He was on a promise: this girl had been throwing herself at him, and had made it blatantly clear the last time he had seen her that she was up for it. Not really his type, a bit podgy and not as great looking as he was used to, but he knew that her shortcomings would work in his favour. She would get a good seeing to and be grateful to him for giving it to her.

5

It was late morning, and Kate had been ringing Jay's phone all night. She paced the house, worried sick that her brother had caught up with him. There was no point thinking about going to bed as until she knew Jay was okay she wouldn't be able to sleep. She picked up the phone to call Emma and started dialling her number, before chucking the phone back down on the table. She decided to go around there; she would go mad if she stayed in this house for much longer anyway.

Grabbing her jacket and keys, she started walking. Emma only lived a couple of streets away, that's how they had met when they were young. She and Emma had spent countless summers hanging around the estate with the other kids. Emma was always getting them into mischief; it had been part of her charm, at first. Kate had always been a shy girl and Emma had seemed to be everything she was not. Kate was not afraid to speak up for herself, even against some of the older rougher boys on the estate, but many times Emma had gone too far and caused trouble for them both and Kate had always been the one who tried to get them out of it. Mind you, that probably had a lot to do with the fact that Kate's brother was the toughest boy around, and no-one wanted to mess with him. Emma didn't really care if she caused trouble, she knew that Kate would always be her back-up and even if things did ever get out of hand, she had no reason to be bothered, she knew her parents wouldn't say anything to her.

Emma's mum had left it until she was in her late forties to try for a baby, and unfortunately she had an early menopause shortly after Emma was born. As having another child was never an option, Emma had been spoilt rotten by her parents. She was their precious little girl, and in their eyes could do no wrong. To make up for her not having a brother or sister they bought her everything: the latest toys, clothes, DVDs and CDs. Kate didn't recall Emma wanting for anything; if she even so much as looked at something then it was hers. Most people where they lived were poor, so Emma had an awful lot in comparison, and Kate wasn't always sure Emma appreciated what she had.

Even now Emma was twenty one, her every whim was still pandered to; no matter how old she got she was always their little girl, as they constantly reminded her. Emma's dad had even bought a flat for her last year, and Emma had rung Kate excitedly to tell her the good news. They were both even more excited when Emma asked Kate to move in with her, as this was something they had talked about the whole time they were growing up. They had spent hours in their own little fantasy land, thinking that they could spend every minute together, there would be no need for jobs or bills or men as they had each other: best friends forever. They wouldn't have to cook, as they would get takeaways every night, and when they weren't out shopping and partying they would have friends over all the time; maybe they would even get a puppy.

The day Emma got her keys she had knocked on Kate's door and they continued their little-girl fantasy once again, but this time they could actually put it into play, they could be real flatmates.

"Just think of the parties we can have, babe," Emma had squealed.

They thought of colour schemes and planned lots of girlie nights... they were both so excited. Then Kate had told Billy. "No fucking way," he had said. "She may be your friend, Kate, but she is also a little slapper, I can just imagine the sorts she will have round there, no fucking chance." It had been embarrassing because Billy had said it in front of Emma, who had tried hard to hide her feelings and shrugged it off afterwards, but Kate knew that Billy's comments had hurt. Billy had always had a problem with Emma, and Kate had never really known why. Of course she had her issues, but she was a good friend to Kate: the best in fact. He was probably just jealous. Kate had often thought that his friends were hardly the trustworthy type.

Kate's mum had passed away only two months before Emma had got her flat, so Kate thought that maybe she should stay at home with Billy for a bit. They were both grieving and very much needed each other; she couldn't leave Billy to fend for himself. Maybe after a few months Billy would change his mind about her sharing the flat with Emma; maybe he would realise that Kate was grown up. He hadn't changed his mind. Kate had justified it to herself; they would have probably fallen out if they had moved in together, as Emma was a complete slob, and Kate knew that she would have been left to do everything around the place. She liked going over there and staying the odd night, Emma was such a laugh to be around, a tonic, but Kate was always happy to come home to her nice, clean, and when Billy wasn't home, peaceful house.

Kate reached Emma's flat and knocked on the door, waiting for her friend to answer. She waited a few moments and then knocked again, this time a little bit louder. Kate looked down at the black rubbish bag by one of her feet; animals had obviously dragged out the contents and there was food and rubbish everywhere. Leftover Chinese takeaway lay scattered along the pavement, and the smell was making Kate feel sick. Mind you, it didn't take much at the moment. Since being pregnant, every smell had seemed to set Kate off. She had heard of morning sickness but she reckoned she had morning, noon and night sickness; still, it would be more than worth it. She smiled, thinking of the baby growing inside her.

"Hey." Emma yawned, as she opened the front door to her flat, wearing only her dressing gown. It was clear that she had been in bed, although it was after eleven: nice for some, Kate thought.

"I've been up all night, Kate, couldn't sleep; I'd invite you in, but I'm just going back to bed, I'm absolutely knackered."

"Oh, okay, Em... I just wanted to talk; the shit has hit the fan at mine."

Emma looked at Kate's puffy, red eyes and realised that her friend had been crying.

"Oh shit, Kate, you told him, didn't you? You'd better come in." She led Kate into her lounge, kicking a couple of empty cans on her way and a pushing a pizza box under the sofa. The curtains were still drawn and the air smelt of stale cigarette smoke. Kate felt the urge to vomit at the sight and smell of a half-finished mug of coffee with fag butts floating in it.

"Sorry, babe, let me move that out the way." Emma picked up the mug and went into the kitchen. "Do you fancy a cuppa?" she called, hoping that Kate wouldn't: then she would be able to go back to bed.

"Yeah, that would be great." Kate did not feel like having a cup of tea, but she wanted to chat to her friend; she was so worried about the whole situation between Jay and her brother, and she didn't want to go home just yet in case Billy came back and started his stupid shit again.

Kate sighed, as she looked around Emma's flat. She couldn't believe her friend could be such a slob; the place was one step up from a squat. Emma had trashed the place; it had gleamed when she had first been given the keys.

God, Kate thought, when she and Jay got their own place it was going to be like a palace. She was sure that Jay would let her decorate however she wanted, and she would cook him lovely dinners and run him nice baths when he got home from a long shift. It would be a proper home, clean and tidy, oh and of course there would be a nursery for the baby.

Oh, the plans she had, she couldn't wait. He hadn't mentioned them moving in together but he would soon, she was sure; after all, they were having a baby.

"There you go, babe," said Emma, interrupting Kate's thoughts as she plonked a mug of steaming tea down in front of her.

"Now, tell Aunty Ems all about it," she cooed, desperate to find out how Billy had taken it all.

"Billy just went mental; I think he's going to do something really stupid." Kate started crying, she had almost no energy left in her now. She relayed the whole thing to Emma: how her brother had gone mad, smashing everything up, and how she had spent the rest of the night trying to put the house back together.

"The worst thing is, Em, I can't get hold of Jay. I've been trying his mobile all night, but it's switched off. I'm so scared Billy is going to see him before I do." Kate was crying harder now, really worried for her boyfriend's safety.

"Hey, come on… stop crying, Kate, it won't be good for the baby," Emma said, stroking Kate's arm. "He'll probably be trying to call you any minute now, hun. You know what men are like. If he was working at the club all night he probably went straight home to his mum's for a kip. He's probably in bed right now, none the wiser; you know what he's like."

Kate took her first sip of tea and quickly placed it back on the table. It was like luke-warm milk, making tea certainly wasn't one of Emma's strong points.

"Yeah, you're probably right, Em; I'm just panicking, that's all."

Kate knew that her hormones were probably making the whole thing worse. Maybe it wouldn't be that bad, maybe Billy would calm down, and once he thought about it all, maybe he would be happy for her. He would be the baby's uncle, after all. She just needed to hear Jay's voice to make sure he was okay. She felt her coat pockets, worried that she had left her mobile at home. She needed to get to it in case Jay had been trying to reach her; like Emma had said, he may call at any minute. She stood up and kissed her friend on the cheek.

"Thanks for the tea, Em, you're a star, but I've got to go, my phone's at home, and you're right, he might be calling me right now," she said, as she made for the front door.

"I'll call you later," Kate called, as she quickly made her way back out of the flat.

Emma lifted the curtain and looked out the window, and seeing Kate practically running off down the road shook her head at her friend's desperation. Kate didn't have a clue when it came to men.

She tipped her friend's tea down the sink then looked at herself in the mirror in the hallway, running her fingers through her matted hair and wiping a black mascara smudge from under one of her bloodshot eyes. Having made sure she looked presentable, she walked into the bedroom. Closing the door, she let her robe fall onto the floor. Then, she climbed onto the bed.

"Did you hear all that? You're on the missing list, you naughty boy," she teased. "Now, where were we?" she asked, as she slipped her lacy knickers off.

Jay had heard every word of the conversation, and he really didn't give a toss if Billy had finally found out and lost it, in fact he was enjoying the drama of it all. Feeling horny at the site of Emma gagging for it once again, he smiled.

"I think you were just about here," Jay said, as he pulled her naked body down on top of him for the second time that morning.

6

The Dog was empty. That was a good thing; Billy needed time out to sort

his head. He sat in his usual seat and gulped his whiskey in one mouthful.

He looked around the pub, at the patches of mould on the ceiling and the

wallpaper hanging off in places. The whole thing could do with being

knocked down and re-built. It had been here for years, this place. It was

definitely the atmosphere that brought customers through the door. If

you wanted a nice quiet pint and a few familiar faces, you came

here. There was cold beer and a friendly staff, and that was all that

mattered in a local.

It was only early afternoon, so Billy was grateful that the place was so

quiet; he could sit and think. Billy was at a loss about what to do. All he

knew was that Jay would be enjoying every moment of this situation. He

felt that he could quite happily go round to his enemy's house and

kneecap him, and he would have done under normal circumstances, but

these weren't normal circumstances. This circumstance involved Kate,

and Kate's baby. Whatever his sister thought she might know about Jay,

she didn't know him as well as Billy did. He was a real dog. He shagged

anything in a skirt, and his sister was naive to this, she believed in fairy

tales for fuck sake. Billy knew there was no such thing as a happy ending

where that man was concerned.

"Can I get you another, love?" Norma had been working behind the bar for years and had been serving Billy alcohol since before it was legal for him to drink. He was always so tall and stocky, how was she to know he was still at school back then? He had fooled the local shopkeepers, though, being sold cigarettes from the age of twelve.

Billy nodded, and she took his glass and went off to the bar to fetch him another. Norma was a gem, despite having a face like a pit-bull chewing a wasp and the dirtiest loudest laugh you'd ever heard. She ran the place on her own, which was unheard of in these parts; landladies normally had a landlord in tow, but not this one, and she did alright. Norma had dealt with all kinds in her time, but no-one in this pub intimidated her, she was thick-skinned and could hold her own and had earned respect for that.

"Here you go, darling; I put a large one in there for you." She placed the glass on the table.

Norma had a lot of time for Billy. He and his mates used this place like an office. They had had plenty of lock-ins over the years until all hours of the mornings, and once the alcohol was flowing, their tongues loosened. She'd heard all sorts, but she was good at keeping her mouth shut, and it did her well.

Billy and the others always made sure she was looked after; there was never any trouble if they were in, or not unless it was among them. Often Norma would find a wad of notes under the till for herself, on nights when it did kick off. They looked after her, and in return she looked after them. That's how it was in these parts; it was who you knew, not what you knew, that got you by. Norma had never had kids, which was something she had sorely come to regret over the years.

"Thanks, Norma; you want to join me?" Billy asked.

The place was quiet, and she could do with putting her feet up, last night had been a late one. Norma was feeling old; she didn't have as much energy as she used to. Fifty was the new forty, or so all the magazines would have you believe, but lately she was having trouble convincing herself of that.

"Go on then, love," she smiled, plonking her bum on the seat next to him. "I could do with a fag break."

She could see that he was troubled, and her heart went out to him. She knew about his temper, she had witnessed it directed towards others on many occasions, but she could see more than that in him, which most others couldn't. He had a vulnerability that he tried to hide.

"You want to talk about it, Billy?" she asked, blowing smoke out, aware that she could be overstepping the mark by prying into his business. But, for once, Billy did want to talk; he just couldn't find the right words.

"It's my Kate," he said, looking up from his glass, "she's pregnant."

"Oh, right." Norma knew Kate well; lovely girl she was. She knew that Kate was seeing that one from the nightclub, what's his name, Jason, no, Jay. She had heard his name thrown around this pub a lot over the last few years. Norma had never mentioned that she knew about Kate seeing anyone to Billy though, as she knew Billy would not be happy about it. He was protective of his sister and as this Jay seemed to be his enemy.

"Well, is she happy about it?" Norma asked.

"Yeah, stupid cow is over the moon, says she's in love too." He took another sip of his drink.

"Thing is, Norma, she doesn't know the half of it. She can't have this baby, she just can't."

"Look, love, I know you are just looking out for her, but she is going to have to make her own decisions. You can't make her do anything she doesn't want to do," Norma advised, taking another long pull from her cigarette. "You may not be happy about it, but this is not your mess to sort out."

Billy was quiet for a long time. Then, and he didn't know what came over him, but maybe it was because Norma was like his mum, so easy to talk to, or maybe it was the years of bottling up all his torment, he found himself telling her the whole story.

It had all started with Den Shaw, Jay's dad. Den was one of life's freeloaders, a nasty scumbag. He would literally take from the poor in order to give – to himself. He called himself a "financer", but he was actually just a thieving bastard who specialised in lending to those that couldn't get credit from anyone else, desperate people on the dole mainly. He would offer them a loan at a good rate: too good to be true. Because it was such a good rate he would persuade them to borrow an extra bit more. Then a few months down the line, he paid them a little visit, letting them know about the new interest rates due to "inflation". He wouldn't elaborate any more than that, but by his snide tone and the look of the two apes he brought with him as heavies, people knew they had no choice but to pay whatever he asked.

Billy's mum had had dealings with Den. As a child, Billy used to see the way Den would walk into their house and intimidate her. Knowing she had no husband to back her up, he had taken advantage of the fact that she was on her own, thinking she was an easy target: things were tight back then and there were days when there was little if any food in the cupboards.

When Billy was twelve, he had been lying in bed one night when he heard a knock at the door. He had heard voices, then people arguing heatedly. He had heard his mum pleading, begging for a bit more time, asking Den for a few more days.

After a few minutes, it had gone quiet, and Billy had got out of bed, curious now at what had been said. He tiptoed down stairs. He could hear his mum crying quietly in the kitchen and wondered when Den had gone, as he hadn't heard the front door when he left. He wanted to make sure that his mum was okay. As he went towards the kitchen door he heard a funny noise, and his intuition told him something was wrong.

Billy had peered through the crack in the door to see Den pinning his mum's hands down on the table. Den's jeans were around his ankles and he was laughing quietly whilst thrusting on top of her. Den pulled Billy's mum top up, exposing her breasts, and bit them, sinking his teeth in hard. She was struggling for him to get off her but she was helpless. She was crying quietly in pain, begging him to stop, pleading with him that her kids were upstairs. He ignored her cries as he bent down over her and put his mouth over hers, forcing his tongue inside, thrusting harder and harder. Then it all stopped, and shuddering, he lay still on top of her. Billy, who had never seen his poor mum look so scared, stood paralysed with fear at what he had just witnessed.

"Now then, Helen, if you don't have the cash for me next week," Den sneered, as he pulled his jeans up, "this little arrangement would suit me just fine. Okay?" he said.

Then he looked over to where Billy was still standing and winked at him. Billy felt as if he was going to be sick, he put his hand over his mouth and tiptoed as quickly as he could upstairs. Stupidly, he thought that perhaps if his mum didn't know what he had just seen, and then somehow it wouldn't have been real.

Billy had lain in his bed and a few minutes later the front door had closed so he guessed Den had left. He heard his mum crying herself to sleep: that night, and for the next few nights. He had never spoken about what had happened to his mum, but it played in his head for years like a movie, tormenting him. No matter what they had had to go without in his childhood, from that day on his mother always had the money for Den. As he grew up, he got angrier and angrier about what had happened. *If only I had burst through the door and stopped him, got a knife out the kitchen draw and threatened him, or better still stuck it in him,* he had thought, but Billy knew he was kidding himself, a boy back then would have been no match for Den.

Norma placed her hand on top of Billy's as he spoke; she had never heard him say so much, it was like a floodgate had opened. Norma's heart went out to him. All his angry thoughts seemed to pour out of him. How he had been so scared and shocked that he hadn't helped her; how his mum had looked so frightened. When he stopped talking, tears streamed down his cheeks. He wiped them away and gulped down the last of his drink.

"Den is Jay's father," he finished, "this baby is going to have that rapist's blood in its veins, and I'll put money on it that Jay is no better than his old man was."

Norma knew there was nothing that she could say that would help to take away the hurt that Billy was feeling. She had listened, and she had a feeling that that was all Billy had wanted her to do. He was going to deal with this regardless; there was no point in trying to make him see reason.

There was someone waiting to be served. Norma knew what a private man Billy was, he would want time on his own now to gather his thoughts after being so honest with her.

Norma got up and bent over towards Billy and kissed him on the cheek.

"You know where I am Billy, if you ever need an ear. I am always here for you, darling."

Stubbing her cigarette out, she walked off to serve her customer.

Billy was embarrassed that he had been so open with Norma, but at the same time it felt as if a bit of the weight had been lifted from his shoulders; he had finally said what had happened out loud. Norma wouldn't tell a soul, he knew that. He hadn't told her everything though; it wouldn't have been fair to burden her.

Billy may have just been a boy back then, but the bad news for Den was, little boys grew into men. Den had been found in a skip just over two years ago, someone had cut his dick off. He'd been slowly tortured too; his body had been a real mess by all accounts.

Billy had been questioned about the murder, but as far as the police could tell he had no motive and a strong alibi, thanks to some of Billy's very loyal mates. Den had lots of enemies and the case was left unsolved. Another piece of shit disposed of, not even worth the police manpower.

One of Den's sons, Jay, had taken over Den's little empire shortly after his death. The apple didn't fall far from the tree, it seemed to Billy, who had put the word out that from then on, any shit that went down with Jay, he wanted to know about. Billy had collected a lot of information over the last two years, and he wouldn't be standing by to let that piece of scum anywhere near his sister.

How he hadn't heard about his sister having a relationship with Jay was beyond him. He was seriously fucked off. Picking up his jacket as he stood up, he decided he was going to find Jay. Kate had no idea what she had got involved with, so it was up to Billy to sort it out for her. He knew he would have to play this one carefully or that little fucker would ruin Kate's life for good.

7

Kate couldn't believe it when she saw her phone flash up with Jay's name, every time it had rung she had jumped on it and each time it hadn't been him. She had been checking it all day thinking maybe it had rung and she hadn't heard it, or maybe it was broken. She had been driving herself nuts, and now finally he was ringing her.

"Jay, where the hell have you been, I've been worried sick, and I've been calling you all day!" She looked at the clock, frowning now: it was almost four pm.

"I'm so sorry, babe, I had a real shit one last night, some fight kicked off at the club and it got really out of hand."

"Oh my God; are you okay, babe, you're not hurt are you?"

Jay smiled; he knew that he already had her onside again. God! This was just too easy.

"Yeah, babe, I'm good, nothing I can't handle. It was just a long one you know, so I went back to my mum's and slept for England. I think I must have switched my phone off and then just zonked out."

Kate felt guilty, she had started to worry that maybe he was elsewhere, she knew what that club was like, she saw the way the girls all looked at him, and some of them threw themselves at him. He was a man, as much as she knew that she could trust him, sometimes when it's all around you…. No, she pushed the thought from her mind. Jay wasn't like most men, he was better.

"What's happened, I've got like a thousand missed calls from you, are you okay?" Jay asked.

"Billy knows about us, Jay, he knows about us and the baby."

Jay already knew, from earlier at Emma's. He grinned, thinking about the day he had just had; that girl was one dirty bitch, and she had all but worn him out. He had only meant to stay for a bit but they had been at it for most of that night and the best part of the day. He had never been with a girl who was hungrier for it than him, she had shown him positions in bed that he didn't even think were possible, and that was saying something, as Jay had been around the block more than a few times! He seemed to have met his match in the bedroom department, who'd have thought?

Deciding to play dumb, he used an exaggerated shocked voice. "Shit, you're joking! What did he say?"

"He went mental, Jay, absolutely mental; he said he was going to break your legs. Said I had to stop seeing you, I just don't understand what his problem is, Jay? I mean, if he really got to know you like I do, he would know what a nice guy you are."

While Kate started to cry softly, Jay was smiling. He could imagine that Billy was doing his nut; he only wished he had seen his face when he had been told: it must have been like a giant kick in the balls.

"What are we going to do, Jay, I can't stop seeing you, you and this baby are my life."

Jay knew that Kate would do whatever she could for him; she was that kind of girl. Not desperate to please like a lot of the others, but she was definitely loved up; he knew that she would pretty much do anything to keep him happy. He decided that he would try and make this situation work to his advantage.

"Hey babe, stop crying. It's going to be okay, Kate, I'm going to lay low for a couple of days, but I'm going to sort something out so we can be together, okay?"

Kate stopped crying. "What do you mean?" she asked.

"We're having a baby, Kate, and it's none of your brother's business. The sooner he realises that the better. Give me a bit of time, babe; I'm going to see what I can do, but I think it's time me and you started making plans, proper plans for us, and our baby."

When Kate finally put down the phone from Jay she felt over the moon with happiness. He had talked about making a commitment to her, said he was going to sort things. Oh my God, she thought, maybe he was he going to ask her to marry him. Kate hoped so, maybe then Billy would leave it all be. She skipped around the tiny kitchen, trying to contain her excitement, saying aloud: "My name is Mrs Shaw, Mrs Kate Shaw."

Laughing, she felt calmness wash over her; maybe things were going to be okay.

Kate hoped they would be married before the baby arrived, give the little one a stable family – and so that she wouldn't look huge as she walked down the aisle. It was the way she had always imagined it as a girl. She knew lots of girls that had had babies on their own, and she couldn't imagine going through all this without Jay by her side. She felt dizzy with excitement, as she pictured in her head her big day. Her dress would be beautiful. Kate could see herself now dressed in a beautiful white dress, all chiffon and lace, Jay on her arm in a lovely suit looking as handsome as ever. She was almost bursting with excitement. If Jay said that he would make it right, she knew that he would. God only knew what Billy would say, but Jay was right, it was none of his damn business. He is my brother, not my blinking dad, she thought; her loyalties were with Jay and the baby now.

Kate decided to have a hot bath; last night had been a long one and had taken its toll on her. Kate was feeling knackered. Climbing up the stairs she saw her haggard-looking reflection in the mirror, she had bags under her eyes bigger than suitcases and her hair looked a greasy mess. A nice, hot bubble bath and a whole lot of beauty sleep were definitely called for. Mrs Jay Shaw would need to look her absolute best.

8

Billy was riled; if that prat behind him bumped into him one more time he was going to lamp him one. Saturday night, as always, was heaving at Goldie's. It was gone midnight and Billy had never seen the place so busy. There was a group of men behind him, and one of the idiots had obviously had more than he could handle to drink and was constantly brushing up against Billy and knocking his arm as he stood waiting for his drink.

Billy swung round as the man trod on his foot for the umpteenth time. "Do you want a fucking smack, mate?" Billy snarled. He could do with a bit of venting, and this little prick was a good place to start. Billy glared at the drunken man who seemed completely oblivious to his fiery mood.

The man shrugged and turned his back on Billy, infuriating him even more.

"I was fucking talking to you," Billy yelled, as he grabbed the man's arm and swung him back around to face him.

Paul, who had been watching the scene, walked briskly over to the bar, interrupting the men.

"Hey, why don't you go and take a seat, Billy, I'll bring you and the lads some drinks over, yeah?"

The two guys standing with the drunken man seemed to grasp the heavy mood and could see that Billy was more than up for inflicting a bit of damage. Apologising for their friend's drunken behaviour, they skulked off with their staggering mate in tow.

Billy, seeing the stern look on Paul's face, decided that the man wasn't worth kicking up over, he liked Paul and he wasn't going to cause trouble for him over some drunken twat. He went to the table where his friends were sitting. They were upstairs in the private members club, which was just as well he thought, looking at the TV screen in front of him displaying the dance floor. Downstairs was looking manic, there were so many people dancing, he was surprised any of them could actually move.

"Here you go fellas." Paul put a tray of shots in front of Billy and his mates and then pulled out a chair and joined them. Billy handed the shots to his mates, Jonny, Lee, and Ryan, who were sitting around his table. The four were thick as thieves, and had been friends since as far back as Billy could remember.

These were Billy's main men, there was nothing that they wouldn't do for each other, and he trusted them with his life. The Ellis brothers, Johnny and Lee, were a feisty pair. They were very clued up on business and had helped bring in a lot of money over the years. Ryan was the muscle, a big bastard and vicious with it. He had to be reined in a lot of the time as he easily lost it, but when he helped to inflict 'persuasion' he did the job as quickly and brutally as possible. If you heard that Ryan Clarke was looking for you, your best bet would be to fuck off on the next plane available, as there would be no time for reasoning with the man, Ryan was evil. If someone needed sorting, he didn't bat an eyelid: torturing was like a hobby.

Billy was the main man, the brains behind most of their business; he had the ideas and the nonce to pull stuff off, and he had nice little deals going on all over town, most of it dodgy: import, export, that kind of thing. Billy always had everything well thought out with all angles covered, so no one would ever catch them out on anything, he made sure of that. He was doing well for himself, had invested wisely in lots of properties over the years, and he definitely wasn't short of a bob or two. They were a good team, no-one with any sense fucked with them.

Although Billy needed to get wasted tonight, he would have avoided Goldie's at all costs at the moment with everything that had been going on, but he'd heard it was Jay's night off. He hadn't wanted to bump into him just yet, knowing the more he drank the more he knew he wouldn't be able to resist doing him some damage. If he saw him face-to-face he'd lose it and fuck his plan up completely.

"How's things?" Billy asked Paul, as he downed his shot, starting to feel a bit calmer as the liquid warmed the back of his throat and start to take effect.

"Things are really good; business is booming so I have no complaints."

Paul could see Billy was still on edge, but no harm had been done. Although he and his friends were generally okay guys, he made a mental note to make sure he kept an eye on this lot tonight. He hadn't done much business with them but their reputation preceded them; if you needed a job done then these boys came up with the goods. There was very little that they couldn't get hold of: motors, guns you name it. Not that Paul was into that sort of thing, but he liked to have contacts.

"Good, that's what I like to hear, let me get you a drink, Paul." Billy lent over to the tray of shots.

"No thanks, Billy. I don't drink while I'm working; I like to keep a clear head."

Billy looked at him and smiled. "It's a shame all your men here don't think that way, Paul; some people can't help but indulge themselves, even while they are on the job."

"What do you mean?" Paul could sense by Billy's tone that he had a bee in his bonnet about something, the comment had been loaded. He was intrigued. Billy obviously thought that he knew something Paul didn't, and like Billy, Paul liked to know everything where his business was concerned. He was a control freak when it came to his club, he could admit that. Knowledge is power, and therefore he had always made it his business to know everything that was going on around him.

"You got something you want to tell me, Billy?" Paul was getting a bit pissed off with the way this conversation was now going.

"Yeah, I have as it happens. Your man on the door, Jay: some of my men have been keeping an eye on him for me, and it's a good job too as it turns out." He paused for effect, enjoying the look on Paul's face, there was something going down right under his nose that he didn't know about it.

"Go on." Paul had a feeling he should have taken that drink he had been offered.

"He's a dealer, and he dabbles himself, I'm told. He's been using your little club here to build a nice little clientele for himself." Billy watched for a reaction then seeing there was none, he continued, "China White? You heard of it? Real lethal shit it is."

Paul felt as if he had been punched in the chest. He had heard of China White. It was a type of heroin that you could snort; a bit like coke, but twice the strength of normal heroin and much more addictive. There had been loads about it in the papers recently; only last week, a kid in this area had died whilst using it. If that fucker Jay had been selling it to his punters there would be murder. A bit of coke flying around his club was one thing, but heroin, and China White at that, was a whole different matter. He didn't want that on his conscience, when the shit hit the fan and where drugs like that were concerned it would only be a matter of time.

"Why are you telling me this? It's not like you to be telling tales, Billy; what do you get out of it?"

"Just think about it for a second, Paul, some young girl in your club snorts some of that shit he's throwing about, ODs on it. Your name will be linked to it, and if you lose this place, where the fuck are we gonna go for a bit of entertainment?" Billy laughed now.

"I'm letting you know Paul, because you're a nice bloke, and he's a fucking waster, simple as."

Paul was trying to take in what he was hearing. He paid Jay to man the door, not to stand there and make a killing off the back of him. He knew that Jay must have been taking the piss out of him and his position at Goldie's for the entire time he worked here, and he knew he would have to make an example of him. Paul wondered who else knew about it, but he was well aware that he could be also doing a bit of Billy's dirty work for him. There was no way Billy was tipping him off out of the goodness of his heart.

"I don't know what your problem is with Jay, Billy, but I'll tell you something, it's got fuck all to do with me! I appreciate you letting me know about what he's doing in my club and I will be sorting that out myself, make no odds about that." Paul got up, nodded to the men around the table and walked off.

"You've fucking set the cat among the pigeons there, Billy mate," laughed Jonny, "what do you think he's going to do with that snippet of information?"

"Well, let's just say that we have just taken Jay out of this little scene for starters, he's going to have to find somewhere else to sell his gear now, and his going to have fuck all back up from any of these boys," He looked over to where Paul was now standing deep in conversation with a couple of the security men.

It was a start, thought Billy, as he looked over to one of the escort girls heading towards him. She was wearing a skimpy red miniskirt and tiny bra that barely covered her breasts. Catching his eye, Candice wiggled over. She was five foot nothing, but stunning, like a tiny doll. What she lacked in height she made up for with her big personality.

Billy always paid her well, so she gave him all her attention. Candice always made him, like she did with all the others, feel like they were her one and only. That's how she managed to rake in almost double what the other girls earned each night. If you made a man feel special, as if you had been hoping and praying that he would even glance in your direction, made it all about them, they were putty in your hands. She had figured that out early on, it wasn't rocket science, and she couldn't believe that some of the other girls hadn't caught on. She was certainly not just a pretty face. Candice placed her arms over his shoulders and started kissing his neck, whispering into his ear. Billy smiled and then standing up grabbed her small pert arse.

"Back in a bit, lads." Billy winked at Jonny, as he strode off with Candice to one of the private booths. Still thinking about how he was going to put Jay in the gutter and how he was going to enjoy every minute of it, he closed the booth door behind him and grinned at Candice. She had a cracking figure and tits to die for: she was the best-looking girl in the club. He thought she had a thing for him, she always made herself available to him if he was around, always went out of her way to please him.

There was no need for small talk. Knowing exactly what Billy liked, Candice dropped to her knees. She had figured Billy out a long time ago; he had a girlfriend that gave him more chat than he could listen to: he liked a bit of light relief now and then. Billy felt himself getting hard as she undid his belt. Taking his cock in her hot, wet mouth, she began teasing him gently, licking slowly and then going deeper and deeper down his shaft. He groped her breasts now, feeling their fullness through the tiny silk bra, she started sucking him harder and faster then, her mouth really wet. He took her long, blonde hair in his hands and pulled hard as he came in her mouth, shuddering intensely. After pulling up his trousers, Billy put some notes on the table. Wiping her mouth, Candice smiled; she knew she was good. Billy normally took ages, tonight she had barely got started, and he had paid her the usual amount too: result.

9

The two men had been sitting in the van for over two hours. It was only a little escort van, no room to swing a cat, especially with two huge men inside it.

It was a chilly morning; March was normally a bit milder than this. The street was quiet, which was to be expected as it was now almost three am. Just the flickering of a streetlamp and a scrawny white cat walking along the path broke up the darkness of the dull, rundown street. The people who lived here weren't exactly house proud, looking around the men could see the front gardens of most looked as if they were being used as dumping grounds. There were overflowing rubbish bags, old rusty bikes, broken flower pots, an old bath leaning up against a fence. It was a dump!

Carl, the larger of the two men, shook his head in wonder.

"The people around here may not have a lot of money but it doesn't cost much to be fucking clean, does it? Lazy fuckers: probably too busy sitting on their arses watching Jeremy Kyle while waiting for their dole checks to clear."

He thought of his missus, who always kept their home lovely and clean. She would be there now, in bed. He couldn't wait to be under the warm duvet and feel her snuggled up next to him, but he had to finish the job first. He looked over to Tommy next to him, who was tapping his fingers on the steering wheel.

"Where the fuck is he?" Carl asked.

Tommy sighed; he was also fed up of waiting around. Just like his mate he wanted to get home to his bed. It had been a long day and he wanted a bit of shut eye.

"Fuck knows, mate. He may not even go straight home; you know what he's like."

He looked over to the house that they were watching; it was the only one that looked half-decent. It was still rundown, and the garden was full of crap, but it had a big solid door on the front, not a typical white council one like the rest of them, and thick windows, which judging by the gleam had only recently been fitted. The driveway was empty and all the lights were off, just the flicker of an alarm system flashing intermittently. It stood out because of the alarm system, made you wonder what would need protecting in a shithole like this. He obviously had something of some value, Tommy thought. Round here people had no call for security alarms; most would sooner put their last fiver on a few bottles of cheap cider rather than in their gas meters, let alone install an expensive alarm system.

Suddenly, they saw the bright headlights of a car coming towards them; finally, it was him. They watched as the beamer drove right past them and turned slowly onto the driveway. Taking their chance the two men quickly grabbed their bats and made their way over to the car, quietly, undetected like the true pros that they were.

As the man got out of the car they saw the shock on his face at the sight in front of him, shock mixed with genuine fear. Who wouldn't be scared? They were both over six feet tall, and armed with baseball bats. The worse thing was he knew them, and knew what they were both capable of.

Before he could even take in the scene before him, the man found himself lying on the floor, the bats raining blows down on him, over and over again. He didn't beg or plead, he knew he deserved this, this was his lesson, he was well aware that it would come to this. Feeling blood pour down his face, and the sound of a bone crack above his stomach, he felt an almighty pain wash over him before he passed out.

A light came on in an upstairs window above them, the two men decided to make a fast exit. Jumping into their van they sped off, just in time to avoid the plump lady opening the front door and screaming hysterically at the site of her son's broken blood-soaked body lying in a heap on the cold floor. People peered out of windows, having a good look, taking it all in so that they could have their own piece of gossip for the morning.

Tommy put his foot down; the police would be called, and they needed to get themselves and the van out of sight. Carl made himself useful, picked up his mobile and tapping in a number.

"It's done," he told his boss. "The smarmy little fucker has just considered himself told."

"Good," said Paul. "I'll see that you both have a little extra in your wages."

Paul put down the phone. He had left it a few days after he had been told of Jay's little side-line, and tonight it had been put to bed. It seemed Carl and Tommy had done well. From what he had just been told, Jay wouldn't be working anywhere, anytime soon. He'd got what he was owed, as far as Paul was concerned. No-one took the piss out of him. Paul had worked too hard, for too long, to risk his club for someone like Jay to ruin it all.

10

Sonia was sitting in a dull-grey cubical, at her son's bedside. They had been at the hospital for over twelve hours and although the doctors had told her that he was not critical, she felt heart-broken. Following a thorough examination and numerous x-rays, they had given him some high dose painkillers and something to help him sleep. Several of his ribs were broken, along with his nose; although looking at all the congealed blood and cuts and bruises all over him, it had looked much worse on first glance.

Sonia looked down at Jay's swollen face and wondered how it had come to this. Sonia knew that he was no angel, far from it. In fact, she knew a lot more than she would ever let on even to him, or anyone else for that matter. Even so she couldn't help feeling guilty; maybe that was why she always made excuses, always trying to justify his behaviour. She should never have left him with Den, she should have taken him with her, brought him up properly. This was her fault.

Sonia had walked out on Den when Jay was just a baby, after one too many beatings and endless mental abuse. She had nothing back then, and reasoned that when she sorted herself out she would go back for her son. But it had never quite worked that way. She seemed to be out of work more than in it those days. Sonia had always suffered with depression but Den had really knocked her confidence out of her and after finally realising she couldn't go on, knowing that if she stayed with Den she would probably end up dead, she had packed her bags and left her son behind. She had never felt so lost and alone until then. The more she had sunk into her dark thoughts, the harder it had been for her to try and claw her way out of it. There were days when she couldn't function at all; she hadn't been able to physically tear herself from her filthy bed. Popping anti-depressants as if they were sweets, Sonia had spent a good few years walking around so dosed up that she may as well have been the walking dead.

The longer she had stayed away from Jay the harder it had been to go back for him, and she convinced herself that it would be better for Jay to stay put with his dad. She could barely look after herself, let alone another human being.

Thankfully, with a lot of help from a very good doctor and counsellor, slowly over the years Sonia had sorted herself out and had been over the moon when her son had started visiting her a few years back, feeling proud almost of the big stocky man he had grown into. Slowly, though, she had learnt the details of his sordid lifestyle. He lied to her at first of course. He had pretended his endless amounts of money were savings but the truth had come out eventually. She knew about the debt collecting, and the stealing, but the thing she hated the most was the drugs. Thankfully, after one or two occasions of some real dodgy people turning up at her door he had moved that side of the business somewhere else. She didn't want him dealing drugs at all, but at least now if he was going to do it, he did it as far away from her home as possible, sparing her from having the dregs of society turning up at her home at all hours, for a fix.

He was her son, and she was aware that she was partly responsible for the man that he had become, but she also knew that he was his father's son, of that much she was certain.

Sonia touched Jay's hand, thankful that this time he was going to be okay, but she was worried sick that next time he might not get off so lightly.

Kate pulled the cubical curtain open. She put her hand over her mouth: the sight of Jay, black and blue, was clearly too much for her. Her poor baby, lying there all battered; she felt bile rise up in her throat, but thankfully she managed to keep it down.

"Who did this?" she cried, her hands trembling.

"He hasn't spoken yet." Sonia patted the chair next to her and gestured to Kate to sit.

Kate was a good girl and she loved Jay deeply, Sonia could see that, but she couldn't help feeling that Kate just wasn't enough for Jay. He was rarely home and Sonia had lied to Kate when she had phoned on many occasions; he had all sorts of girls at their house.
Sonia had spoken to her son about it once, after she asked him to move in with her when Den had died. Said she didn't want her home to be used for his sordid one-night stands with random girls. He had laughed in her

face. After that, when he did bring girls home, he was even louder with his goings-on, for her benefit.

Sonia felt that she couldn't ask him to leave; she had only just got him back. She also knew that Jay sensed this and played it to his advantage. Kate stared at Jay lying in the hospital bed, silent tears sliding down her cheeks. She felt sick. She knew her brother was after Jay, but he couldn't have done this, not with her being pregnant: surely not?

"Stop your tears, honey," Sonia said, in a voice that sounded more confident than she really felt. "We need to be strong for Jay now."

Kate nodded and took a couple of slow breaths; she couldn't get herself into a state; she had to think of the baby, something she had to keep reminding herself of lately. Poor Jay, she'd had enough, knowing that she couldn't go back home and carry on as normal with her brother now, not after he had done this to Jay.

"The police are looking into it," Sonia informed her, as she pushed the curtain slightly so that Kate could see the two male detectives at the front desk talking to a female doctor. The younger of the two was writing information in a notebook, as the doctor spoke. The doctor pointed over to the curtain, seeing them look over at her. The older of the two men pulled the curtain across as the two policemen entered the now crowded cubical.

"Mrs Shaw?" He addressed Sonia. "I'm Detective Carlson, and this is my colleague, PC Fowler. I appreciate that you are with your son now, but we need to start our investigation as quickly as possible, so I hope you don't mind if I ask you a few questions?"

The two woman exchanged glances, both knowing that Jay wouldn't want the police involved. Sonia knew that a number of people could have done this to him. Like his father before him, he had pissed enough people off. Kate, however, was sure that it was her brother, but as much as she could kill Billy right now, she knew if she so much as hinted at his involvement, then there would be a whole world of trouble in store for her. As angry as she was with Billy for what he had done to Jay, she would deal with him herself. The police didn't get much information from the two women: they hadn't expected to. This sort stick together, Detective Carlson thought, after he had asked several questions and got nothing much from them.

Kate decided that she would go to Emma's place for a couple of nights. She couldn't face going home to her brother, not now. Seeing Jay in such a bad way had knocked her for six, and what if it was all down to her? She watched as the two policemen walked off and then looking back at Sonia's pale, worried face, she knew she had to tell her the truth.

"Sonia, I don't know how to say this but I think I know what this is all about," she said, looking over at Jay again.

Sonia looked at the girl with doubt, she was sure that Kate didn't know half of Jay's business; if she did, she wouldn't be sitting at his side.

"I doubt very much that you do honey, Jay is a very private man; this could be down to any number of things."

Kate looked puzzled by Sonia's matter-of-fact tone, there was an under-current to the reply, like she was hinting at something, but Kate continued regardless.

"I think Jay needed some time to get his head around the idea before he told you, but I should tell you now. I'm pregnant Mrs Shaw: Jay and I are having a baby."

It was the last thing that Sonia had expected Kate to say. Jay was not the type to want to settle down and knowing how unfaithful he was to Kate, Sonia couldn't believe he wanted to stay with her. She let the enormity of what she had just been told sink in. A baby: she was going to be a nan, bloody hell. This girl was going to need her. Thrilled at the idea of having a baby around, she couldn't help but wonder whether Jay was going to do right by this girl. She very much doubted it.

"The thing is, my brother had a real problem with it, said he was going to kill Jay. What if it was him that did this?"
Kate looked at Sonia with such fear and sadness in her eyes that Sonia couldn't help but think that maybe Kate was right, maybe it was him. She had heard people talking after Den's death about Billy being involved, but it had never come to anything; even when the police had looked into it, rumours were often just that, rumours.

"Hey, don't you be upsetting yourself honey," she said, resting a comforting hand on Kate's arm. "Until Jay comes around and can tell us what happened, we should keep our assumptions to ourselves."

Knowing that people around here often had nothing better to do than talk about other people's business, whether it was true or not, Sonia had dismissed it as spiteful gossip and lies. Could there be an element of truth? No doubt she would find out.

Kate wanted to stay at Jay's side, but Sonia insisted that she go and get some rest; if not for her sake, then at least for the baby's. She fancied a bit of time on her own, to get her head round the fact that she was going to be a grandma, and she also wanted to be there on her own when Jay came round, she knew it was a bit selfish, but she was his mum after all.

Kate reluctantly agreed to go, she was totally exhausted and could do with some rest, and her pregnancy was making her feel sick and drained all the time, she felt as if she had no energy at all. After making Sonia promise to call her the minute that Jay was awake, she made her way to Emma's; she would stay there for a few days, and sort out what to do about Billy.

11

Billy was sitting alone in his office at the warehouse. He yawned loudly; it was only two o'clock but he was knackered, what a day it had been. There had been a few shipments in today and it had been a busy one. He wasn't complaining though; he smiled as he reminded himself about the wedge they were earning. This warehouse was just one small part of their empire, and it was a nice little earner. He took a sip of his tea, which was now as he discovered with distaste, cold. Then he checked his emails once again, he hoped that all was going well for Lee and Jonny. They were both in France sorting a very lucrative business deal out, the guy they were dealing with was working for customs and excise, he was the ideal answer to a shipping problem they had concerning getting packages that were a bit dodgy to say the least. Keeping this greedy Frog happy was paramount for their business.

Jonny and Lee had very professional business heads and could basically sell ice-cubes to the Eskimos, so if anyone could strike a deal, these two were the ones to do it. Billy was sure it would go well; after all, they were offering this guy a nice little earner. All he had to do was keep his eyes open and his mouth shut; not hard really.

Hearing his mobile beep with the sound of a new text message, he grinned as he read it. One of the lads, Gerard, who worked the door at Goldie's, had told him that Jay had got done over last night. No guesses about who was behind that: a very unhappy nightclub owner. Now he was officially away from the club, Billy's plan was to fuck up every aspect of Jay's life, he was going to teach that sorry fucker a lesson for daring he think that he could muscle in on his sister. He had already looked into Jay's other side-lines and was feeling very smug with himself for gathering so much information. He knew about the debt collecting, which was common knowledge, but had also found out from a few sources that Jay often went round to the local parade of shops at lunchtime and gave kids as young as twelve drugs. Apparently he was handing them out like Sweets. He was like the fucking Pied Piper, befriending kids just to get them hooked; the kids always came back for more, once they were well and truly addicted he was no longer Mr Nice Guy. He was no longer so friendly to them, he'd make them pay up front, or do little "jobs" for him, like mugging people, or breaking into people's homes or cars, whatever it took until they had paid off their debt. Jay even had a couple of girls making money for him, in a couple of grubby little flats nearby, flats that belonged to the birds he was making earn for him. He was scum, making money off those with fuck all, bullying young girls and innocent kids, ripping off anyone he came across.

Billy was far from being an angel himself. He knew that if the police ever raided this warehouse or found about their little shipping arrangement, he would go down for years. Billy played with the big boys, ripping off the police and the government, half of whom, let's face it, he knew were doing a lot of dodgy shit themselves, which made his activities more than okay. If you don't take it, no-one's going to just hand it to you, right, he would say. But he would never take from his own, and selling drugs to kids was just the lowest as far as Billy was concerned. Not only was he going to fuck up Jay's life, he was going to enjoy every second of doing it.

12

Kate just could not get her head around Emma's weird behaviour; she was shocked as she made her way back from Emma's to her own house.

Her visit to Emma's on the way back from the hospital hadn't quite turned out as she had wanted, so now she was walking home to sort out her options. She wouldn't be staying at home if Billy was there. Not if she was right and this was all down to him, she couldn't, it would condone his behaviour. And now Emma had let her down too.

Emma had been in an absolute state. Her eyes were sunken and dark, her skin grey and dull, and in the five days since Kate had last seen her it might as well have been five months, by the state of her, she looked as if she had lost about a stone, her cheeks looked so gaunt and hollow.

"What the hell has happened?" Kate asked, looking around the flat as if searching for a clue when she had first arrived.

Emma didn't seem to want Kate to be there, she had seemed reluctant to let her in, and Kate could see why now. The curtains were drawn, making the room dark. There were cups filled with cigarette butts, mouldy food on plates on the floor, it was much worse than normal. The place stank. Her friend was sitting there, strewn over the armchair, her legs dangling over the arm; she didn't even bother to look at Kate, just sat there trance-like and inhaling long drags from her cigarette.

"What do you mean 'what's happened'? Nothing's blooming well happened," Emma smirked. She knew what Kate was getting at, but she couldn't be arsed to go into it. It was her house and she could do what she wanted. She didn't have to explain herself to anyone, as far as she was concerned. Kate was too boring for her own good, Emma thought, as she put her fag out on the side of a dinner plate on the table next to her. Then, picking up her fag packet, she immediately sparked up another.

Kate could see her friend was on something. She knew that some of Emma's friends smoked a bit of weed now and again, but Emma had never done anything other than that as far as she knew, and it had been a sociable thing when she had done it in the past. Now, Emma's eyes were glassy, her pupils dilated.

"Are you on something, Em; have you taken anything?" The concern in Kate's voice turned to anger. What the hell was Emma playing at?

"Oh, chill out, Kate; it's just a bit of coke, nothing to get so het up about." Her friend laughed at her.

Kate was furious; since when did Emma start using coke, if she had seen her in a nightclub dabbling in it, she still wouldn't have been happy about it, but it would have made more sense. Emma was easily influenced and would have tried whatever her mates were doing; Kate would have put it down to being a one off while she was out drinking and not thinking straight. It was two o'clock in the afternoon, and Emma was sitting in her dirty flat alone and clearly she was off her face.

"Emma, what the hell is going on? Since when did you start doing coke?"

Emma was bored of Kate's tone: she may be her friend but she wasn't her mother, and Emma in no way had to explain herself to her.

"Kate, I don't know if you're aware of this or not but I'm a fucking adult and I don't need to explain myself to anyone, I'm having a shit day so I've done a bit of coke, no big deal. Okay, Miss Goody-Two-Shoes?"

Kate couldn't believe it: what had got into her friend? Emma hadn't seemed herself at the beginning of the week when she had come around either, she realised; what was she doing?

"Emma, I came to speak to you about Jay." Kate spoke quietly. "Jay got attacked last night, he's in hospital." Kate fought back tears as she spoke, then she felt anger bubble inside her as her friend had no reaction to the news.

Emma sat there quietly, tapping her foot whilst focusing on the picture frame on the window ledge; she wanted to ask how he was, what had happened, but she knew if she spoke about him now she would give the game up. She knew that she had started to fall for Jay herself, and right now Kate didn't feature in the bigger picture. She was sure Jay felt the same way about her, but giving the game away to Kate would fuck things up for them before they had even started. She continued to stare ahead blankly, and didn't appear to react to the news.

"Don't you give a shit, Emma? My boyfriend is lying in hospital as we speak. He's black and blue, he could have been killed. Don't you even care?"

Emma stared at Kate. She was feeling higher than a kite, which was the only thing allowing her to keep herself together. She had only just snorted a couple of lines five minutes before Kate had knocked on her door. She had been looking forward to the feeling of complete oblivion that she was craving more and more as the days passed. She hadn't realised how addictive the stuff she was taking was, but she knew that when she wanted to she could give it up easily: it was only coke. Jay had given her a few lines the night he had stayed, and they had had the most amazing sex. Emma was hooked. She had always been good in bed, it was her thing, and she wanted so badly to be wanted, needed in fact, that she would pretty much do anything. Jay had been persuasive, told her a few lines would loosen her up, and even though she knew that she would do almost anything to please him regardless, she took it anyway. She had never felt such a high, and they had fucked all night. He had been nice enough to leave her a few bags when he left the next day, but this was her last one and Kate was putting a real dampener on her high now; she wished her friend would just go.

Emma was staring at the floor once again, looking as if she were in a trance. Kate knew she had to get out of there before she grabbed her friend and shook some sense into her. She had taken one last look of disgust at the squalor Emma was living in then made her excuses and left. Not that she had needed to make any excuses; Emma had acted as if she couldn't wait for her to leave, quickly showing her the door and slamming it almost off its hinges behind her. She could have really done with a friend today, she thought sadly, as she put the key in her own front door. For the first time ever, her friend wasn't there for her.

Kate breathed a huge sigh of relief as she looked around the lounge and kitchen once she was home, thank God Billy was still out. She went upstairs to her bedroom, picking up a large bag from the landing cupboard on her way.

Her bedroom was bright pink, as it had been since she was a little girl. Her mum had painted it after she had begged and pleaded to have a 'princess's bedroom'. Her room was the smallest of the three in the house, but neither she nor Billy could bring themselves to sleep in their mother's room after her death; they had left it exactly as it was, although Kate had washed the bedding and made the bed neatly, as her mum would have. Often, she would go in there and sit on the edge of the bed. Sometimes it almost felt like her mum was there, she felt closer to her. The room still felt as though it belonged to her mum. Kate wasn't ready to disrupt that, so she stayed put in her pink bedroom. It had always made her feel safe. Some mornings, she would wake up here and forget, and for a few minutes she would feel that nothing had changed, that her mum would be downstairs making tea and toast, grilling Billy at the breakfast table about whatever trouble he'd been in the night before. It only lasted a couple of minutes, and then it hit her: her mum was gone.

When it had happened, her mum had been walking back from the market. It was her Friday morning ritual, Kate and Billy used to joke about it; they had stopped offering to go with her on the basis that she was so shameless with her haggling, they had both been embarrassed. She would go down there first thing every Friday morning and barter with all the stall holders for the best prices she could get. She always came home with bags full to the brim of every bit of fruit and veg imaginable, and generous cuts of meat at probably half the going rate. She was well liked, being a regular, but due to having hardly a penny to her name, she would try to get the stall holders to give her the cheapest deals possible, sometimes verging on begging.

That morning had been different. She didn't come home with her bright smile and her arms full of groceries. Kate remembered it like it was yesterday, although it had been just over a year. Her mum had been coming back from another of her "shopping sprees" and had keeled over: gone, just like that! Heart attack, they said later. She was only fifty four: too young to die.

Kate wondered what her mum would think of her pregnancy. She would have been a brilliant grandma, she thought sadly. If ever there was a time when Kate needed her mum the most it was now; she knew having this baby was going to be the toughest thing she had ever done. She didn't have a clue. Nappies, feeding, the constant care a baby required, sometimes if she dwelled on it too much the fear overwhelmed her. Kate glanced around the room. It was purely due to Billy that they were able to stay here. He had taken over the mortgage long before their mum had died. He continued to after too, trying to keep them together as a family, but she knew they could never be that now, not after what he had done to Jay.

Kate opened her wardrobe and started filling her holdall with clothes and shoes. She wasn't sticking around here for Billy anymore. Jay and this baby were her family now, she was sure that Sonia wouldn't see them on the streets.

Taking one last look around the house, she closed the front door behind her and picking up her pace in case she bumped into anyone she knew, she made her way to Sonia's house.

13

Jay's whole body ached. He knew he must look a right state, but there was no point looking in a mirror if he didn't need to, it would only depress him.

He had been given a warning. He knew that if they had wanted to kill or seriously hurt him they were more than capable of doing so. Jay had instantly known who they were and why they had come to issue his reprisal. He had worked on the door with both of them for the past year, and he had watched many a beating dished out by the two men, mainly to unlucky troublemakers too stupid to realise with whom they were messing. Tommy and Carl were old school, a real force to be reckoned with, and they had a good ten years on Jay and were probably both double his size. He had respected them both when he had worked alongside them at the club, knowing that with their backup, he was as safe as houses, should any trouble come his way. He had always been careful when doing any deals on the door, and apart from a couple of close ones, he'd managed to keep both them and the other doormen from knowing about his little money-making set up.

The doormen randomly searched people as they went into clubs, so slipping gear into a punter's pocket with one hand and removing the cash they had ready in the other pocket with his other hand was child's-play. His gear was good, so he rarely had complaints in that department. The thing that had always made him laugh was that he was actually being paid to stand out on the door, the prime location, and paid to sell his drugs; it had been perfect. Jay sighed now as he realised Goldie's was over for him; he would be avoiding Paul Goldie in future, he should have realised that you don't mess someone like Paul about. In fact he had known it from the beginning, but it was just too easy. Punters came to him, he had the best location, good backup on the door if anyone tried to mug him off, he had made good money, and had been getting paid a wage while he was doing it. He wasn't sure how Paul had found out, as he was always so careful, but he guessed it was bound to come out at some point. He would have to find somewhere else to do his deals, his contacts had been supplying him with some shit-hot gear, and he was making a fortune.

He had enough of the debt-collecting, which was too much like hard work, whereas dealing was easy money. He loved the power he had over his regulars; some were so hooked on drugs that they could barely see past their own noses, they would give him pretty much anything he asked for. Not that they had much he wanted, but he felt so in control, these weak pitiful messes begging him to give them a couple of ounces on tick, the vulnerable young girls wanting to pay him in kind, which depended on his mood and the state of the girl he often indulged in. He was on top of his game, so okay, he wouldn't have his prime spot at the club anymore, but it was a bit of an inconvenience and not the end of the world. He would have to lay low for a bit, let things cool off, but his little empire would soon be back up and running, of that he was sure.

Jay looked up at his bedside table and could see that his mum had been in; he could see his wash bag from home and a few other bits that only a mother would think of. He could only use one arm as he reached over to get his drink off the side, his mouth felt swollen, and he felt so thirsty. Trying to undo the bottle with one hand was proving to be a bit of a mission, as the lid was on so tightly. Jay couldn't even put much strength into trying to open it, as his ribs and stomach hurt so much. After a few minutes, he gave up, letting the bottle of water fall onto the floor.

"Jay darling...." Sonia beamed, as she came back into the cubicle with a plastic cup full of hot tea in her hand. "How are you feeling, my boy?" she asked quietly, picking up the bottle of water.

"I'm fine, Sonia," he replied, as he snatched the now open bottle of water from her hands, even though he was in agony, there was no way he would let his digs to his mother slide. He knew that calling her by her Christian name always hurt her. But then she had hurt him, and in return he owed her a lifetime of hurt. What sort of a mother walks out on their baby, and never bothers to look back? Jay had often wondered as a child how his mother could have just upped and left him like that. It had bothered him for years as a boy, but as Jay grew into a man he realised that he didn't actually care anymore. She was filled with guilt and that he could tell her to jump and she would ask how high, pretty much every time. She would go out of her way for him, cooking, cleaning, fetching, and why not? After all these years of being abandoned by her, she bloody well owed him, he figured.

Jay swigged his water; it was lovely and cold, although his body hurt when he swallowed and when he tried to sit up.

"The doctor said you have a couple of broken ribs, you've been lucky really Jay, it could have been much worse," Sonia said.

"Yeah, I'm well lucky me, beaten up by some baseball-bat-wielding thugs, in the middle of the night, on my own front door step, lucky old me!"

"So," strained Sonia, deciding to ignore his sarcastic tone, "do you remember much about what happened, Jay? Did you manage to see who they were?"

"It was dark, I didn't see anything. Let's just drop it, Sonia; I was probably just in the wrong place at the wrong time. You know what some of the little shits are like in our neighbourhood; half of them do this sort of thing just for kicks."

Sonia had a feeling that her son knew who had beaten him. She knew that half of the scumbag kids that hung around their neighbourhood were scared shitless of him. He had made a name for himself. This wasn't kids, she was certain. She had no choice but to drop it, though; getting information out of Jay was like getting blood from a stone, there was no chance. Sonia could tell that Jay was in one of his foul moods so she decided to keep the fact that Kate had turned up at theirs with her suitcase in tow, to herself. Sonia hadn't had the heart to say no to the girl when she had opened the door to find her there in tears, with her bags in tow, and she hadn't known what to do for the best. She wasn't sure that she had done the right thing by saying that she could stay for a bit, she had a feeling that Jay would not be happy about it at all. Most people wouldn't want to see their pregnant girlfriend out on the street, but then Jay wasn't most people. Sonia knew that the hospital wouldn't let Jay go home for at least another couple of days, so she figured that she'd bide her time, who knows, once Kate calmed down a bit she may just go back home. Sonia had a feeling that that wasn't going to be the case at all, however. The poor girl had been so upset, convinced that her brother had done this to Jay.

"Any news?" Jay sighed in a bored exaggerated tone interrupting Sonia's thoughts.

"No news, love. Your Kate's a nice girl, though, isn't she? She was here all day yesterday, seems to really care about you, Jay, you want to look after her."

"Yeah, no offence, but the last person in the world I'd take relationship advice from is you, Sonia."

Sensing Jay's mood turning, Sonia chose to ignore his narky tone and smiled at him.

"Shall I fetch you a cuppa love?"

"Actually Sonia, you could do me a favour, I need you to go back home and get me my two mobiles from the cabinet in my room, I need to sort some stuff out."

Glad to finally be of some use to her son, Sonia agreed, she also wanted to make sure that Kate was okay, and to warn her that it might not be a good idea to tell Jay that she had moved in, at least not yet. The boy seemed to have other things on his mind.

Sonia hurried off, leaving Jay to mull over what he was going to do once he was out of hospital. When he did get back out there he would be on his own, there would be no more backup for him, so he needed to get things organised.

14

Tanya had a major hump again. She felt as if she had the permanent hump. Billy had been out every bloody night now for the best part of this week, and she was fed up.

Scraping yet another of his dinners into the waste disposal unit, she looked at the clock above the oven; it was ten o'clock. She wasn't the best cook in the world but she had made a real effort with dinner tonight, making chilli con carne, which was Billy's favourite. She had mentioned to him earlier that she was going to cook for him tonight, and still he couldn't be bothered to come home to eat with her. No guesses as to where he would be tonight, she sighed. Looking around her gleaming kitchen, Tanya felt depressed.

It had been a month now since Kate had moved in with Jay and his mum, and for the entire time Billy had been like a bear with a sore bleeding head, he was moody, on edge and had been down The Dog every night not coming home until the early hours.

Tanya scrubbed the already gleaming kitchen sides, taking her anger out on her pristine Italian marble worktops, forgetting in her anger that they had cost a fortune, just like the rest of her designer kitchen. Throwing the sponge into the sink, Tanya sighed to herself loudly. The night that Billy had the row with Kate had been unbearable. Apparently he had gone home to find that Kate had packed her bags and left. Fuming, Billy had called her mobile at least twenty times, although it kept going to voicemail. Pleading with her to answer her phone, she had finally done so and told him that she knew it was him who had beaten Jay up, and as far as she was concerned she had to make a choice for her unborn baby: Billy or Jay. She had chosen Jay. After informing Billy that he was no longer anything to her or her child and that she never wanted to hear from him again, she had hung up on him.

Billy couldn't believe the way Kate was acting. He hadn't laid a finger on that piece of shite. Billy was sure that Jay loved this. The smug bastard was probably laughing his mug off.

Even Tanya had to admit, only to herself of course, she wouldn't dream of voicing her doubts to Billy, that she had her suspicions that Billy was behind Jay's beating, especially after the way he reacted to the news of Kate being pregnant, but she knew that if Billy had done it, despite Kate's reaction to the whole situation, Billy would have confessed to them both by now if it had been him. He was the type to stand by his actions, and Tanya knew he was genuinely upset by his sister's reaction to him, because he really was telling her the truth, he really hadn't dished out the beating to Jay. When he had found out that his sister had then gone and moved into Jay's mum's place he felt sick to his stomach, imagining that she would be round there attending to that scumbag's every whim. He realised now that he had played it all wrong, now his sister had chosen that piece of filth over him. Hoping that in time Kate would calm down and reconsider, Billy had left her alone. He had no other choice, he didn't want to lose her forever so he thought he would bide his time, although inside he was stewing. It had been a whole month now and there had been no word from Kate at all. His sister was all he really had, he had always been so protective of her, and growing up as the only man in the house he had kind of taken on the whole provider/protector role too. He wasn't very good at being on his own, like most men, there was too much shit going round inside his head, being on your own meant that you had to think about stuff, and who could be bothered with all of that? So he had stayed most of the month at the flat with Tanya. He was getting in the way though, and she often had an irritated tone to her voice when she spoke to him. He just wanted to lounge around, chill out a bit, smoke a few joints, but Tanya was clean and tidy and organised, and she knew it was driving him nuts. He sometimes said she had OCD. He wanted her to be more chilled, loosen up a little. After this month living together, the cracks were definitely starting to show.

Tanya had been made up when he had turned up with a bag of his stuff in tow, she thought that maybe now Kate had pissed off and become someone else's problem that she would have Billy to herself. She had planned quiet little dinners in, thought she could light a few candles, put on a nice bit of music, she couldn't wait to spend every minute with her fella. But Billy was driving her crazy with his grumpiness and short-temper. When he was at home he mainly sat around making the place look untidy, constantly banging on about Kate, almost as if he were obsessed. He was her brother, but the way he had been acting you would have thought that he was her poor jilted lover. And he was getting worse.

Tanya sighed; she knew that Kate meant a lot to Billy, but this was unhealthy.

Calling him and giving him agro wasn't Tanya's style, she would bide her time, she knew that she wouldn't be able to take much more of this from him, but was well aware that this was actually his place at the end of the day, and she loved this flat, it was her very own little oasis. If things carried on the way they were going and Tanya lost it, Billy would just end it with her, and she'd lose it all. She had no intentions of going back to nothing. She had a status now, when she went out with the girls, which wasn't very often these days, she had got into the habit of being home in case Billy wanted to come by. She was treated like royalty when she was out though. They knew she was Billy's girlfriend, and as everyone wanted to keep him happy, they knew they should keep her happy too. Tanya was sure that her beauty also played a part in the attention she got; she couldn't help but notice the looks she got from other men when she was out. It was a shame Billy didn't appreciate what he had.

Tanya was glad when Billy did finally bugger off out to The Dog in the afternoons, she was enjoying the peace and quiet. Reaching for her glass of wine, Tanya gulped it down, loving the coolness and the feeling of familiar numbness taking over. She had felt more and more like a kid lately, having to sneak a drink whenever Billy wasn't looking. She was careful when Billy was home, he didn't mind her having a drink, and in fact he had commented a couple of times that she was more chilled when she'd had one. What Billy didn't know was that she could quite happily do a whole bottle in an evening just to herself and sometimes if she was having a shit day she did have the odd glass, even if it was still morning, though that had only happened a few times. Well, maybe more than a few, but she wasn't addicted or anything like that, she wasn't an alky. Alcoholics sat on benches drinking Special Brew, they were low down in the food chain. She was in control. No, she didn't have a problem; she just enjoyed a few drinks every now and again. After another long swig of wine, her mood started to lift. She loved the calm that swept over her. At least when Billy wasn't here, she could have as much as she liked without feeling guilty or having to justify it to him. Pouring another glass, she smiled to herself as she remembered a saying her nan used to say to her all through her childhood: "Be careful what you wish for; because one day, Tanya, you might get it". She finally understood the meaning, taking the rest of the bottle into bedroom Tanya prepared herself for yet another fun-filled night of watching telly in bed, alone.

15

Kate smoothed her crisp white shirt down over her tiny bump, smiling as she felt the flutter of movement. She had had a good pregnancy so far, her skin was glowing, her energy was high; she was quite enjoying it. She was over four months gone, and she loved that she now had the tiny start of a little baby bump. No one else had mentioned it but Kate could clearly notice it, especially as her trousers were becoming so tight she was worried that if she sat down, she might split them. She needed some new clothes.

Mentally adding trousers to the long list of everything else she was going to need to buy, she looked into the mirror again, giving herself the once over, and began to worry that perhaps she was a little over-dressed. She looked as if she was going for a job in a law firm or something, very formal and well turned out, maybe she was overdoing it a little. The job advertisement had been for a cleaner, it was part-time hours and cash-in-hand, and most importantly it was local. Kate knew that in her present condition she would be lucky if she could get the job. A lot of employers wouldn't employ a pregnant woman if they could help it, especially someone halfway through their pregnancy; it wasn't worth all the hassle. So she figured that for her interview this morning she needed to make an extra good impression.

Kate had been at Jay's house now for a month, and to say that it hadn't been going that well would be an understatement. He claimed that he didn't know who had attacked him that night. Kate had even started to think that maybe she had been wrong, maybe her brother hadn't been behind it after all, that perhaps she had over-reacted.

Kate missed Billy so much, and sometimes really needed him around. But on speaking to Jay one night after a very rare early night together, he had all but implied that it had been Billy who had attacked him. He wouldn't discuss it with her, and he didn't actually say the words, but he had implied it clearly enough to her. Maybe that was half of Jay's problem with her at the moment, she thought, he had been really funny with her when he had first come home from hospital, he had gone nuts at Sonia for letting Kate move in without consulting him, and Kate had felt very unwelcome. Then he had spent the next few days constantly telling her not to go through his stuff, and that she wasn't to be poking around, he was acting very odd.

At first Kate had put it down to her being a little over-sensitive, with her hormones and everything, but it had just gone from bad to worse. Then she had thought that maybe some of it was resentment for what her brother had done to him, that they were just experiencing what most couples did from time to time, a rough patch. It was all new to both of them, this baby stuff; Kate was more than aware of just how scary it all was. Perhaps Jay was scared of becoming a dad, settling down, and supporting them all. Kate just wanted to see him smile at her like he used to, and to want her like he used to. Jay seemed not to be that bothered at all by her, and he didn't seem to be interested in the baby either, but after long talks with Sonia, Kate felt a bit more reassured about that one. Sonia and Kate had become good friends over the past few weeks and often spent the mornings gossiping over mugs of tea and buttered toast. Sonia was obviously excited about being a grandmother; she was forever coming up with cute baby names, hoping to inspire Kate, and making suggestions about places they could take the baby once it was born. She was a tonic and Kate would have felt lost without her. When Kate had been close to tears one morning because of Jay's total lack of interest in the baby's first kick, Sonia reassured her that while women feel an instant connection with the life that was growing inside them, men sometimes didn't have any feelings towards the baby until it was actually there. That was when the baby became 'real' to them. It made sense in Kate's mind, and she hoped that when they did have the baby, Jay would be a good dad.

There were times when loneliness washed over Kate. She hadn't heard from Emma now for five weeks, the last two times she had been round there Emma had been acting really oddly, and now Kate knew for sure that she was taking something, she decided to keep away, she didn't want anything happening to her baby and hopefully Emma would realise that if she wanted to see her then she could, but only if she wasn't off her head on drugs.

The biggest hole had come from cutting Billy out of her life, and now Jay was becoming even more distant, Sonia seemed like Kate's only friend, and as nice as that was, Kate needed more. She didn't want to burden Jay even more than she already had, so she had decided that she needed to make her own money. Kate was bored of sitting around all the time, she was pregnant not ill, so when she saw this little part-time job advertised, she decided that she would apply for it, earn some cash to buy her baby some nice things, and get out of the house for a bit too.

Kate had decided not to tell Jay about the interview yet, as she wasn't holding out much hope of getting it, but she was sure that he would be made up for her if she did get it. He would be pleased that she could pay her own way. Sonia had insisted that she needn't worry about paying rent while she lived there, and Kate had decided to earn her keep and help out around the house, washing dishes, doing the laundry, whatever needed doing, it was the least that she could do.

Kate had never realised how lazy Jay was; most days he laid in bed until midday, then he would slob about for a couple of hours, drinking strong coffee and chain smoking, despite her asking him to stop because of the baby. Then from about three o'clock most afternoons he was gone, "doing business," he would vaguely add when asked, and Kate rarely saw him again until the early hours when he crawled into bed next to her.

Things needed to change; this wasn't how Kate had seen her and her baby's future, and fingers crossed if she did get this little job, things would be better for them all. Maybe she would treat Jay to something with her first pay to show him that she really loved him. Once they were back on track things would be fine.

Feeling better, Kate picked up her bag and made her way to the interview; she was going to arrive a few minutes early, to show willing, she had loads of time to get there; besides, Goldie's nightclub was only a few streets away.

16

Opening her eyes, Emma looked around the room. Had he gone? The bedroom door was open, and she couldn't hear anything in the house. Relief washed over her; he had gone, thank God. Emma was aching all over, her head was pounding and she felt as if she had been run over by a truck. Emma rolled over on her bed and tried to sit up but pain seared through her. Reaching over to her side table, she saw the fifty pound note on the side; biting her lip to stop the tremble, she couldn't help but feel the insult. She reached down to the drawer in the table and took out her little bag of gear and struggled to keep from crying, it was almost empty. Snorting the contents and laying back against the stale, grey sheets, she felt the drug run through her body, helping to block out the last few hours of torture she had to endure.

Last night had been a bad one, a fucking bad one. The guy Jay had sent had been a nutcase, a proper loon. He had tied her up to start with, using black masking tape, and at first she had made a few light-hearted jokes about him being kinky, but he had breathed really heavily and stared at her, hate gleaming from his eyes. She'd started to get scared then, asked him to untie her, told him that this was not how she did things. But he had bound her even tighter. She had begged him, but he had just covered her mouth with the tape too. He had whispered in her ear, while he gagged her that she was a dirty slag and he was going to teach her a lesson. After dozens of punches, he grabbed her so tightly around the throat that Emma passed out, and then he brutally took her while she was out cold. She was sore beyond belief, looking down at her top she saw that it was torn almost in half and winced at the sight of one exposed breast, covered in bite marks and bruises.

He hadn't looked odd when Emma had first let him in. He had said his name was Alan. At first, he had been very quiet, and on first impressions, Emma would have had him done as some sort of nerdy train spotter. Guess you never can tell about people on looks alone. She rubbed the red marks on her wrists; the binding had been so tight. She had never been so scared. The reality of her ordeal was sinking in; he could have killed her. But then to leave money, Emma couldn't believe it. He had paid to rape her. And somewhere in her mind, to leave only fifty pounds was an added insult.

Emma was out of her depth. God knows what she would do next. She couldn't work out how she had let it get this far. One minute she was in bed with Jay, thinking that she had a chance with him and doing her upmost to please him, the next thing she knew, Jay was persuading her to "entertain" one of his wealthy "friends". Jay had made it sound glamorous. He said that he had "friends" who would pay good money for Emma's company, "friends" who wanted someone young and eager like Emma. Not only would she make lots of cash, but he promised that he would keep her in a constant supply of coke.

The first time it had actually gone quite well, it was a businessman from the USA, he was gorgeous, loaded, and in fifteen minutes Emma had earned two hundred pounds. He hadn't really spoken to her, he had just got what he wanted and left. Not the most mind-blowing sex she'd ever had but definitely the quickest money she'd ever made, and with the guy being so good looking it was hardly a chore. Jay had given her a big bag of gear as a thank you and told her there was more where that had come from. It had seemed so easy. Emma thought that she could handle it, and that with Jay by her side she would be okay. That was the plan, anyway; the reality was far from that.

Jay had sent her some real weirdoes lately, lots of them. She had told him that she wasn't doing it anymore. It had been a novelty at first, but she was beginning to feel used and dirty, but Jay wasn't having any of it, he stopped giving her the gear knowing that she had become totally addicted to it now.

When she had tried to score coke elsewhere, she had found that it wasn't the same as Jay's stuff, it wasn't as potent; it didn't give her the hit she craved. So after a bit more persuading from him, she had agreed to see some of his "friends" again, but this time Jay said he would make things easier for her, he'd deal with the money, and arrangements, look out for her, but he would also be taking a cut.

The condition was that she would have an endless supply of gear and still make good money. She didn't really feel she had much of a choice; she was desperate to get some decent gear off Jay again, and to feel that buzz once more. She knew what she was doing, knew what she had become, but she didn't care; all she could think about was getting her next hit. She had no idea that the coke she had become hooked on, was actually China White: a form of heroin, she was completely oblivious. Emma had done a bit of speed and a line or two of coke when she was out with mates in clubs, and she had indulged in the odd joint, all pretty harmless. But this stuff was different, she craved it. She felt that she needed it as much as, if not more than, food and water. It was the first thing she thought of when she woke up, and the last thing she thought about when she went to bed. Jay had convinced her that it was well-cut coke, but she had tried coke from some of her more generous clients and nothing compared to the stuff Jay gave her. Emma had her suspicions that it was cut with something else, but no idea that it was heroin that she was now hooked on: he had her right where he needed her.

Getting up to go to the toilet Emma saw blood trickling down her thigh. Fucking bastard, he really had been rough with her. She had almost passed out from the pain. Feeling totally alone, Emma started to cry. There was nobody who would help her. No point calling the police, how can a prostitute, who's been paid, have the cheek to cry rape? She knew she needed to go to hospital, God knows what damage this sick bastard had caused.

Picking up the phone, Emma decided to call Jay. He was supposed to be looking out for her; this would be one mess that he could help her out with. He owes me big time for this one, she thought. He could take her to hospital for starters and she was sure that after what she had to suffer because of him and his dodgy fucking "friends", he owed her a big bag of gear too. She was going to use this to her advantage. As he picked up the phone, Jay could hardly make out what Emma was saying through her sobs, the last thing she had heard him say was that he would be there in five before he hung up on her. Now she just had to wait.

17

Paul Goldie didn't quite know what to make of his morning, but it had just started to improve, and greatly. For starters, he wasn't even supposed to be here. Suzy, his promotions manager, was supposed to be here doing all these interviews for him. They had had a good night last night, the place had once again been packed, and Paul knew that his staff had been working extra hard lately, and extra hours, as they were short staffed due to illness.

The place was making a real name for itself, he had lots of new faces using the gentlemen's lounge upstairs and even a few celebrities treating Goldie's like their local haunt.

Goldie's had been mentioned loads on Twitter and had a massive following on Facebook too. As great as it all was, Paul was knackered; he had got home at three thirty this morning, and had only put his head down for a few hours when Suzy had rang him to say she couldn't come in. Her son was sick, and as Suzy was one of his best workers she would have felt terrible about calling him.

He had needed to sort some paperwork out anyway, so when he got Suzie's call he thought that instead of doing a ring around and seeing if he could get one of his senior members of staff to do the interviews, he may as well do them himself: keep an eye on who was being employed.

They only needed cleaners for the morning, a couple more dancers/hostesses for the gentlemen's lounge, and two more bar staff.

Paul had done a few interviews already this morning, employed a couple of girls who had just starting out dancing: they were pretty and young, and seemed naive, but then they usually all were to begin with. Then they wised up and got shrewd, earning some decent cash. The gentlemen's lounge was proving to be a real hit, his regulars loved it. He wanted to keep it fresh; get a few more girls up there. A couple of older girls had come about the cleaner's position; they seemed to be hard workers who said they wanted regular money. Up until about five minutes ago, the morning had been a bit of a chore. Now that had changed. Sipping his coffee, he looked across the table to where Kate was sitting; yes, now things were looking up. She was gorgeous. He looked her up and down once more, taking in the view; she was very classily dressed, Paul had thought that she was here to apply for a dancer or hostess position at first, she had the looks and figure for it, and Paul could see that she would get a lot of attention from the gentlemen, but once he started talking to her, he realised that he had got it wrong. There was an air of innocence about her, not only that, she seemed smart. Kate had come about the cleaning position, which Paul couldn't understand. She had been speaking for a couple of minutes now and he could tell that this girl had little idea of just how stunning she was.

"I'm happy to work whatever hours you have going, Mr Goldie, I'm a really reliable worker." He didn't doubt that. "You can even put me on a trial or something, see how I get on?"

Paul smiled and wondered why such a beautiful girl would want to spend her time picking up empty bottles and scrubbing toilets, when she could be out there doing anything she put her mind to. "I hope you don't mind me asking, Kate, but why exactly do you want to work here? Obviously Goldie's is a great place to work, though." He laughed. He didn't want to say that cleaning was beneath her.

"You could do pretty much whatever you wanted," he added.

"I just need the money, Mr Goldie."

Kate fidgeted in her chair. She had decided against telling him that she was pregnant, she thought that if she could get her foot in the door, she would tell him then, and hopefully by then he would have seen what a great worker she was and would let her keep her job. She really needed a break, and she wasn't sure how the man sitting opposite her now would respond to her situation; most employers would rather do without the hassle, and then there was health and safety, etc.

Paul wasn't convinced that it was all about the money for Kate; there was something not quite right here; she seemed like an intelligent girl, why was she aiming so low? She was so young, didn't she have greater ambitions?

"So, do I have the job, Mr Goldie?" Kate interrupted his thoughts.

Paul made up his mind. The girl intrigued him.

"I'm sorry, Kate, I'm afraid that the cleaning position has already been taken."

"Oh!" Secretly, she was a little relieved, maybe it just wasn't meant to be.

"But, Kate, there is something else I could offer." Paul grinned at her, and she could see his laughter lines, which made him more handsome.

"Oh?" Kate was more than a little surprised, and she was starting to regret coming for the interview now. She hated lying and felt that Paul knew her secret.

"I need someone to do some of the paperwork... make calls, help organise stuff a little better. I need an assistant." The more Paul spoke, the more he realised that he could do with things being a bit more organised. There were piles of paperwork and contacts scribbled on bits of paper lying around the office, so many things that he didn't get round to doing himself. There was just something about Kate that made him want to help; something in her tone that was more determined than desperate. She sounded as if she could do with good luck.

Kate's eyes lit up. This was so much more than she could have expected.

"There is one condition though, Kate, and it is quite an important one," Paul said seriously.

Go on, thought Kate; what's the catch?

"You must call me Paul; all this Mr Goldie is making me feel really old." He laughed now, and relieved, Kate laughed too.

She left shortly afterwards, and Paul was surprised at how grateful Kate had been, she had seemed over the moon at getting the job.

Paul smiled, feeling very happy all of a sudden. Kate was starting on Monday, so he could leave all his paperwork until then, seeing as he was going to have to find things for her to do. He was still smiling, as he locked up as he left, thinking: if this is how it feels to do a good deed, I should do one more often.

18

Jay lost his grip on the sill and fell back down onto the muddy verge beneath him. It was dark now, particularly around the warehouse where there were no street lamps. He got to his feet once more, pulling himself up again to the window. He swung his leg up and this time he was in: fancy having electric gates and fancy alarm systems set up and then going and leaving a window open. Jay tutted; he's almost invited me in, he laughed, although it was more of a nervous chuckle. He knew he had to get in and out quickly, because if Billy or one of his lads turned up he would be dead this time.

Looking around, he didn't know where to start. He hadn't really had a plan; he had been getting high with a couple of mates at one of their flats, and on his way home had kind of just stumbled this way. The open window had seemed a sign, enticing him in; too easy, he thought.

The warehouse was huge. Looking at all the boxes and containers, he could see that the men must be busy. He knew the lads did run a legit business, shipping goods overseas and providing a courier service and storage. But Jay also knew that if he looked hard enough he would find out the not-so legit goings on, then he could play Billy boy at his own game.

Billy had put the word out on Jay, he had been collecting information on him, but unfortunately for him he had pissed a few people off himself along the way, and not everyone was as loyal as he would have liked to think. Lifting up the lid of a big box, Jay whistled. It was full of what looked like very expensive jewellery. Dipping into the box, he picked up a long gold chain with a butterfly pendant embedded with crystals. Jay put it in his pocket, hoping to get cash for it later. He put the lid back on and then made his way to the office. Jay looked about, impressed. The office was every guy's dream workplace, decked out with the state of the art gadgets, a big plasma screen on the wall, leather sofas, expensive Macs. Jay was envious. There were days when he would be rolling in dough and other days when he had to trawl through shit to get what was owed to him. He had cash stashed away, but nothing that could set him up like this. This was what he wanted. Billy must be rolling in it; his legit business alone must be bringing him and his lads in a fortune. There was a lot about Billy that Jay envied, not that he would admit that to a living soul. Billy had had a proper family growing up; he had his lads to back him up, ones that he'd been friends with since he was a boy. You couldn't buy that kind of loyalty. He had all of this, too. Jay looked out to the warehouse floor once again. It was filled from floor to ceiling with all sorts of things. But most of all, what Jay envied the most was that people feared Billy; respected him. Jay could scare people, he could bribe and blackmail them, threaten and rob them, but that was as far as it went. He was a dealer, and no-one respects a low-life dealer, they feared him but they had no respect for him. People were only nice to Jay when they wanted something, and if he was honest with himself he would admit that he used them too. Even his dad had used him, teaching him all sorts of corrupt stuff, putting him in dangerous situations as a child. His dad hadn't encouraged him to do well at school, or have a better chance at life in any way, but to act as his own accomplice, and now he was dutifully following in his old man's footsteps.

Jay sat down on an office chair and booted up the Mac. He spent the next half an hour going through files, looking for something that Billy had not hidden, but the boy was good and he couldn't find anything. Billy had what appeared to be a lucrative warehouse. Whistling to himself, as he switched everything off and made sure that everything was exactly as he left it, he made his way back to the window, which was ajar. He would have to come back another time. Jay would stop at nothing until he had it. Let them all think what they like, he thought, because that would be their downfall.

Reaching up for the window pane above him, Jay was startled as the warehouse lights flickered on, blindingly bright.

Shit!

He was too scared to move, physically frozen to the spot.

"You think you're so fucking smart, don't you?" a voice bellowed. Startled, and feeling his heart beat ten to the dozen in his chest, Jay turned to see who had caught him. Not believing his bad luck, Jay saw Ryan: he was one of Billy's boys, and the worst one of the lot. Then, he realised Ryan had his back to him and was shouting down his phone rather than at Jay.

Slowly dropping down, Jay cowered behind a box and listened to Ryan bellowing down the phone:

"Well, let me tell you now, you cunt, if you don't deliver it to me in the next half an hour, I'm going to pay your wife a little visit, mate, you got that? Bet she likes a bit of cock, huh, your missus? If you're not here in thirty minutes I'll go round to yours and find out for myself." Laughing then, he hung up the phone and he stumbled towards the office.

Jay was crouching behind a box on the floor. Of all the people to walk in, it had to be bloody Ryan. He was a first-degree nut job, and Jay was betting that whoever he had spoken to on the phone was probably shitting themselves at the moment and rightly. He was a nasty bastard at the best of times, and tonight he looked worse for wear, like he had had a skinful.

Jay sat against the wall and reached into his pocket to switch his phone off; then, having second thoughts turned it onto silent mode and got the video settings up. There was no way he was chancing getting up and making a jump for the window, not while Ryan was about. If he caught Jay snooping around he would string him up by his balls. He would have to wait it out. He angled the camera towards the main door. It may even turn out to be good entertainment; some poor sod was probably running here to Ryan's beck and call as we speak. Let the show begin.

19

There was blood everywhere; she had never seen so much. She thought she would pass out. She thought that she had already done so, but everything was blurry.

This can't be real, she thought, and maybe it wasn't, perhaps she had not yet woken up from a sick nightmare, and this was just a bad dream. It felt real, though. As yet another searing pain ripped through her, she realised that she was kidding herself; it was real, it was happening.

Tears were running down her face. They were hot tears. She was not sure how long she had been crying, she had not realised she had been.

She tried to get up, but she was too weak. The pain in her stomach was ripping through her body. Her T-shirt was soaked in thick, dark blood. The duvet, which was also covered in blood, would be ruined. Why was she even worrying about the bloody duvet at a time like this, she thought, sod it. Writhing in agony once more, she called out just before darkness swept over her for a second time.

She wasn't aware of Sonia's finding Kate lying in a pool of blood and screaming; she wasn't aware of the two paramedics that were at her side within minutes, or the panic in their voices as they rushed her to hospital, and she wasn't aware that the tiny life she had been carrying inside her for the last four months was slowly slipping away from her.

20

Billy had been sitting at his sister's bedside all night; she had a small room in intensive care. He had never felt as scared as he did right now: his poor baby sister.

The doctors had said that the miscarriage was more complicated than most, and they had had to operate on Kate. In order to save her life, the doctors had no choice but to remove her uterus, to stem the bleeding. She had not only lost her baby but any hope of mothering a child in the future.

Billy had told the doctors that he wanted to be the one to tell her, he didn't want her to find out from a stranger, whether they were a doctor or not; this was going to rip her heart out.

He looked down at his sister and willed for her to be okay. He knew she was over the worst, although she had lost six units of blood and he was just realising now how close he had been to almost losing her. Watching her lying there with tubes and monitors around her, Billy felt helpless. His beautiful sister. She had been so happy about being pregnant. He shouldn't have over-reacted; he should have been there for her. Next time he would be there for her, whether he liked what she did or not. He would make it up to her. He wasn't sure how she would react when she heard the news, and he felt scared for her. The last time he had felt so vulnerable was when he had lost his mum. God, he missed her. He wished she was here to help him, more than anything. She would know what to say, he thought, his mum always knew the right words to say.

Billy could see Sonia in the corridor outside. She had bags under her eyes, as she had also been there all night. Billy had been rude to her, made her feel unwelcome, but he had only done it because of who she was. He could see the worry and grief in the woman's eyes, she genuinely cared for Kate; he was sure. He thought about warning her to keep Jay away from the hospital, but he knew if he did he would have no chance of Kate forgiving him. As it stood, no-one had heard a dickey bird from him, anyway, causing Billy to have a conflict of feelings. He was glad that the prick was nowhere to be seen but fuming that the bastard didn't care one fucking bit about Kate.

Kate had moved around in the night but had yet to come round. The doctors had warned him that she was probably exhausted and when she did come round, she would feel very weak.

Getting up to buy a coffee, Billy passed Sonia. She was surprised when his eyes softened and he offered her a cup of tea. Smiling gratefully, Sonia accepted. She guessed that the gesture was a lot more than a hot drink, it was a peace offering, and she was not going to be stubborn and refuse. Billy had been damn-right rude when he had first arrived. He had almost barged past her and looked at her like she was to blame for the situation, but she knew deep down that he just cared about Kate, it was all probably a fright for him.

"What's your cunt of a son done to her?" he had snarled, and not believing her reply that Jay had been nowhere to be seen that night had given her daggers for the rest of the night. She had known to stay well clear. She knew that Billy would have been worried sick seeing Kate in the state that she was in. She felt upset for the poor thing too. Billy was the first person that Sonia had called, they may have not been on speaking terms, but Sonia knew from many a conversation with Kate how close the two of them had been. If Kate needed anyone now it was her brother. Sonia had also rung Jay as soon as she had arrived at the hospital. She had come with Kate in the ambulance, and was more concerned about looking out for Kate than ringing Jay, as it was her call went straight to his voicemail. He was probably up to no good as usual, she sighed. That was seven hours ago now, and he still hadn't got in touch. She didn't need to feel guilty about him not being the first person she had contacted; she knew she was right to think he would have let Kate down. Billy was who Kate needed.

Billy was standing by Sonia's side now, he passed her a cup of tea and then sat in the seat opposite her. The ward was busier now; nurses were changing shifts.

Billy put his coffee on the floor and rested his head in his hands. After a few minutes, he looked up, his eyes showing his pain.

"What the hell am I going to say to her, Sonia?"

"You're just going to have to tell her the truth, Billy, there can be no skirting around it; the girl needs to be told."

Billy shook his head, wondering if he would be able to find the words that he knew would break his sister's heart.

"She loves you, Billy; you know that; despite it all, you have to be strong for her."

"Have you got hold of Jay yet?" he asked, trying not to spit the man's name as he spoke it.

"His phone is off." She looked down, not meeting Billy's eyes. Typical, Billy thought. Where the fuck was he then, fucking waster. Kate was lying in hospital; her whole life had just been ripped from her and no sign of lover boy. Well, hopefully Kate would realise she would never be able to count on a man like Jay. Billy would keep out of it for now, he promised himself, but he would be there to pick up the pieces; he just hoped that Kate would come to her senses sooner rather than later.

"You should go home, Sonia, you look knackered." Sonia noted that Billy's tone was softer towards her; what he said wasn't a dig or a command, more of a suggestion. She was exhausted, but she really wanted to be there when Kate woke up.

"Do you mind if I stay, Billy?" She looked at him. "I just want to see that she's okay; just let her know that I'm here for her. Me and Kate have got really close these past few months, and you know, as her mum isn't around I thought maybe she might need someone... woman to woman like."

Sonia was right. He hadn't thought about it, really, what would he know about losing a baby and never being able to have another one? Kate was going to be a mess; he was going to be the one to tell her, but his sister would need this woman sitting opposite him even more over the next while.

As Billy walked past Sonia to re-join Kate, he put his hand out and touched Sonia's arm. "Thank you," he said quietly.

That was a very rare moment, Sonia thought; she wondered how many people were lucky enough to see the softer side of Billy O'Connell.

Sonia heard an alarm in the room a few minutes later. Jumping to her feet, she saw Kate had come round, and that Billy was leaning over her, holding her and speaking softly to her; she couldn't make out Kate's expression, as Billy's stocky shoulders were blocking her view, but as a nurse came running she heard Kate's heart-breaking sobs.

21

Tanya looked at her reflection in the mirror, as she applied the last of her makeup. Pure perfection, she thought to herself. She knew her looks got her plenty of male attention, and she could do with a bit of an ego boost tonight, as Billy acted like she was invisible.

She had gone all out and bought a fantastic dress for tonight, all shimmer and sparkle, with a very low-cut neckline that should guarantee some admiring glances. She was almost ready.

Tanya hadn't really wanted to go at first, the thought of sitting opposite a teary-eyed Kate all night really didn't appeal. But the more Tanya thought about it, the more she had decided that she could do with a night out. A nice meal and a few bottles of wine would go down nicely.

Billy had been acting funny these past few weeks, since Kate had lost the baby. He was worse than ever about his sister, trying to do everything and anything that he could to help her. Tanya played it cool, but she was seething; he had never made this much fuss over her, and these days to say she got little attention from him was an understatement. It was like she didn't exist. He was so busy helping Kate that he hadn't noticed Tanya losing her patience with him, their sex life had dwindled into nothing, and she was drinking more than ever.

Well, tonight she would make him realise what he had been missing. Her hair had been highlighted and twirled into a French pleat by one of the best girls at the salon, her dress had cost a bomb and was so low cut at the front that her ample cleavage was spilling out, and she had waxed, scrubbed and tanned every part of her toned body. If nothing else came of this circus of a meal, she would use it to get his attention tonight, she grinned, as she squirted her favourite perfume onto her cleavage and the nape of her neck.

Billy had arranged tonight and Tanya didn't hold out much hope for how the evening would pan out. This was a big deal to Billy, and how he had the willpower to go through with it was beyond her, she was shocked that he had suggested it.

They were going to La Riviera, an exclusive restaurant in Notting Hill. It was a very swanky place, with a waiting list of a month or two for most people, but Billy was friends with the manager. He always said to her "it's the people you know," and she guessed he was right, he had managed to get a reservation for the best table at a moment's notice. Tanya was looking forward to the food, it was to die for. It was her favourite restaurant. Tonight, though, thanks to Billy losing the plot they were going to be joined by not only Kate, but Sonia and Jay.

Tanya had thought, when Billy had told her who he had booked a table for, that it was Kate's idea: there was no way that Billy would have thought of this, let alone organised it. He may have been jumping at every one of his sister's pathetic whims at the moment, but this was too much. The more Tanya had stewed on it all, the more okay she had been with the whole charade; of course it was all going to go tits up, there was no way after everything that had happened that the two men would ever genuinely get on, and Tanya was now looking forward to the shit hitting the fan and blowing up straight in Kate's face. Poor little Kate, she couldn't have kids, big deal, loads of women couldn't have kids; they coped… book a holiday, buy new shoes: life goes on. What about the kids with no parents, the orphans? There were options. It was so annoying to watch everyone running round after Kate, who was playing the victim; it was wearing a bit thin with Tanya.

Billy had brought Kate to the house almost every day and the two had put their falling out behind them. They had spent so many hours talking things through, crying and laughing. Tanya had sometimes felt that she was in the way in her own bloody house.

Kate needed her brother more than anyone, but she had made it clear to him that he needed to make peace with Jay, for all their sakes.

Jay hadn't been that upset when he had finally rolled in and been told, by Sonia, about the baby. Sonia had been shocked by his reaction: or lack of one. He had played up his feelings when he had seen Kate in the hospital, and Sonia had watched as her son had stood at Kate's bedside and made up lie after lie of where he had been that night, and how he was feeling about losing his child. Sonia could see straight through him as only a mother could; she knew that her son had no real feelings for Kate and she had seen the look of relief in his eyes when she had told him that Kate had lost the baby. Billy had made himself scarce by then; he knew that he had to give Kate time.

Billy had sobbed when Kate rang him a few days after she had left hospital, to thank him for being there for her. She said that that was what was important and that she wanted to stop arguing with him. She told him that she loved him, and she had cried. Every day since then, he had been there for her.

Kate had suggested that Billy and Jay bury the hatchet, and even though there was only one place that Billy would have liked to bury it, he had smiled and nodded and agreed to do whatever it took, for her sake. This was a big deal for Billy, never in a million years would he normally consider giving Jay the time of day, let alone eating a meal with the guy, but he would do this for Kate. She didn't need to know that it was going work in his favour; he was going keep Jay closer than ever, and watch the bloke's every move, all the time knocking up brownie points for being brother of the year. Never again would he let anyone get between them, and next time his sister needed him he would be there.

"Come on, Tan, we need to be making a move," Billy shouted up the stairs.

Tanya tottered down the stairs in her four-inch Jimmy Choos, waiting to see Billy's face.

"Fucking hell, you women take ages getting ready, we're going to be late." He reached for his keys and was out the door before he could see the rejection on Tanya's face turn to pure hate.

Kate convincing Jay to come to the meal was another story.

Kate was also running late. She and Sonia both looked lovely. Sonia was wearing a hot pink dress that made her look radiant, while Kate had opted for an understated black shift dress. They had practically had to force Jay up the stairs to have a shower and put on a clean shirt.

"What's the fucking point, Kate? He hasn't got the time of day for me, and I can't fucking stand him," he had protested, just to make a fuss really, to make Kate think that he was putting himself out for her. Actually, over the last few days, since Kate had first mentioned the dinner to him, Jay had come to the realisation that if Billy boy was on a mission to keep Kate happy, then Jay had him where he wanted him. Maybe he too could pretend that it was all forgiven, left in the past. Maybe this could be his 'in': people would think twice about fucking with him if they thought he and Billy were tight. As he ran the shower and waited for the water to heat up, he thought of the old saying: "Keep your friends close and your enemies even closer".

Sonia smiled with relief when she saw her son come back into the lounge twenty minutes later, dressed in his best suit and with a look on his face that suggested he may actually be able to enjoy the night. Maybe tonight,

123

after all that had happened to poor Kate, the boys could put their problems with each other behind them and make a fresh start.

22

Guzzling down a cold glass of chardonnay, Tanya was feeling tipsy. It was her third glass and had already had two at home while getting ready. So far, things hadn't been bad. The food was gorgeous, as always; the fresh lobster Tanya had ordered had been cooked to perfection. It was just a shame about the company. There was no big drama, no daggers being thrown, it was all very civilized, or should she say very fake. Tanya could see by Billy's body language every time he answered Jay that he was struggling; to everyone else around the table, Billy smiled and looked like he was enjoying himself... but Tanya knew.

Jay was off his head. Tanya could see his pupils were dilated, and the guy had a real nervous energy. Constantly babbling on about crap, he had given Tanya the once over a few times. She knew the effect she had on men, especially weak ones like Jay, and he was good-looking. She glanced around to see if anyone else had spotted his leering. No-one had reacted to it, so she doubted that anyone else on the table had even noticed, especially Billy who had shown her absolutely no attention whatsoever. Fuck him, she thought, as she looked around the restaurant at the male eye candy.

The restaurant was packed, waiters wearing white gloves running around at everyone's beck and call, sucking up to the rich businessmen that were dining their wives or mistresses. One table near the cocktail bar had caught her eye, there were five guys having a meal; by the way they were dressed and acting, Tanya guessed that it was a business dinner. One very hot, tall blonde man kept meeting her eye. Tanya smiled at him. That's a bit more like it, she thought, maybe someone else in this room appreciates beauty.

"Tanya." Billy nudged her. "Wake up, Sonia's talking to you." Interrupting her thoughts of the tall blonde guy ripping off her lacy knickers with his teeth, Tanya blushed.

"Oh sorry, I was miles away... what did I miss?"

Sonia put her cutlery onto her now empty plate. She had had sea bass on a bed of lentils. She felt very out of place in this restaurant, where there were too many glasses and too much cutlery, and the main meal had been so small that her stomach grumbled for more. Still, the evening so far was going quite well, although she could tell that her son was on something, and this annoyed her, for once why couldn't he just make the effort? He was fidgety and his eyes were like saucers, she hoped he could behave himself for the rest of the meal. She could see that Billy was trying really hard with Jay, really making an effort.

"I was just saying that I like your dress, honey," Sonia smiled at the frosty-looking Tanya, "is it designer?"
Looking flattered that her beautiful dress had finally been noticed, Tanya nodded to indicate that it was; she didn't bother giving Sonia the designer's name, as by the look of what she was wearing, she probably

wouldn't have heard of him, much less appreciate the amount that the dress had cost, which had been charged to Billy's credit card: the least he could do.

"Her dress designer? Of course it is. Probably had a designer price tag, too." Billy looked at it now and had a feeling that his credit card had been given another bashing: Tanya had expensive taste.
Tanya bristled at his disapproving look.

"Well, it's nice to make an effort sometimes, and for someone to actually pay me a compliment," she threw back. She added a little chuckle, but the stiffness of her mouth indicated to everyone at the table that she was gritting her teeth.

Kate was having a lovely evening; it had gone much better than she had hoped. The food had been good; she was getting her appetite back, which was just as well as since she had lost the baby, she had lost so much weight that her clothes were loose. Billy was making an effort, she couldn't believe that she was sitting between her brother and her boyfriend having a very lovely meal. She had had the toughest few weeks of her life. She had thought that nothing could come close to the pain of losing her mother, but this had. She was heartbroken and still in shock, she was finding it hard to take in the fact that she would never properly be a mother herself.

When the baby had died, so had Kate's dream of her and Jay's little family. But tonight was helping, she had never thought that Billy and Jay would be able to sit at a dinner table and share polite conversation and a meal. She appreciated what her brother was doing and was so grateful to have him supporting her the way he had the last few weeks, he had been a pillar of strength to her and she would have been lost without him. Things were finally going to be okay.

"Well everyone, I've got some news for you all." She smiled, looking around the table. "I've got a bit of good news. I've got a new job, starting from Monday."

She had been saving this news for the meal. She knew that the people around the table cared for her and worried about her, and she wanted to let them know that she was okay and moving on.

"Well done, babe." Sonia beamed; she was glad that Kate was making plans for herself.

"Where?" asked Jay, barely hiding the fact that he was a bit miffed that Kate had left him in the dark about her plans; surely he should have been the first person that she told.

"You are now looking at Paul Goldie's personal assistant." Kate grinned, feeling proud that she was going to be able to stand on her own two feet. Hopefully Jay would see now that she didn't want to live off him and his money, but earn her own. She was supposed to have started her job weeks ago but what with losing the baby and everything, it hadn't happened. Paul had been good about it. She had rung him a few days after she had been discharged from hospital and explained why she hadn't turned up on the original Monday that she was originally supposed to start. She had been completely honest with him, and had told him everything; she was surprised at how easy it was for her to talk to him. He had told her to take all the time she needed, and that there would be a job for her when she was ready. She had felt bad about lying to him in the first place, and she was glad that they now had a clean slate; work would be just what she needed to help put all of this behind her.

Jay went very quiet at the news. He decided not to say anything, but he was not a happy man. Paul had it in for him: what the hell was he playing at offering his bird a job?

Billy was happy enough: he respected Paul, he was a decent guy, and Kate need never find out that Paul had organised Jay's beating. Knowing that Paul felt almost the same as he did about the guy made him feel better about the whole thing. A personal assistant: the guy must be moving up in the world; he chuckled to himself and raised his glass to everyone at the table.

"To Kate. Well done, little sister; you'll do a cracking job for him. Knowing you, you'll be running that place alongside him before long." Everyone smiled and chinked glasses. Looking over at Jay, Billy smirked, although it was obvious enough for only Jay to see it, and he did.

After desserts and coffee had been had by all, except for Tanya who insisted she was watching her figure but kept the wine flowing, Billy said that he would call a couple of cabs. He was glad the night was over. It hadn't been too bad, but he didn't think he could stand being in Jay's company for another second, how he had hidden his feelings this long he didn't know. Sensing this, and trying to make Billy's life harder, Jay piped up: "Oh, but the night is still so young... why don't we come back to yours for a nightcap?"

Before Billy had a chance to make an excuse and get rid of this waster, Kate smiled at her brother, happy that this was all working out so nicely between them. "I don't mind, Billy; it's only early, what do you say?" He couldn't refuse his sister. Sonia made her excuses and got her own cab. She was going to have a nice cheese sandwich and a cup of tea when she got home, this posh food wasn't enough to keep her full, no wonder all the celebrities that ate here were so skinny; poor buggers were living on child-sized portions.

Kate and Jay got in a cab with Tanya and Billy and headed to their house. Billy was going to have to let Jay into their home, and he would grin and bear it even though he was not happy about it. Tanya didn't give a shit by now, she had had a rather good night herself, the blond guy in the corner had been giving her the eye all night, and the more she had drunk the hornier she felt. She gave him a look of regret as she brushed passed him through the restaurant and out to the waiting cab. She planned to have a few more glasses of wine at home and hopefully then pass out, as there would probably be no chance of any bedroom action with Billy, again! Kate was a bore, but Jay she found quite amusing. He was a cocky little shit and she could see through him, but she was finding it highly entertaining that he could so easily wind Billy up.

"Nice gaff," Jay said, looking around the designer kitchen, this was exactly what he wanted, state of the art, really modern, a far cry from the shithole in which he lived with Sonia and Kate. This house was plush, if small.

"Tanya designed it, fancies herself as a bit of a Linda Barker. Spent a small fortune, didn't you, Tan?"
Tanya smiled back at Billy, but her smile did not meet her eyes. She was close to losing it; why did things always come down to money with him? Okay, so it was his money, and she had indeed blown a small fortune on the flat, but he had told her to get what she liked so why was he being sarcastic?
Sensing the atmosphere, Kate went to use the bathroom, leaving the room quiet, with the three running out of things to say.
Going through to the lounge with some glasses and a bottle of chilled wine, Billy's mobile buzzed on the table.

"I've just got to get this," he said, as he picked up his phone and left the room; his calls came through at all times of the day and night because of his dealings abroad and the time differences, so his phone was never far from him, which was another thing that pissed Tanya off.

Kate came back to find Tanya and Jay laughing at some joke that Jay had made. Tanya had her feet up on the chair and you could practically see her knickers, she was definitely pissed. Tanya got up to fill her glass again, but stumbled and ended up in a heap on the floor, laughing and struggling to stand. Jay put his hand under her arm and pulled her to her feet.

"I think I need my bed," Tanya slurred.

"It's upstairs on the right, Jay, you'd better help her,' Kate said. 'I'll go and get Billy, I'll ring us a cab too, babe, maybe it's time to call it a night."

Kate looked at Tanya, slumped over drunk and shook her head before heading off to get her brother.

Jay almost had to carry Tanya up the stairs, as her legs didn't seem to want to go in the same direction as her body. Laying her down on the bed in the darkness, Jay was stunned by the strength of her when she reached up and pulled him on top of her. Her mouth reached for his, and he could taste the wine she had been drinking. He felt himself getting hard. She reached inside his trousers, laughing quietly. He realised then that she had not been as drunk as she had made out; realising that maybe she had planned this, he felt the urgent need to take her. He could feel her warm hand gripping him tight and he wondered how she would feel and taste. She was obviously gagging for it. Looking down at her, he saw she had tits to die for. What is it with the women in Billy's life: they just can't resist me... He kissed her hard and his hands cupped her breast, feeling his way down her body, almost making it to her thigh, and then jumping from the bed as he heard Billy coming up the stairs; he went to leave the room, reaching the door just as Billy did.

"Fuck me, she is in a bad way, gone and passed out," he whispered to Billy, who was poking his head into the room and could barely make out Tanya's silhouette on the bed through the darkness.

"Yeah, she knocked them back a bit tonight, silly mare." Billy was physically holding himself back; Jay was standing in his bedroom, in his fucking house. It was taking all his willpower not to throw the fucker out. Jay stepped out of the room, and just as Billy closed the door out, they both turned as they heard Kate calling up the stairs that their taxi had arrived.

23

Emma was a mess. Her hair was greasy, her breath stank, she had big sores all over her chin and her sunken eyes had large bags under them. She was rock bottom, and she knew it, and worse than that the punters knew it too.

When she had first started out doing this, apart from the nutter who had attacked her, she had been treated like a sex toy; she was desired; the men had taken her body but in a strange way she had felt that they had almost been grateful to her, impressed by her eagerness and willingness and, of course, her womanly curves.

Of course there had been a few weirdoes, and a few of them she wouldn't have gone near for any amount of money, but her standards were slipping. Emma thought she could handle it at the beginning, thought she could stay in control, but the drugs had taken over. The lower she sank so too did the quality of men she entertained. They were as filthy as she looked, and they just used her like she was a piece of meat, like she was nothing in fact. She had lost so much weight that her ribs were sticking out, her womanly curves had gone. She looked pale and gaunt, like a skanky druggie, which in fact was exactly what she had become.

The only thing that was of any concern to her these days was where her next bag of gear was coming from; first thing in the morning, last thing at night, these were her only thoughts.

Emma knew where it had all gone wrong; the turning point had crept up on her slowly and then smacked her straight in the face. She thought that she had him right where she wanted him, but she felt stupid now that she had even considered blackmailing him and telling Kate what her precious Jay had been up to. Stupidly, she had said to Jay the night she had been attacked, when he had come to help her, that she could tell Kate at any minute what had been going on; her threat had been loaded, but Jay hadn't risen to the bait, he had just ignored it, or so she had thought.

Jay had looked after her, he had sorted her out when that nutter raped her, he had cleaned the place up for her, spent a bit of time with her, and he had been nice to her. She had begun to think that he might have feelings for her. One night he had given her so much gear, she felt as if she was flying. He had told her that they were going to a party and that he had some special friends that he wanted her to meet. He had even brought her a new outfit, a very slutty looking one, a black silk babydoll with lace around the plunging neckline, it looked more like lingerie, but she just thought that that is what a typical red-blooded male would chose, and she was happy that he wanted to show her off. She had made a real effort, looked really sexy for him.

He had taken her to a dingy little flat, which she really didn't think much of, the things he had told her about these "friends" of his didn't add up to a pokey little flat in Vauxhall. They had money, they were supposed to be high flyers, men who knew what they wanted and got it; it just really didn't make sense.

As soon as she walked through the door and saw the five men, she had known. She was at a party all right, only she was the main source of entertainment. Emma had felt scared, and had kept looking to Jay thinking that even though he had set this up, he was going to be her saviour.

Someone had given Emma a whiskey, and then she had a few lines of coke, or what she thought was coke. It helped, as she began to relax a little, helped by another whisky. The men were smoking: gear, cigars. She was feeling out of it, she had only had a few drinks but then she suddenly felt as though she were losing consciousness.

She had slipped in and out of what had happened next. She recalled lying on a big bed, faces near her, bodies on her: touching, pawing. She couldn't stop them, she was too weak. She felt as though she were floating, like she were asleep, but she could hear them laughing around her; strangely, they sounded far away.

Even the next day, when she had woken back in her own bed in her own flat, she had no real memory of what happened, or how she had got home. She was sore between her legs and felt sick with fear, used and dirty. She didn't have to wait long to find out what had happened.

Jay had been sitting in her lounge with two spotty boys, who looked no more than fifteen. She didn't recognise them, but that was nothing new, there were more people in and out of there on a daily basis than Emma could keep up with. She saw that they were looking through some paperwork or something. They sniggered as she stumbled past them to get a drink of water. Jay glared at her; she had a miserable expression on her face and this riled him.

"Morning!" he had chirped sarcastically. "What's got your knickers in such a twist?" He smirked at the two lads, and they both laughed as if sharing some kind of private joke between the three of them.

"I'm fine, just need a drink." She fought back the tears; she felt humiliated, she couldn't understand why he was acting so nastily.

"We're just going through a few photos, Emma,' Jay said, 'you should have a look, there's a few gorgeous ones here, bet your mum and dad would love a few of these for the family album."

Her heart pounded in her chest. She knew even before she looked down at the coffee table what she was going to see, although never in a million years could she have imagined that the images would have been so graphic. The pictures were sickening. She looked at a photo of three or four men groping her, doing horrible things to her, including having sex with her. It was like looking at somebody else in the photos, the girl in the images had a blank expression and glassy eyes; she looked like a hollow shell, someone who wasn't really there. Emma knew, looking at the photos, that she had been drugged last night. Running to the bathroom, she threw up. The vomit burnt her throat. She dry-heaved for a few minutes. When she looked up, she saw Jay in the mirror; he was standing behind her.

"Don't ever try and blackmail me again, do you hear me?" His voice was low and heavy, and Emma knew he meant it; he could cause her a serious amount of grief.

"You think I'm going to feed you the best gear going for the last few months for nothing? You're having a fucking laugh. You're nothing but a dirty slag, love; you owe me, and you're going to start paying me back. Any grief from you, and I think Mummy and Daddy may stumble upon these." He tapped the envelope in his hand and looked at Emma in disgust, as he left her to cry her tears to herself on the bathroom floor.

That had been a few weeks ago. Now, she was desperately lonely; she had no-one to talk to or to help her. He had her now, she knew that. She had thought she had it all under control, sure that if she played it right Jay would see that he would be lost without her. He had just been using her, like the rest of them. Firstly, for his own dirty needs, and now he was done with her purely to line his pockets.

She hadn't heard from Kate in months, and couldn't bring herself to call her. What would she say; where would she start? It was all too much. She was ashamed of what she had become.

Her parents had called a few times, and she had made up a lie about landing a good job as a flight attendant. Emma made up stories to tell her mum on the few occasions that they had spoken since then. She had described the glamorous locations to which her job was taking her, and her mum had hung on to her words, glad that her little girl was making her own way in the world at last. As Emma made up lie after lie about the hotels she stayed in and the people she had met, she had almost started believing it herself. Her own fantasy world sometimes had herself convinced, letting herself float away in the pretence of it all, even if it was just for a few minutes. Emma had almost convinced herself, and her parents had seemed to buy it completely.

24

Kate was beaming. She had made it to the end of her first week in her job, and was actually looking forward to the next one. She had really got stuck in; busying herself with sorting out the office for Paul had been her main challenge to start off with and after spending hours putting contacts into his database and filing paperwork and invoices and making things a whole lot easier to find, she had been over the moon to see Paul look impressed with her efforts. Then she had sorted out the rotas for the staff; she could see straight away that there were a few shifts not covered well enough by the bar staff, and then as if that wasn't enough she had even suggested a few promotional evenings to Paul to bring in more money.

Paul had been very impressed. Kate was a breath of fresh air; he was surprised at how she had thrown herself into the job. It wasn't a glamorous high-profile career, but that was how she was treating it, she was putting in one hundred and ten percent. He liked that about her. She was a diamond. He found that he enjoyed being in her company, too. They had sat in the office together several times over the week. He could have been doing other things but found himself drawn to her. Kate often sat on the floor sorting through piles of paperwork, and chatting away about anything and everything, while he sat at his desk, not really doing much, looking up stuff on the Internet, just so he could be around her.

Paul had been shocked when Kate had said that her boyfriend was an ex-employee of his, he hadn't realised initially that she was Jay Shaw's girlfriend. Kate was obviously kept in the dark about her boyfriend's dealings, she seemed to have no idea that there was any bad feeling between Jay and Paul, in fact she had even said that Jay had no choice but to give up working at Goldie's, as he was so busy with his own business.

Paul decided that it was best to keep quiet; he couldn't get his head around how someone as beautiful and intelligent as Kate could have ended up with a lowlife scumbag like Jay. Kate must be really naive, he thought: but then he too had been taken in by the bloke. He realised that someone as decent and trusting as Kate would have no reason not to believe every line she had been spun by Jay. Paul was also impressed that she hadn't tried to use her brother's name to get herself a job; most girls that had a relative with as much clout as Billy would have done, but then Kate wasn't "most girls". He could see that she was determined to make her own way and she certainly was doing that.

Paul liked Kate, she was a nice girl; he could see half the reason that she threw herself so passionately into her work was so that she didn't have to think about losing the baby. He felt pleased that Kate had confided in him about that, she had done so well holding herself together and he had offered her whatever support she needed. At first, he thought maybe she could have done with a bit more time off, but soon realised she needed a distraction and the club was ideal for that.

Kate was just leaving for the day when she overheard Paul on the phone to Suzy, who seemed to be saying that she wasn't coming in to work again tonight. She could tell Paul was stressed about it, as he was tapping his foot impatiently on the floor as he sat on the edge of his desk.

"Problem?" Kate asked when Paul had put down the phone.

"Suzy isn't coming in again tonight; that's the second time this week." He sighed. "I think you've put her nose out of joint a bit." Kate felt awful, the last thing that she had wanted to do was to come on board and tread on someone else's toes.

"Don't worry," Paul reassured her, as if he could read her thoughts. "If she had been doing such a great job, I wouldn't have needed you, would I? I thought she had the place running great, but you have done more in one week than she has for months."
Paul hoped Kate felt better at his words, and as he said them he knew that they were true. Suzy had seemed to have done a good job up until now, but thinking about it the place was so much more organised thanks to Kate. She had only just started but she had made a real impact already. Kate hadn't really taken to Suzy; she had been the only person in the club who hadn't made her feel welcome. In fact, Kate thought that Suzy had gone out of her way to make her feel very unwelcome, with her glaring, steely looks and her harsh tones, which left Kate feeling like a silly child.

"Only problem is, there's going to be no-one to run the bar in the gentlemen's lounge upstairs tonight, I'll have to close it and stay down here, the guys can't be down here on their own, it will be too busy." Paul rubbed his forehead, as he tried to work out the best plan of action. Kate didn't need to think twice before she spoke, she loved being at the club, there was a real buzz about the place and she enjoyed working there.

"Well, why don't I stay?" She knew she would only be going home to an empty bed until Jay crept in, in the middle of the night, and she thought of the extra cash too, which would come in handy. "I can help you out down here, and you can run upstairs as normal." She smiled at him eagerly.

After a bit more persuasion from Kate, Paul agreed. He hadn't wanted to take advantage of her good nature, but he could see that she was happy to help out so he showed her the ropes. The bar staff were friendly, showing her where everything was, how to use the till, and the general running of the bar. It was funny, Kate thought, as she poured the pints and lined up the shots later that evening, she had spent hardly any time with Jay this week, and she was starting not to mind so much. In the past, she had been on his case, especially when she had been pregnant; she had wanted him to give her more affection, a little bit of his time, but he had seemed disinterested. Even after she had lost the baby, she could see that he wasn't that bothered about her or the loss of their child. Losing their baby had affected her more than him. She had thought at first that helping to sort out the rift between Jay and her brother might change things, but still they weren't quite right; in fact, during the short amount of time she had spent with Jay that week, he had seemed irritated. Oh well, she thought to herself, at least she could keep busy with this little job.

Kate smiled to herself as she passed some shot glasses to the two pretty girls she was serving, she was really enjoying the hustle and bustle, the club had a good vibe, and it was proving the place to be. You could hardly see the dance floor for people dancing, and the bar was so busy she doubted she would even get a two-minute break, not that she minded.

Paul had been upstairs for most of the night and the place had again been packed, there had been no trouble up there, but then there rarely was, as the guys in the gentlemen's lounge always seemed quite happy with everything that was provided for them. The new girls were grinding to the rhythm of the music and were having lots of admiring glances; it always surprised Paul how fickle men could be, flash a bit of tit and arse and the loving wife or girlfriend waiting at home was forgotten in an instant.

Sure, Paul could appreciate beauty when he saw one, but he wouldn't go as far as leering or pestering. He felt very old-fashioned in that respect: if you have a nice bird, look after her was his maxim; he had been brought up to believe that you don't truly love someone unless you have that respect for them. He was a rare breed, he knew, most men in here had and would pay for a blowy behind their women's back in a heartbeat.

It was getting late. Paul, in a rare quiet moment, nipped downstairs to see how Kate was getting on. He peeped through the swing doors, not wanting her to see him and think that he was checking up on her; it wasn't that he didn't think she could cope: he just wanted to make sure that she was okay.

He could see her laughing and joking with the other bar staff and going from customer to customer serving drinks, smiling and chatting away. She was seemingly unaware of the admiring glances she was getting from the men around her. Paul could see the looks that she was getting and he was surprised when he realised that he was feeling jealous. Kate was having a very strange effect over him; he had decided a long time ago that women were best left alone. At least in a long-term relationship sense, he had plenty of offers from young gorgeous girls, but he could see them for what they were and what they were after, which didn't interest him. Sure, he had a few flings, he was human, but beyond that there was no real interest. He had been hurt before, and could just about admit even to himself that it had cut him really deep. That was years ago now, though, and despite the heartache he had felt at the time, he had got something special out of that relationship, something that was worth every second of the heartache that he had endured.

He wouldn't be making the same mistake again. He was a bit old-school like that, call it old-fashioned. He wanted more than a fling; he was waiting for someone with something special about. Shaking his head, as he went back upstairs to the bar, he wondered if he was going soft in his old age, as Kate had really got under his skin. Pushing the double doors open, he tried to put her out of his head: no doubt, he would have a long queue of thirsty customers waiting for him.

25

Jay had a thumping headache; it was probably from the stress of running around making drops for fucking Billy-boy all week. He had been given an "in", or at least that's how Billy had made it seem. Jay wasn't happy though: he was talked down to and he had to swallow his pride and just get on with everything he was told to do. Being treated like a dog's body was wearing thin.

He knew that Billy still hated him, but he also knew that Billy was trying to do his upmost to please his sister; Jay had been given the job for Kate's benefit only. Jay knew that he had not been accepted by Billy, or Billy's cronies, he was barely tolerated by them. He could see that by the way they looked at him, like they all had no ounce of respect for him. Billy made sure that Jay was kept busy running around doing jobs like an errand boy, and it was starting to grate. He had a few ideas of his own as to how to change that, though.

Jay pulled up outside a block of flats; he had just dropped off a package for Billy round the corner, about the fiftieth package this week and while he was in the area, he figured that he may as well make a bit of wedge for himself on the side. Stepping out of his beamer, he locked the doors and did a quick scan of the road. If there were any little hoodies hanging around he would make sure that they wouldn't dream of touching his car, but it was a quiet day. The car was alarmed up to the bollocks anyhow so he thought it would be fine.

One of the guys on the top floor of the flats, Robbie Challis, had created a mini-Kew Gardens: except the only bit of greenery on display was of the ganja variety. Jay knew that he would be able to shift a bit of his own gear through him; Challis knew most of the junkies in the area. Before, he had been reluctant to do any sort of business with Jay; he didn't like the idea of the pills and the harder stuff, he just liked to deal in weed and on several occasions it had got a bit heated when Jay had tried to muscle in on his little money making machine. Jay had tried to persuade Challis, and had cut him a good deal, but he had proved to be a stubborn one; Jay had finally offered a deal so good that he thought even Challis couldn't refuse, but the fucking cheek of him: he did refuse it. It was like he was making a point, the fucking mug. What sort of bloke doesn't want to make a few quid, huh? Oh well, today would be different: today Jay wasn't going to take no for an answer. Word had got around that Jay was working for Billy, and Jay was going to use that to his advantage. He wouldn't be offering any sort of deal today; Challis has been given a chance and he had blown it. Today he would be told. Jay wanted some serious money, and this little fucker would help him to make it.

No one need know that Jay and Billy's relationship wasn't as cosy as Jay pretended. Because he worked for Billy, no-one in their right mind would fuck with him.

An hour later, Jay opened the door of his car a grand richer and a lot happier. He had his blade in his pocket, and was pleased on this occasion he hadn't needed to use it. In fact, he had seen by Challis's face when he had opened his door that he wasn't going to have any problem getting him on side, fear and defeat had been written all over the other man's face.

This was going to be a lot easier than Jay had thought: as far as Challis was concerned, if he didn't shift a couple of grand's worth of gear each week, Jay would be back, this time with Billy and some of the other boys. Jay liked the power Billy's name had given him; he guessed that there were a few more little arrangements with people he could set up. Before long he would be sitting around, living the high life; everyone around him would be busting their arses to make money for him. Starting the engine, Jay smiled; he was chuffed, this was going to be too easy.

Jay thought that a little surprise visit would be right up Tanya's street, would relieve the boredom she must feel just sitting at home looking pretty. He liked Tanya, she was a stunner, a bit feisty, she wouldn't take any shit, but there was something a little unhinged about her, and he couldn't wait to see what she was like in the sack; he imagined that she could be a very dirty girl. He expected that she would be pleased to see him, as the other night she had made it clear that she was up for it, and shagging Billy's missus would be a giant notch on his bed post.

26

Kate stretched out her long legs in the bed; reaching for the alarm clock, she was amazed to see that it had gone ten, not only because she never slept in this late, but because she was surprised that Jay was actually out of bed before her. Normally on a Sunday, she would have to creep out of the bedroom once awake, trying not to disturb him, as he would only be angry with her for waking him, especially as most nights he wasn't back until gone three or four in the morning.

She heard the water in the shower running and the sound of his whistling filling the hallway. He sounded like he was in a good mood, which pleased Kate; maybe today they could spend time together. She had hardly seen him over the past few weeks, between Jay working with her brother and her new job at Goldie's it was almost like they were living separate lives. Kate knew that things were strained between her and Jay, but she was convinced that if they just spent some time together and talked, they could be okay. Jay sounded like he was in a good mood, and Kate decided to keep it that way. Throwing off the bedcovers, she stood and wrapped her dressing gown around her and put on her slippers; then, she went to the kitchen to make him a fry-up.

Jay scrubbed himself clean under the hot shower; good mood was an understatement, he was flying. Yesterday, with Tanya, had been unbelievable. He had got up early to see her and was hoping that if he planned things right today, he might be in for round two. Tanya had been insatiable, X-rated, he guessed it was true what they said about those bored and ignored housewife types; he smiled to himself; they went all out to please. When he had arrived at her flat, they hadn't even bothered to talk: they didn't need to, they had both known what he was there for, and it wasn't a cup of PG Tips. Tanya had known that Billy wouldn't be home until late, as always, and that at some point Jay would be paying her a little visit, she knew he wouldn't have been able to resist the play she had made for him on the night of the meal. Tanya wasn't quite sure why she had done it, if she was honest with herself he wasn't her usual type, but she was drawn to the danger of him; it excited her, and she needed that excitement.

The sex had been amazing: hard and rough and most of all vengeful for both of them. She had half-hoped that Billy would come home early and catch them at it, and that thought had turned her on even more. They hadn't even made it up the stairs; Tanya had made him take her in the lounge. It had been as quick as it was intense and Tanya had been left wanting more. She knew that she would be seeing Jay again and that pleased her. She was sick of waiting for Billy to notice her; she wanted some fun, and Jay could give it to her.

Jay knew that he sometimes got infatuated with his conquests; he lived for the chase: the games and, of course, the sex. The hardest case that he had ever cracked was Kate, but he could admit to himself now that she bored him. She was just Little Miss Average in the grand scheme of things, she was always blabbering on about useless gossip that he couldn't give a shit about, and lately she didn't stop talking about her poxy job at the club. Jay had less and less time for her and no interest in her in bed. It was only the fact that he was still using Billy's name as a tool to help him move up the ladder, so to speak, that he hadn't told her he wanted out of the relationship. For now, he would keep the feeling to himself, he was playing a waiting game.

Following the smell of bacon into the kitchen, he found Kate cooking a mountain of food for him, and she had a nice hot cup of tea waiting.

"Cheers, babe." He smiled at her, sitting at the table and noting that she did have some uses: he loved a fry up and loved being waited on hand and foot even more. Jay had always prided himself on his acting skills; he had had to blag his way out of so many situations in the past that he was sure he could handle keeping Kate sweet for a bit longer, just to give him more time to get a real in with Billy. It pained him to even think it, but Billy had it sorted, he was running a very smooth and very profitable operation and had a great front, with the backup he needed and the right contacts.

Jay knew it would only be a matter of time until he got something out of it: whether it was given to him, or he had to take it, he was going to get something out of Billy, no matter what. He was kept in the dark about the ins and outs of the business, but he would bide his time.

Placing a plate in front of Jay, Kate smiled.

"This is nice, isn't it, babes? We hardly ever get to sit and have breakfast together." She was curious as to why Jay was up early, and why he seemed to be so happy, but she knew better than to quiz him: a bit of gentle prodding should do the trick.

"Yeah, well, I've got lots to do today, you know, thought I'd make an early start." He saw the smile fade on her face, as she realised that he would be off out shortly, and yet again they wouldn't be spending time together. Changing the subject, before Kate could start whining on about living separate lives, he quickly asked, "So, how was last night, was the club busy?"

He only half-listened to her answer, whilst chomping on his food, then his ears pricked up at the sound of Paul Goldie's name. When he was mentioned, Jay noticed that Kate spoke fondly of him; knowing that Kate was not the type to do the dirty on him should have made him feel a bit better but it niggled at Jay that maybe Paul would try to muscle in on her just to piss him off. Kate babbled on and on, loving that Jay was asking about her job, oblivious to his staring.

"Paul this, Paul that, anyone would think you'd been screwing the fucking bloke," Jay said, his joking tone not hiding the spite behind it.

"Don't be silly, Jay, Paul's a lovely man, but it's nothing like that. I'm with you, I wouldn't even look at another man, babes." She was hurt that he would even think like that: what did he take her for?

"Yeah, but that doesn't stop them from looking at you, though, does it?" He looked at her accusingly. "A club is no place for someone like you, Kate; I should know, I worked there too, you know. All those leering drunks trying it on, seeing if they're in with a chance…." He did know; he had been one of them.

"It's not like that, though, Jay, really; I go in, do my job, and then come home."

"Yeah, well, that Paul better not try his luck with you, or he'll have me to deal with, and he better not be taking the piss out of you either, making you work all hours."

"Paul's not like that; he's very professional, and he thinks I'm a great worker. Not all men perv, you know!"

Angrily, Kate began clearing the table, her appetite gone. Why couldn't her boyfriend just be happy for her: she was doing a job she enjoyed and he wasn't interested in the slightest, all he seemed to care about was his bloody ego: typical. Turning her back on him, she began to wash up the plates, splashing water all over the place and clanging the cups; she knew her stropping about the place was petty, but she was so angry. Jay noticed her mood change, and rolled his eyes, he was glad he was going out as he couldn't be arsed with Kate's tantrums. He had better things to do.

Sitting in his car, Billy tapped his fingers on the steering wheel. He felt sick, not in a gut-churning jealous way, which had initially surprised him.

He had assumed that would be how he would feel; he had always thought if Tanya ever thought about cheating on him, he would kill her and whoever the bloke with a death wish that was cheating with her was. Billy hadn't expected to feel like this, it was a different kind of feeling, more of a realisation. He had now come to the conclusion that he didn't give a toss about her anymore, they had just been 'going through the motions', he realised.

Billy had been outside Tanya's flat for over forty minutes; he was supposed to be sorting out some business at the warehouse, but had nipped back to get some paperwork he needed just in time to see Jay going into the flat. No need to be Albert Einstein to work out what was going on. He waited and tried to get his head together.

He could have gone in and caused merry hell, but something made him wait. God knows how he had managed to sit so calmly for so long, all the while guessing what was going on behind the curtains in the bedroom. Tanya must be crazy if she thought she could do this to him, he had paid for the roof over her head, given her everything she wanted and this was her repayment, and with that skank of all people.

Thinking back to the night he had walked in on Jay in their bedroom, his intuition had told him something was up, Jay had looked shifty – but then, thought Billy, when didn't he? He wondered if it had started then or if it had been going on for longer. How had he not noticed before?

Tanya was easily sorted. Billy frowned: Jay was another matter. First his sister, now his missus; Jay was proving to be a fucking piss-taker. If this got out, Billy would look like a mug, and his poor sister's heart would be broken, God knows why, but she loved Jay, and after everything that happened with her losing the baby, she didn't need any more problems. Jay didn't give a shit about Kate. Realising this, Billy could feel his blood boiling, he was fucking raging, but he knew that he would deal with it once and for all. He was no-one's mug. He was done with Tanya, and it was the excuse he had been looking for, if he was honest.

Jay, on the other hand, deserved something a bit special, he needed to be shown the error of his ways. Billy had kept the peace for his sister, but now he would do what he should have done in the first place. Kate might not thank him for it, but he would be doing her a bigger favour than she would ever know, he thought. Picking up his mobile, he couldn't believe it when he heard Tanya's voice.

"Alright, Tan, you sound out of breath? Didn't make you run for the phone, did I?"

"Oh hi, Billy; yeah, you did, actually, I was... downstairs, sorting out the kitchen, I must have left the phone upstairs... had to leg it up here."

Billy could picture Jay, looking like the smug slimy bastard he was, lying next to Tanya as she lied out of her skinny arse; Billy betted he loved every minute of this.

"Oh well, best you run back downstairs and put the kettle on then, Tan, 'cause I'm going to be home in five."

"Oh… okay, babe; see you in five."

Billy hung up. He had noted the panic in Tanya's voice that she had tried to hide and could imagine the pair of them were running about like headless chickens, trying to get dressed so Jay could leave before Billy got home and found out about their dirty little secret. Two minutes later a very worried-looking Jay left the flat, looking as if someone had just shoved a rocket up his arse.

As Jay drove off, Billy started his own engine, and picking up his phone once more rang Tanya.

"Change of plan, Tan, I've got a bit of business to attend to, looks like you'll just be making tea for one."

Not waiting for her reply, Billy hung up. Tanya looked at the dead handset wondering what the hell that was all about.

Although Tanya was relieved that Jay hadn't been caught, she was a little bit put out that they had been rudely interrupted, especially as she had been almost at the point of no return when Billy had called her. Smiling to herself as she put the phone down on the side she was blissfully unaware that Billy was on to her and at that particular moment was following Jay's beamer down the road.

Billy had decided that he would tail Jay for a bit, check out what the guy was up to; he wanted to get all the pieces in place before making his move.

27

Looking around, Paul was pleased to see that again they were in for a busy night. The club was packed and he had heard from a few little birdies that Goldie's was becoming more and more well-known, and because of the great DJ line-ups that they put on, people were coming from all over. There were a lot of celebrity faces about most weekends, which of course was great for business, in one way, but in the beginning had been hard work, Paul had had to extend his security and hired a PR girl. It had been manic trying to calm down punter's reactions to certain celebs. He wanted them to have a great night out, not to be pestered by mad drunken fans. Kate had suggested cordoning off an area for VIPs near the DJ box, and that had proved a success. Paul hadn't originally thought about a VIP area as such, he had figured at first that the private members' lounge upstairs would be enough. But this way, people could hear the latest tunes whilst checking out celebs from afar, which suited everyone. He had decided that because it was Kate's idea and because she was proving to be an asset, that she would be in charge of the VIP bar, it would be her baby. He had pretty much let her set it up and run it however she wished, although he had made sure that she had another member of staff with her at all times to ensure the quickest service. Paul continued to run the members' lounge upstairs; it made sense, as Paul could keep all the big wigs happy and keep an eye on the entire club as the security room was up there too; he often checked out the monitors to make sure everyone was happy and doing their jobs. The rest of the staff ran the other main bars, and everyone seemed to be happy, and it was just the way Paul liked it: smooth and controlled.

He spotted Billy pulling up a stool at the bar and decided to go and join him; he could do with a drink and five minutes off.

"It's on the house, and I'll have a Jack and Coke," Paul interrupted, as he caught the end of Billy's drinks order to the bartender.

"Cheers Paul, nice one; thought you didn't drink while you were working, though?" Billy smiled.

"Well, that was the original plan, but every now and then won't hurt, huh?" Paul could see all was not well with Billy; the bloke had worry etched on his forehead.

"How's my little sister doing?" Billy tried to make conversation to take his mind off the shitty day he had had. Following Jay seemed to have opened up a whole can of worms, Billy had seen a few things today, and to say he was annoyed was a massive understatement; he didn't know how to play things, the rules had all changed today.

"Kate's a little diamond, Billy; she has the punters eating out of her hands."

Billy smiled, nodding in agreement. Kate had a way of being liked by everyone, he just hoped that no-one took that the wrong way and overstepped the mark.

"She's no pushover though; she can shoot a man down with a stare if he crosses the line you know." Laughing now, Paul said, "I should know, I've had the pleasure of watching the poor wounded guys' faces that have been on the receiving end." As if he had read Billy's mind, he continued. "She won't get any trouble in here, Billy, I'll personally make sure of it mate, besides she is actually a lot stronger-minded than she looks."

Paul looked over to the bar where Kate was working; he could see her smiling and chatting away to Lucy, the other barmaid on duty. They were both laughing and joking as they poured drinks; being careful to include the punters in their banter, they had everyone smiling. Turning back, he asked,

"So how are things with you, Billy? You look like you have the weight of the world on those shoulders of yours, everything okay?"

He nodded to the barman to top up their glasses, as Billy sighed; he did have the weight of the world on his shoulders. He had been following Jay for a few more days now and had been to more hovels than the average rat; the guy had fingers in many pies, each and every one of them as cheap and nasty as the next. Billy had just seen him go into Kate's friend's Emma's flat; God knew what the guy was playing at. He had decided he would lie low here for a bit and then go back and pay Emma a little visit when Jay had gone, see what the girl was playing at.

"Nothing that can't be sorted out," Billy replied; he had every intention of doing so later on.

"Anything I can help with?" Paul was intrigued.

"Nah, this is something that I should have settled a long time ago... something long overdue, besides, I think you've already had a bash at "it", so to speak, a while back."

Suddenly realising who Billy was hinting at, Paul could instantly feel his hackles rise; he felt his body tensing just at the thought of Jay's name. He could handle that the guy had taken the piss and used the club to deal his crap from; it went on, it wasn't such a huge deal, Jay had been given a hiding: job done. But more and more, as Paul had got to know Kate, he had grown more and more to physically hate Jay. Kate never said anything outright about Jay's behaviour, or not the bad side of it, but he could sense that the whole thing just wasn't right. Jay wasn't capable of seeing how amazing Kate was, he certainly wouldn't be capable of doing right by her. By the sounds of it, Kate knew he was generally up to no good, but she couldn't have the slightest inkling of what he was actually up to, or there would be no way she would be with him: he was sure of that. Paul had decided when she had first mentioned being Jay's girlfriend that he would keep quiet about what he knew. He would let Kate work it out in her own time; he had hoped that would be sooner rather than later.

"I'm sure that whatever needs doing, Billy, you're more than capable of sorting it out, but if you need me, you just say the word," Paul said.

"Cheers mate." Downing his drink, Billy gave Kate a nod and indicated that he was going upstairs; he had just come to see her, but she was busy, and he hadn't wanted her to feel like he was keeping tabs on her.

"See you later, mate, cheers for the drink."

Billy made his way to the gentlemen's lounge. Paul watched as he walked upstairs, he was a big bloke, as broad as he was tall. He felt that he had witnessed the calm before the storm. Billy was never a man of many words, but Paul could tell that he was troubled. He liked Billy, he always had. Since Kate had started working for him, she had done nothing but sing Billy's praises, the only negative thing she had ever hinted at about Billy was that he was very over-protective but that she knew he had her best interests at heart. Paul couldn't help wondering about that, though, how could Billy stand back and watch his sister be with such a lowlife? He imagined that it must take a lot for him to remain calm and controlled. It just didn't make sense, surely he wasn't happy about the relationship. Paul had heard that Billy had even let Jay have a small hand in his business dealings. Maybe it wasn't as simple as that, though, he knew the theory behind the old saying "keep your friends close..." and all that. Something was definitely up, he was convinced that it involved Jay, and if he was right he had no pity for Jay, the guy had a lot coming to him. Paul could see there was something unhinged in Billy, something in his eyes, he was not a man to be crossed.

28

She pulled the thick blue rope up and reached up on her toes to make it tie around the light fitting on the ceiling; it was a big wrought-iron light fitting so it had seemed strong enough. She had already made a big loop on one end of the rope. She had only ever seen this sort of thing in films, and had up until now thought that attempting suicide was done by somebody using it as a pathetic cry for help, to gain attention. Well, that wasn't an option for her anymore, she had no-one who could help her and attention was the last thing she needed, she had had enough attention to last a lifetime: all of the wrong kind.

She stood on a chair and pulled down hard on the rope, she could feel a rope burn on her right palm as she tugged tightly and knew it was strong enough to hold her.

She looked at the brown wooden chair she was standing on, at her pale, grubby feet, her scuffed toenail-varnish; her feet were as neglected as the rest of her. She didn't care about herself anymore, she had let herself go. She wasn't sure whether she should have written a note, but looking over at the dining room table she was glad she had now. There were two envelopes, one addressed to her parents, letting them know that it wasn't their fault and that she loved them and was sorry. Her mum would be devastated, but she wasn't sure if she would be more upset that the illusion of her successful daughter was shattered more than finding out the truth of what her daughter had actually become. Her dad would be disgusted and very disappointed, he had bought and paid for her to have the best throughout her childhood and he would not have understood how she had come to this at all. They lived in another world, most of the time, they had bridge afternoons and dinner parties; they had no idea of how everyone else lived, struggling to get by and doing whatever was needed to pay the bills. There was a time that she had been tempted to call and tell them everything, sure deep down that they would help her and take her away from it all. Something had stopped her, though: a combination of shame and fear, as over the months she had sunk lower and lower. Even the punters knew it. She was a mess, a down-and-out, there to be used and abused, and for practically pennies now as she was so far out of it these days she would just mainly lay there in her own little dream world, hardly even acknowledging whoever was grinding and panting away on top of her.

The other envelope was addressed to Kate, apologising for everything, confessing about what she had done behind her friend's back with Jay and how he had got her hooked on drugs and prostitution. She had cried when she had written it. She had thought about how upset her friend would be once she heard she was dead and felt even guiltier for the pain she would cause. She thought about all the memories of them growing up together, the laughs and the mad nights out clubbing. Kate had been the only person that had ever really cared for her, and she was beside herself at how she could have treated her like she had, she could not forgive herself for that.

Next to the envelopes was her empty bag of gear. She had summoned every bit of strength not to take anything this morning, to remain clear-headed while she sorted out the last few things she had to do, which had been so hard; she didn't normally have to deal with her feelings and writing the letters had brought them all out; she had had to be strong and find the right words, she wanted to do that much at least, she felt that she owed them that.

She had waited until Jay had paid her his nightly visit to collect his money and had sniffed the gear as soon as he had left. She knew now that it was a form of heroin that Jay had been supplying her with, she had loads of it from punters too, not China White like Jay had got her hooked on, just normal street stuff. She had realised she was a druggie the first time she had stuck a needle in one of her veins to take it; until then, even though she used drugs several times a day, she had convinced herself that she wasn't an addict, that she had it under control. But she didn't, she knew that now: she was a druggie, and a whore, and worse than that, she was trapped, and she didn't want to be where she was anymore. She didn't want some dirty unwashed man forcing himself into her, while she laid on the bed with her legs splayed open, or to be strangled or used as a punch bag as some of the dirty fuckers liked, she hated being used and feeling filthy when they had taken from her what they wanted, fed up of waking up in the morning and thinking about gear, craving it so much that it physically pained her. More than anything else, she was sick and tired of feeling alone. Loneliness washed over her every second of every day.

She didn't want to be alone anymore. Placing her head in the noose and feeling a tear roll down her cheek, she kicked the chair. The rope tightened around her neck and she struggled for breath; she writhed around kicking her legs in the air then finally she gave in to unconsciousness.

Emma didn't hear the front door open, or her name being called, she didn't feel a pair of big arms wrap themselves around her as she was lifted up and the rope loosened. She was out cold.
He hoped that he had reached her in time. He called an ambulance after making sure that she was breathing, he saw the envelopes on the table. He put them in his jacket pocket, then went and sat next to her until the ambulance arrived.

29

Billy was ready. He had followed Jay for the best part of a week and was sure he had seen it all; it was time to put things into motion. Today was Jay's day of reckoning. Billy had everything he needed on the guy; he had had to call in a few favours, but now it was all in place. He thought he deserved a fucking Oscar for his acting skills with Tanya, but he knew that if he waited it out, she would dig herself into a deeper hole. Well, she was going to be wishing that she could jump in the bloody hole too in a moment. He grinned as he got out of his car and walked around to the passenger side; opening the door for Candice to get out, he took another look at her and smiled. Seeing her dressed like this of an evening in the gentlemen's lounge was the norm for him, but at this time of the morning, in his street, she looked obscene, like she had just finished filming a porno. He had told her to wear the most provocative outfit she owned and had laughed when he picked her up from her flat this morning. She had tottered towards him in six-inch heels and the smallest bit of fabric Billy had ever seen, which had the cheek to label itself as a dress; it was way too much for this time of the morning, in fact for any time of the day full stop. As well as looking very slutty, she was tanned and glossy, just as they had discussed. Tanya would go nuts when she saw Candice.

"Okay, babe; I'm ready… let's do it." Candice winked as she took his hand, and they both walked towards the front door.

Hearing a loud, squeaky laugh coming from her hallway and the front door closing loudly, Tanya sat up and pulled her robe around her; she had been chilling out to a bit of Jeremy Kyle on telly whilst lounging on the sofa, enjoying her first coffee of the day. Billy hadn't come home again last night, but by the sounds of it he was now and he had company. She could hear the laughing in the kitchen now; getting up, she decided to go and see who was making that awful noise. Laugh: it sounded more like a fucking cat getting strangled.

Walking into the kitchen, a gobsmacked Tanya was not sure exactly what was going on but had a feeling that Billy had lost the plot.

"Oh hi, Tanya, do you fancy a coffee? I was just making one for Candice here. Oh, actually, I expect you'd rather a glass of wine, wouldn't you, I mean it is after all almost ten in the morning." Billy had the kettle on and was acting as if nothing was up, but his shirt was undone and so was his belt, she noticed, and he had bright pink lipstick marks on his cheek. Looking at the tart sitting on her granite worktop Tanya's blood started to boil.

"Who the fuck are you?" she glared at Candice, sitting in her kitchen with everything hanging out, like some kind of slapper; well, at least the girl was wearing knickers, thought Tanya, noting that they, like everything else this girl had to offer, were on display.

Candice looked Tanya up and down as if she were a five foot seven, walking, talking turd.

"I'm Candice." Short and simple: no explanation.

Something was not right.

"Well, Candice, what the fuck are you doing sitting in my kitchen looking like a dog's fucking dinner?" Tanya bellowed now, starting to feel really unsure of what was going on.

"Ah, Tanya, Tanya, calm down will you." Billy passed Candice a cup of coffee.

"Told you she could be a narky bitch in the mornings, didn't I?" He winked at Candice now. "Don't listen to her, I think you look fucking tasty, babe, good enough to eat." He licked his lips and the room was once again filled with Candice's loud dirty laugh.

"What the fuck?" Not being able to finish her sentence Tanya lunged for Billy, her cheeks were flaming, how could he try and humiliate her like this, bringing this cheap little slut into her house and talking to her like this? Billy grabbed Tanya's wrist, just in time to stop her fist coming down on him.

"Get her out of my fucking house, Billy, how fucking dare you." She was so angry, she could feel tears stinging her eyes; she was determined not to cry in front of them both, especially not Candice who was sitting there looking like the cat that had got the poxy cream.

"That's just it, though, Tan, it isn't your house, is it? It's mine, isn't it? On paper." He looked at her seriously.

Tanya felt sick. He knew. She didn't know how or when it had happened, but he had found out. It was the only explanation. As if reading her mind, he grinned at her, a grin that didn't reach his dark, narrowed eyes.

"You might want to go and get dressed, Tan; you have a busy day ahead of you, love. You're moving out."

She wanted to scream and shout, cry and beg; she couldn't give up everything and walk away. This was her home; she had decorated every room, made it her own, and she loved it. But she was not going to put on a show, not while that slut was watching her, no fucking chance; Tanya would be a laughing stock if this got out. She would keep her dignity and accept it. The game was up, and she would have to leave, there was no fighting Billy once he made his mind up, and the house was in his name, so she didn't have a leg to stand on.

"Oh don't you fucking worry mate, I'm off. You think you can bring some cheap little slut in here to our home? Well, you know what?" Turning now to face the girl on the worktop, she shouted, "You're fucking welcome to him." She glared at Candice who still had the cheek to stare back smugly at Tanya.

"Oh I know I'm welcome to him, babe, I've been "having" him for months now; thanks for your generosity though." She fluttered her eyelashes and blew Billy a big pouty kiss.

Tanya could restrain herself no longer and lunged forward to slap the little tart, but Billy had seen it coming and jumped between the two.

He had warned Candice about Tanya, told her what had been going on with her and his sister's boyfriend, and even though cheating was an everyday occurrence round these parts, even though Billy had been at it with her, Candice was disgusted at what she had been told about the state Billy had found Emma in a few days previously, she found it hard to believe all that poor girl had been through, she knew part of Billy's plan to sort Jay out, and had been more than happy to help him get his plan into action. Sitting here now, face to face, she could see what a cold-hearted bitch Tanya was, and that she also deserved whatever she got; Candice was actually really enjoying winding her up.

Billy took Tanya by the arm and marched her upstairs and stood in the doorway of their bedroom while she packed a few bits into a bag and threw on some clothes. He could see that she was fighting her rage and her tears, but he felt no sympathy for her; they were over, she had treated him like a mug and now she was leaving: end of.

Tanya put as much as she could into the bag then looked around the room, wondering what would happen to the rest of her stuff. She hoped that she would be able to come back and get it when things had calmed down. As angry as she was, she was going to bite her tongue until she had her stuff back. Billy's eyes followed hers around the room, and once again, as if he was inside her head, reading her thoughts, he said in a cold voice: "I'll send it all on to you," then he followed her back downstairs and held the front door open for her.

Candice couldn't resist one more dig; after all it was what Billy was paying her for this morning, to rub Tanya's nose in it.

"Toodle-doo, babe, nice meeting you." She waved from the front doorway, as Tanya walked down the path, then grabbed Billy by his shirt and gave him a passionate kiss, before closing the door with her stiletto-clad foot.

30

She was fourteen, but Jade knew that she looked older than that. Once she had her slap on, with her hair done, and was wearing the right clothes she always got let in to the local clubs. Once she even got into The Manor, an over twenty-ones club. It had been easy. It helped that she was tall and blonde and most of the door staff were men, and men were so pathetic like that. She could have any boy at her school she wanted, but she didn't want any of them, because that's all they were: boys.

Her mum would kill her if she knew half the things Jade did whlle she was slogging away at work all week. Jade had become a master at hiding her secret life from her mum. She rarely bothered going to school anymore, she always got up and dressed and made out she was going, but as soon as she had walked around the block she would go back, reaching home in time to see her mum's car nipping off down the road. Most days Jade would just sit around on her laptop, checking out Facebook or watching crappy daytime TV. She was bored. Bored with her so-called mates who all seemed immature compared to her. She wanted excitement. Maybe, just maybe, she had found it.

Jay was lying in bed next to Jade; he was smoking a joint. Her mum would go ape if she could smell smoke in the house, but she hadn't wanted to sound like a silly little girl and ask him to put it out, she wanted him to think she was grown up. Besides, she would open the window when he left, and spray air freshener, maybe her mum would think she had actually done some housework for a change. Jay rubbed her leg with one hand, and flicked his ash onto her bedside cabinet with the other. Jade's room was a mess, looking around she wished that she had tidied it before he had come around, as it looked like a typical teenager's bedroom. She had told him she was sixteen, although she wasn't sure he believed her, but he didn't seem to mind if he did realise she was younger. Her body still wasn't as developed as she would have liked, and she had thought that that would have given it away. She had boyish hips and her boobs, she was barely filled an A-cup bra. She had also little sexual experience before she met Jay. A fumble with a fourteen-year-old boy behind the bins at the back of the school disco did not count as an "experience". It had all been so quick and awkward, she hadn't really been sure in the end if they'd actually had sex or not. Dean Woods had been one of the hottest boys in school, but lying on top of her on the cold damp ground that night and panting like an over-excited dog he had been anything but hot, at one point she thought she was going to have to stop and draw him a map. The whole thing had been embarrassing, they had avoided each other ever since.

So when she and Jay had first slept together it was a whole different game.

She met him at the parade, across from her school. All the kids in her year went over to the shops at lunchtime and spent most if not all their lunch money on cigarettes or joints or anything else that was on offer. Jay was a bit of a face; if you wanted some gear, he was your man, and all the kids knew it, and if Jay wasn't around he had a few Year Elevens selling stuff for him. Jade had spent many a lunchtime batting her heavily mascaraed eyelashes in his direction, and although she had seen that she had caught his attention, he hadn't approached her, which made her try harder.

It was by chance that they were at the same party on the estate; some lad's parents had gone away for a weekend and the place was heaving. Jay was doing some deals in the kitchen with a few of the older boys from Jade's school; when he was finally on his own, Jade had made her move. She hadn't realised at the time how she seemed like she was offering it on a plate, but Jay could obviously see right through her, and within the hour they were upstairs in a bedroom. Jade had been frightened at first, she had felt out of her depth. He had known what he wanted, and although he asked if it was her first time, to which she told him it wasn't, he must have known.

He had taken her hard on the bed, on top of the coats and jackets that had been dumped on there, at one point she had wanted to ask him to stop, it was hurting her. But she kept telling herself that this is what she wanted: a real man; excitement. It had been over before quickly, then she had come downstairs with Jay, and had been given a few looks from her schoolmates as if she had gained a new kind of respect from them, she was with Jay, after all.

That had been a few weeks ago, and now she was more than used to Jay's sexual demands. She wondered if he was officially her boyfriend, whether maybe he loved her; she was hoping that that was the case, but not wanting to sound childish she didn't ask, she would wait and see where it went. She was far too shy to ask him about his feelings; besides, that was playground stuff.

So far their relationship consisted of being in bed, but that is what all new relationships were like, right? Not getting enough of each other? He hadn't told himself anything about himself, though, and hadn't asked her much about herself, but they had plenty of time for all that stuff, she guessed. He had just mentioned introducing her to some of his friends one night, at some party, so maybe they were in a proper relationship. He wanted to show her off. Smiling, she put her hand under the duvet and rested it on his.

"Make us a coffee, would you, Jadey?" Removing her hand, he patted her naked arse, as she got up to wrap her gown round herself before going to the kitchen to make him one. Seeing his phone flash, he noticed he had three missed calls.

"Alright, Tanya," he said, picking up the call before it rang out again,

Tanya was crying, and he found it hard to understand what she was saying.

"What do you mean, he knows? Who knows what?" Jay asked.

"Billy: he must know about us, Jay, he's thrown me out; I've got nowhere to go."

"Alright, where are you now? I'll come and get you."

After calming her down and getting her to say where she was, Jay put his clothes on. Jade had came back with a mug of coffee.

"Where are you off to?" She couldn't help but sound disappointed; she had thought she would have him to herself for a few more hours.

"I've got to go, babe." He pulled his jeans on and didn't look her in the eye. He had got what he had come for, and she might be a pretty face but she had nothing interesting to say. He would definitely have a few friends who might be interested in her, though; she seemed to be easily persuaded so she should be easy to convince.

"I'll call you in the week, babe. Let you know about that little party I'm organising?"
Glad that he was arranging to see her again, Jade perked up.

"Okay, babe, you do that; can't wait." Waving him off, as he walked down the front path towards his beamer, she felt pleased as punch with herself, already selecting party outfits in her head.

Jay got in his car and drove off to pick up Tanya; he had no idea how Billy had found out, but he knew that if Tanya was in the shit he would be more so. He decided that he would take her back to Emma's flat and she could stay in the spare room; it wasn't ideal, but as he had been given little notice, it was all he could sort out, and he was sure Tanya wouldn't mind if it were just for a few days. Emma wouldn't know what day of the week it was, let alone who Tanya was, the girl was off her head all the time. He would cancel her punters and keep it low key while Tanya was there. He needed to pop back there, anyway, he hadn't been there for the best part of the week and Emma owed him her week's earnings. Driving faster, his head was spinning; he didn't know what to do about his job, or Kate. None of it made sense: how could Billy know? Or maybe he didn't; maybe he had had enough of Tanya? Surely Billy would have had it out with him, too. Jay knew how Billy had had a thing with one of the girls from the lounge at Goldie's when he used to be there; a little blonde bird, Candy or something. Maybe he didn't give two shits about Tanya and had just ended it, or maybe he'd just traded her in?

As he pulled up outside the newsagents where Tanya was standing with a Louis Vuitton suitcase, mascara running down her cheeks, he knew he would soon find out.

31

Billy was dreading this, but he knew it would be the only way, once and for all, that Kate would actually listen. He had to make Kate physically see the damage that Jay inflicted on people, and how that scumbag had no qualms about walking over anyone in his way.

Billy had already spoken to Sonia, and she had agreed with everything that he said; Jay had gone too far and needed to be taught a lesson. Billy had got to her house first thing that morning; luckily Sonia always got up at the crack of dawn, at least a few hours before Kate, so they had had the chance to talk things through, and the stuff that he had told her had shocked her to the core. She had been disgusted by what Billy had told her about the poor girl he had found trying to hang herself, how Jay had drugged her and used her to make money for him, and that he had other girls out there in the same state made Sonia ashamed to be his mother. Sonia had been even more disgusted when she had heard what Jay's father had done all those years ago to Billy and Kate's mother; it made her sick to her stomach. She had known Den had been capable of vile things, it was one of the reasons she had got out in the first place. She could understand now why Billy hated Jay so much. She wondered if when she had walked out on Den all those years ago, things would have been different if she had taken Jay with her. Maybe he wouldn't have turned out as repulsive. She couldn't help feeling guilty, that somehow she was partly to blame for her son's ways. He was Den all over again, so maybe no matter what she had done differently he would have turned out this way, maybe it was in the genes. The apple didn't fall far from the tree, they said, and in this case the apple was rotten to the core.

Sonia had agreed to change the locks, and decided that as of that moment she would disown Jay. Billy had said that he would send one of his guys round for a few days, just in case Jay returned home and thought he would try his luck, and that way he would know that Sonia meant it: he was no longer welcome here; he wasn't her son any longer.

Sonia had suggested that Billy should break the news to Kate and hopefully they would be able to comfort the poor girl. Pouring Billy a mug of hot tea, she placed it down on the table, and sat down to join him as he drank it.

"I honestly don't know where I'm going to start, Sonia, this is going to break Kate's heart. I don't know how much more she can take." Billy had known all along that Jay was no good, but his sister would never hear a bad word said about him. Well, that morning when she finally came downstairs, bad words were all that would be worthy of the bloke. As Billy and Sonia were starting their second cup of tea, Kate did finally come downstairs, wrapped in her dressing gown and yawning.

"Billy?" She looked from her brother's frowning face to Sonia's worried look. "What's going on? Has something happened?" She had been working at the club all evening, and hadn't got home until after three; she would have still been in bed but she had heard her brother's voice and had come down to see what this unexpected visit was all about. He had bags under his eyes and a frown so deep across his forehead it looked like a scar. Worried, she looked at Sonia, who was looking into her tea as she stirred it. Billy should be the one to tell the poor girl, she wasn't getting involved; not until she was needed, that was. Pulling a chair out for Kate, Billy told her to sit down. At first, he didn't really know where to start, there was so much filth and dirt and lies. Then it all just came out, everything he knew. He told her about Jay's dad and what he had seen all those years ago, when he was just a boy. He told Kate how he had caught Jay coming out of his and Tanya's house and that he had followed him. He had done this for a few days and one flat in particular that he kept being led back to was Emma's. He told Kate how he gone to Emma's flat on his own, to find out what was going on, and what he had seen there.

He gave Kate the letter that was addressed to her, which he had taken the night he had found Emma trying to hang herself. He tried to hold himself together, as he watched the tears roll down Kate's cheeks as she read it.

"Where is she?" she sobbed, as she put the letter back into the envelope.

"She's in hospital, Kate; she's going to be okay, but she's in a state right now. She's been there for ten days now. I would have told you sooner, but she wasn't strong enough. The doctors wouldn't have let you in anyway, not until she was over the worst." He touched her hand across the table.

"She is asking for you now, though, and she really needs you, Kate."

"I just can't believe that Jay would do this, I don't get it; I feel like I'm missing something here." It was all too much to take in, she had had an inkling that Jay was up to no good and she had decided to ignore it rather than question it, but this... this was unforgivable. Getting her priorities straight, Kate added: "Can you take me to see her?"

"Yeah, of course I can, go and get dressed, love, and we'll go now."

As she left the room, Kate looked like she had had the wind knocked right out of her.

"What do you think will happen to Jay now, Billy?" Sonia asked.

"My bet is he will try and come back here, Sonia, and knowing him, if you don't let him in, he will try and force his way in."

Sonia knew Billy was right. Jay would always do whatever he was told not to, a trait he had had from when he was a boy. Seeing the anguished look on Sonia's face and as if reading her mind, Billy reassured her:

"Ryan's on his way over, he's going to be staying here with you for a few days, just until Jay gets the message, okay?"

"Okay." Right now, Jay wasn't on her mind; her only thoughts were of Kate: that poor, poor girl, how did she ever go falling for someone like Jay? Right now, more than anything in the world, Sonia would have swapped a million Jays for one Kate. She had grown to love the girl like her own, and hoped that after all this was over Kate and she would remain close friends. Sonia would be there for Kate, no matter what.

32

As he put Tanya's heavy suitcase down in the hallway of Emma's flat, he
wished he had been given more notice before he had brought her here.
She had been crying her eyes out when she first got in the car, but Jay
soon realised they were tears of pure anger. Tanya was angry about the
fact she had had to leave her home. In fact, she was seething.

Jay was pleased that when the shit hit the fan, Tanya didn't have any love
for Billy, he had never been really sure of her feelings for him until now.
Some birds would say anything to get one over on their old man,
especially if they were after money or a bunk up. He had heard every line
possible in the past from every bird he had known. But Tanya was
different. She was high maintenance, that was true, but most women
were these days, they wanted everything they were entitled to and then
some more. He loved the way that Tanya wouldn't take any shit; he could
see how angry she was, and he had no doubt that she would get her own
back on Billy for the way he had treated her.

There was something else he felt too; something he couldn't put his
finger on. He had never been in love, so he was sure that it wasn't that.
But he did feel something: some sort of need for her. He thought about
her all the time that he was away from her; he couldn't get enough of her
smell, her taste, or the way she was in bed with him. He could tell that
she was a bit damaged, though, like himself, she had her issues. He could

see that she had that strength inside her, like he had, no one fucked with her; that's why he felt he knew her so well: she was the same as him. Emma's place was a shithole, and the stench that had hit him as he opened the door nearly made him gag. The curtains were shut, and there obviously hadn't been a window opened for months as the air was stale. Emma was a filthy bitch, and getting her to tidy up every now and again was too much for her by the looks of it. The smell and mess didn't bothered him normally, it was only now as he looked around and saw the flies buzzing around the sink, which was overflowing with dishes covered with dried-on food, and the fag ash all over the carpet, that he realised how filthy the place actually was.

Seeing Tanya's disappointed face and knowing that she deserved better, and that she clearly thought she did too, he decided that he would take her out for something to eat, and get that trampy cow to clean while they were gone.

"Hang on here a minute, babe," he said, leaving Tanya in the grubby hallway, obviously unaware that under no circumstances did she have any intention of stepping another foot forward in this stinking pigsty. She was desperately trying to hold her breath, and only took short breaths through her mouth when she had to. Tanya convinced herself that she was only here because she had nowhere else to go, and she was desperate. Looking at the dirty, stained carpet and the mould growing up the wall, she tried not to start crying again at the realisation of how bloody desperate things were for her now.

Billy would not take her back; she knew that for a fact. He had always said that if she ever cheated she was gone and picking his arch-rival would have just about put the final, rusty nail in the coffin. She had lost it all. Her beautiful house, her designer clothes: everything. She knew she hadn't been happy with Billy for a long time, but her things meant more to her than anything, and she had plodded on in the comfort that at least she would always have a roof over her head. Now her roof was over some little slag's head. Tanya fought to hold back her tears as she thought of that scrubber in her bed, under her Egyptian cotton sheets, using her Jo Malone toiletries; it made her blood boil.

Jay must be rolling in cash, she thought, although looking about it didn't seem like it. Tanya was far from stupid; even though he had never discussed his business dealings with her she had an idea what he was involved in. He would be making a fortune with the drugs side alone, and then there were the debt collecting and the girls. Tanya had made it her business to know what she was getting into. It hadn't made her judge him; at the end of the day, Billy was dodgy, but she had realised early on that Jay must be making some serious wedge, although judging by this dive the question was: where was he hiding it? He lived at home with his bleeding mother, for God's sake; from what she could work out, he had plenty of incomings and fuck all outgoings. Tanya was a cold-hearted bitch: she knew that more than anyone. Money made the world go round; if someone had no money, they were nothing: simple as. Tanya was surprised at the feelings she had begun to have for Jay. She normally went for men with a hard reputation, someone who had all the pieces on the board and who knew how to play the game. At first she had loved having Jay at her beck and call, loved having him come over and fuck her as soon as Billy was out of the house, on the floor that Billy had paid for. He was her bit of rough. She had had her most intense orgasms with Jay grinding on top of her, thinking about Billy catching her.

Something had changed, though, and it had shocked her when she realised it wasn't all about getting back at Billy for not being the man she had wanted him to be and for not giving her the attention she needed; she realised that she liked Jay, and that they could go far together. Jay didn't have the clout but she reckoned with a bit of guidance from her they could be good together, make real money. Tanya had seen enough of Billy's business dealings to recognise that it wasn't what you knew, it was who.

Opening Emma's bedroom door, Jay was surprised to realise that she wasn't at home. The last few times that he had been back to collect his money the place had been empty too, although it didn't look as though anything had been touched and he didn't think she would have the balls to do a runner, so she couldn't have gone far. He was starting to get a bit pissed off now though, and if it wasn't for Tanya standing in the hallway, he would probably have gone looking for her. Thinking that Emma had probably nipped out for some gear, and was probably doing God knows what to pay for it; he tried to put her out of his mind. She didn't have any friends anymore; he had seen to that; her confidence was at an all-time low, too, so she wouldn't speak to anyone even if she did bump into them. He would have to take Tanya to the cafe in the high street and then come back and clean the mess up: he would fucking kill Emma when she finally turned up. Tanya would not be happy about staying there, full stop, but it was all he could do for now. He would have to stop Emma's visitors for the time being for the few days that Tanya was there. His mind was in a whirl, there were so many things all at once to think about. He wondered what was going on: did Billy know that Tanya had been with him? Did Kate know, too? What would happen to his work for Billy? There were too many questions in around his head. He decided to call Kate. Her phone was diverted to her answer phone; he figured she was probably still in bed.

"Hurry up, for fuck's sake, Jay," Tanya called, getting seriously impatient.

"I'm here, babe," he said; returning to her side and then picking up his keys, he put his arm around her shoulder.

"You can't stay here, Tan, it ain't right. I'm going to book you into a hotel." He decided that her staying here with Emma would be more hassle than it was worth.

"Thank fucking God for that," Tanya almost smiled, "for a moment there, I thought you were going to make me stay here with the vomit stains and the cockroaches."

Picking up her bag from the hallway, he trudged behind her out to the car.

"There's a little hotel on the edge of town; a right little posh place it is; I'll stay there,' she said. "Think they have a spa, too, and I could do with a nice massage, my neck's frigging killing me."

Jay wasn't really listening; he was too worried about what to do next. Best thing to do was act normal, he thought; Billy might not know that it was him screwing around with Tanya. For all he knew he was worrying about nothing. He decided that as soon as he had dropped Tanya off at the hotel he would go home, and see what the situation was: surely if Billy was onto him, Jay would have been the first to know. Tanya had said that Billy had brought that bird from the club home, so that had to be it, as simple as that: Billy had traded Tanya in for a younger model. Chucking Tanya's case in the boot he felt calmer: yeah, things would be fine, he was sure. Opening the passenger door of his beamer for Tanya he grinned and winked.

"Your chariot awaits, madam."

33

Emma was a ghost of the girl she had been, seriously underweight, her once full chest now shrunken to nothing and her ribs visible through her nightshirt. She had endured so much for the past ten days and felt exhausted. The hospital had kept her in and helped to wean her off her drug addiction, she had been hallucinating badly for the first few days, and at times she had felt so disorientated she had imagined she was back in the flat with Jay. Thankfully the side effects were dying down, but she felt drained and tired all the time. The doctors had recommended medication to ease the symptoms of going 'cold turkey', but she had refused; she was determined to beat this herself.

The last six months of her life had become a blur and the bits she could remember were so horrible and dirty she didn't even want to remember them. She felt so ashamed by what she had become. Emma understood that Jay had done a lot of it, but she also understood how she had caused it to happen too. She had let him worm his way in, behind her friend's back, and she had put him above Kate, her best friend, and she had got what she deserved and more in the process.

Emma had never felt as happy as she had when she had seen Kate come into her hospital room that morning. She knew that she didn't deserve her friend's kindness after betraying her. She had been stupid. They had spent the last hour talking, crying and apologising. Kate had hugged Emma and promised her that from now on she would be looking after her. Emma had been worried about what Jay would say when he found out that she was in hospital and that Billy had helped her, but Billy was adamant that she shouldn't worry and that he was sorting him out, and even though she was frightened she hoped he was right.

Kate had had no idea of what had been going on; even Billy's words before he had brought her here were hard to take in. It was like he had been talking about a complete stranger, as if he had made an awful mistake. Seeing Emma was the only thing that had helped the reality to sink in.

Jay had done this: to Emma? He was an animal. Kate couldn't understand how he could do this to somebody; obviously his motive was money but surely there were other ways to earn it? She was in shock and felt as if she were going to pass out all the time, but looking at her brave friend in front of her, she knew that if Emma could come out of this the other end then she could. She would be strong, for Emma; she owed her that. Emma had been kept in for ten days, apparently that period was the worst for coming off drugs and she had been given round-the-clock care and regular counselling. After speaking to Billy and Kate, and advising them on the tough few weeks ahead of them, the doctors agreed that Emma could be discharged as an outpatient, but that she was to keep up with her counselling on a regular basis.

Leaving Emma to finish sorting out the paperwork with her case worker, Kate went out into the corridor, where Billy was waiting.

"You okay, babe?" Billy's concern was clear in his voice.

"Yeah, thanks, I guess I'm just in a bit of shock, that's all." Kate didn't know what to make of the whole thing. Jay was a monster. How could she have thought she loved him? How could she have let herself get pregnant by him? Her poor friend had been subjected to the sickest acts imaginable and would probably never get over them; Emma had been brought so low by Jay that she had tried to kill herself. Kate's guilt of not being there for her was overwhelming; a whole six months of being angry with Emma and cutting her off because of her weird behaviour, and her friend had needed her. Kate was determined not to cry, though: not here, not yet. "I don't know what to do, Billy, I can't go back to Jay's, I know Sonia said she wouldn't be letting him back in, but it just doesn't feel right going back there."

"Don't go worrying about Sonia. Ryan's going to be staying there for a bit, so she'll be looked after. Why don't you stay at my house; Tanya's gone, so why don't you and Emma have it?"

Kate knew that Sonia would be safe from Jay's torment with Ryan there; he was not a nice piece of work, and she knew that if he was on your side then you were safe as houses. As much as Kate loved Sonia, she knew she couldn't go back there, it had been her and Jay's place too and with the memories and all his stuff everywhere, it would just be too hard. Besides from now on she was going to be taking care of Emma, being the friend that she should have been all along. Moving into a place where Jay could turn up at any minute wouldn't be wise. Billy's flat would be perfect; she and Emma could move in and start again. Emma would need as much support as possible; everyone, including the doctors, couldn't believe how strongly she was fighting her addiction, they had never seen such determination; yet they had warned Kate that she could relapse, so she was going to keep a close eye on her. The flat would be perfect. Thanking Billy and giving him a hug she looked up at him tenderly.

"You're a great brother, Billy. I'm sorry I let him get in between us, between all of us, I truly am."

Billy shushed her, not wanting to hear another word; he was just glad she had finally seen what Jay was capable of and hoped that she would now move on and be free of him once and for all.

"Let's go back in and let Emma know the good news, bet she'll be over the moon at having you as a flatmate," he smiled.

Back in the room Emma was delighted, she had been so worried at the thought of having to go back and live with her parents, but this would be perfect. She knew that she would have to tell her parents the truth at some point but she decided that she wanted to be a little stronger in her head when she did. Billy had lied to the staff at the hospital when he had bought her in, he had told them that he was her brother, her next of kin. She was thankful for that, as she couldn't bear the thought of her parents seeing her here like this. She was so glad that Kate was here, she really needed her friend more than anything or anyone else at the moment.

She just wanted to get her life back again: be normal and do normal things. Right now the thought of a hot bath and dinner in front of the telly with her mate seemed like absolute heaven.

34

The little hotel was swanky by name and swanky by nature. Fancy chocolates on the pillows, mini-bar full to the brim, the toilet roll was folded into neat triangles. Mind you, none of it was complimentary, as they would have you believe, not at two hundred and fifty pounds a night. They had checked in yesterday and had a little meal in the bar; that had cost a small fortune, considering it had barely been big enough to feed a poxy budgie, but Tanya had cheered up a bit, so Jay thought that it had been worth every penny.

His plan had been just to drop Tanya off, but now as the sunlight beamed through the edge of the curtains he realised that she had had other plans: she had been persuasive last night. He had to get back now though, he hadn't seen Kate in three days, and although there had been times he had been away from home for longer he wanted to know what was going on, if anything. Looking at Tanya lying next to him, her tanned naked body all snug under the sheets, it was hard to drag himself away. Being careful not to disturb her, he quietly put his clothes on and took his car keys from the side table. Leaving a note on the coffee table saying that he would call her later, he left her some cash for pampering at the spa, closed the door gently behind him and made his way home.

Ryan couldn't physically function in the morning without a cup of tea with four sugars, he was like a bear with a sore head most of the time anyway, but catch him before he'd woken himself up with his mug of "cha" in the morning and you'd be in trouble. He glanced once more out of the window, watching the beamer pull up outside.

Billy had filled Ryan in on what had been happening with Jay: not only the drugs and debt collecting that had been done in Billy's name, but the girls, including his sister's best mate, Emma. He had been only too happy to stay at Sonia's and keep the scummy fucker out. The couch had been nice and comfy and Sonia was just knocking up a nice fry up for him, she had been keeping the teas coming since he had arrived yesterday. She was a lovely woman; he could see that. His mum had been a waste of space. She had had no time for him or his brother and they had been left alone frequently when they had been growing up, often nearly starving and having to fend for themselves. How the fuck someone like Jay could have such a lovely mother like this one, God only knew.

To be fair, none of the lads had taken to Jay when he had first come on board. However, they had all been told by Billy that that was the way it was going to be and they were to like it or lump it. Jay had only been given errands, really: nothing major. They certainly hadn't given him any "in" on the real money that there was to be earned.

All of the lads knew that Billy thought the world of his sister, and that was the only reason he had put them in the position of having to work alongside with such a loser, but it had at first made everyone question Billy's priorities. They had worked alongside him for years, and he always came up trumps with deals and connections. He had a real way of talking people into things and getting exactly what he wanted: he was a perfect businessman. Billy had wanted to keep an eye on Jay, and that he had: he knew everything about the crooked little shit now. Billy was currently making sure that Jay Shaw didn't fuck up his sister's life any more than he had already: cue Ryan. After what he had been told about Jay and his scummy ways, it was the least he could do to help Billy out; knowing that none of them had to put up any pretence anymore and be civil to the sly little fucker was the icing on the proverbial cake.

Hearing Jay scraping his key at the front door, Ryan put his cup in the sink, and gave a now pale-looking Sonia a reassuring look; he knew he had the look of a man that could sort anything, and he was in control of this situation.

Trying another key, Jay couldn't work out why he couldn't get in; he only had a couple of keys on the fob, and one of them had to work. Realising he was getting nowhere, he realised that the dozy bitch Sonia must have changed the locks: well, that answered one question then, didn't it? The shit had obviously hit the fan. What Sonia thought she was doing getting involved he just couldn't fathom, he had as much right to be here as her: if it wasn't for him, she would have fuck all to her name. It might be her house, but he had done the place up; he had bought some massive fuck-off telly for her to watch her poxy soaps on: what was she fucking playing at? Jay was about to start booting the door in, when it opened. He was confronted by a large, beefy-looking Ryan. Jay didn't have a chance to ask

Ryan what the fuck he was doing in his house, before he registered what was going on, he was slammed onto the floor, with Ryan's fists raining down on him, blow after blow.

"Next time you show your face around here, boy, I'm going to cut your fucking throat, do you hear me? You're not fucking welcome. If I hear of you even looking at Sonia or Kate the wrong way, I'm going to personally cut you up into tiny little pieces and feed you to my fucking dogs. Do I make myself clear?"

Jay could just about see Ryan's face; it was screwed up and red with hate and anger. Just when he thought the punches had stopped, Ryan leant down and whispered:

"And this one's for Emma, you slimy fucking cunt."

Getting up and launching his size-eleven boot into Jay's stomach, he then spat at him before turning and walking back into the house and double-locking the door, more for Sonia's benefit than anything: he had a strong feeling that Jay wouldn't be so stupid as to come back again.

Jay struggled up off the floor. It had been a pounding all right, but he knew Ryan's reputation, and that was a little tap compared to what that man was capable of. Glad that the warning was over, he scurried back to his car; hoping that as few people as possible had just witnessed his humiliation, he pulled away so quickly that his tyres screeched. He was aware that his own mother had probably stood and watched that whole scene, along with half the fucking neighbourhood, twitching their curtains and probably loving the show. He pulled up a few streets away and, after wiping the blood from his nose, he rested his head on the steering wheel.

Shit, they knew about Emma.

He knew he was up fucking Shit Street without a paddle. Billy has dumped Tanya, now it was Jay's turn to be in the firing line. He decided to make a few calls to his contacts to see exactly how far this thing had gone.

Robbie Challis had been expecting Jay's call. Billy had paid him a visit a few days earlier, after following Jay. Robbie had been very humble to Billy and had explained that he had thought Jay was working for Billy. Billy had felt sorry for the bloke, it was clear Jay had mugged him off and was using Billy's name to do so. He asked Robbie how much he had given in cash to Jay, and Robbie figured it at about four grand; his last lot had been the week before, and they were busting their guts to make the five grand a week Jay demanded.

"Tell you what, mate, you keep it, on the condition that you tell Jay the next time he calls round that you do work for me, and that from now on he'll have to go through me, too: understand?" Billy reasoned.

"Yeah." Robbie was shitting himself; he could see Billy was really pissed off; he was glad that he wasn't his target.

"What about Jay, though, he's bound to kick off, Billy."
Looking around the tiny flat, seeing the scales on the table and the collection of mobile phones next to them, Billy could see that this guy

was out of his depth and just some small-time druggie, Jay always tried to pick on the weak. Billy grinned, deciding that Robbie could keep his money, he wanted no part of it: he had bigger fish to fry.

"If he calls, just pass the message on. Any trouble from that ponce, you call me, right. As far as I'm concerned, you and me have no axe to grind, mate, you get on with your business, it doesn't interest me one bit, but you make sure you tell Jay you're working for me from now on, got it, and trust me, once he hears that you will get no trouble at all, mate." Dropping his card onto the table, he let himself out.

"Right." Breathing a huge sigh, Robbie was relieved that he no longer had to break his neck trying to get Jay's dough together before he could think about his own money. So when the call from Jay came in, Robbie Challis enjoyed every word. As he inhaled one of the biggest spliffs he had ever rolled, this one of course for celebration purposes, he said down the phone:

"Jay? Sorry, Jay who?"
Riled, Jay thought the bloke must be truly fucking stoned to be talking like this.

"You listen to me, you fucking waster," he began, but before he could finish his sentence he was interrupted by a slow cackle.

"Why don't you just fuck off, Jay, you poncing cunt," Challis said, slowly and clearly so that Jay could take every syllable in. "Billy says he's personally collecting the money from now on, any problems with that and you take it up with him. So you, you fucking mug, can do one."

201

Hearing the dialling tone, Jay realised that Challis had hung up. He was shitting himself, his worst thoughts had been confirmed and he had a terrible feeling that this was just the start of things to come. This was turning into a bitch of a day.

35

The saucy brunette was using every trick in the book. She had on a low-cut top and a very pert pair of breasts spilled over of it every time she leaned forward. She had been flicking her hair and pouting for the best part of the evening but, to be honest, Paul found it more entertaining than anything else. She was a very attractive girl, he would be a liar to deny that, and it was good for his ego to know that he still had it, but he had met dozens like her and she was nothing special.

It never failed to surprise him that so many girls tried it on with him as soon as they realised this club was his. He was more shocked that they seemed to be completely unaware of how obvious they were. Gold-diggers of the worst kind, they were more transparent than the fucking windows.

Peeling himself away from the disappointed girl at the bar, insisting he had work that needed his attention, he made his way to the sanctuary of his office. Pouring himself a whiskey, he went through his e-mails half-heartedly. He glanced at the clock and then back at the computer screen; tapping his fingers on the desk, he chuckled to himself. He had just realised that if anyone had been here to see him they would have just witnessed the look of a lovesick man. He knew that he had been doing nothing but mope, he could admit to himself that he was feeling lost without Kate. She was having a few days off, she had rung and explained that she needed to help her friend, and after hearing the story Paul said he would help her in any way possible. Kate had also asked whether, when she came back to work, she could bring Emma for a trial behind the bar to see if she was up to it. He had agreed without question; they could always do with extra hands, the place was booming, and if Kate thought Emma was up to it that was good enough for him. Paul had told Kate that if there was anything she needed she should call him. She hadn't, though. Which was, obviously, a good thing, but he had hoped that she would have called by now. He missed her. She had her brother to look out for her, but Paul was her friend: they had become close. He knew that if he hadn't heard anything from her, though, it meant she was okay.

Paul realised that he wanted Kate to call just so he could hear her voice. He also realised that he had, somehow when he wasn't looking, turned into a soppy bastard. Laughing once again, he knew that at some point he had fallen for her. He hadn't known until now how much he loved being around her, working with her, laughing with her, talking for hours about anything and everything. He hadn't felt like this about anyone for a long time and it had really shocked him. He had only been in love once, and he had been hurt badly: some might say beyond repair. His ex, Caroline, had taken him for a complete ride, she had cheated on him with anyone that had a pulse. He had been oblivious, completely unaware of what had been going on behind his back throughout their relationship. He had been so busy trying to build up his career, working every hour that he could, that he had no idea what she had been getting up to. Paul had wanted desperately to make a decent living so that he could provide for her and for his now broken family. Sophia, his beautiful baby... it broke his heart to think of her, she deserved more than what they had given her. It had been such a mess, when he finally found out the truth about Caroline sleeping her way through the city, through a work contact of all people who was trying to do him a favour, he had confronted Caroline, half expecting her to be sorry. At the least she could have sounded apologetic. He expected her to beg him to stay with her and to say that she had made an awful mistake. Paul had been full of rage at the betrayal, yet somewhere inside, he thought that if she was sorry and if she hadn't meant to hurt him, maybe he could fix things. After all, he had done nothing but work twenty-four seven for months; even if it had been for both of them, he hadn't been there for her. The last thing he had expected when he had confronted her was her laughing in his face and sneering at him that it was entirely his fault. Caroline had blamed him for all of it; none of it had been her fault. She had screamed at him in anger that it was he who had driven her to sleep with other men. He had neglected her; he had never been there; she had been lonely. She reeled off a list of her conquests whilst slugging a gin and tonic, all the time staring into his eyes triumphantly. He had stood in front of her a broken man, realising that this was nothing more than a game. Paul had tried to be a good husband; she had tried to score points. He had known then that it was all pointless; it had been for nothing. Paul had never known her. So he had walked away, and he had never looked back. Since then he had never trusted a woman, and he had thrown himself even more into building his career. He had found success, had more money than he could have wished for, but he had learnt the hard way that there was more to life than money and clubs. If he did get a chance at love again, he would put that first above everything. He wouldn't make the mistake of thinking money was showing your love. Money wouldn't keep you warm after a hard day at work, and he didn't want to grow old alone.

Paul never mentioned his beautiful Sophia to anyone; she was his private business. He had kept her and everything about her close to his heart, but he had felt lately that he could tell Kate, they had become so close; there were times when he almost had told her. She had her own stuff going on, though, what with her losing the baby, and he had never felt it the right time: one day maybe he would.

Deciding rather than moping in the office all alone, he would pick up the phone to give her a call to see how she was doing, he downed his whiskey and dialled.

"Ooh, someone has a little crush on you," giggled Emma. Kate blushed as she put down her mobile phone. She had been on the phone to Paul for at least twenty minutes, catching up on the gossip from the club. Although it had only been a few days, she felt as though she had been away forever.

"Don't be so silly; he's my boss, and he's just checking to see how I am." Kate could feel her cheeks burning and knew that her friend was nowhere near convinced.

"A concerned boss, eh…." Emma was laughing. "Oh Kate, you really are oblivious, aren't you, love?"

"What?" Kate exclaimed. "You have it all wrong, Ems, you really do; he's just a nice guy, and he's just making sure I'm okay. Not all men are after something, you know." Immediately regretting her words, she quickly added, "Oh, Emma, I didn't mean anything by that, honest…."

"Don't be daft, Kate, I know you didn't. I'm sure that he is a lovely guy. I mean, from all that you've told me; not that you talk about him every five minutes, or anything." Laughing even louder, she ducked down as Kate threw a cushion across the lounge; just missing her it landed on the couch next to her. Kate laughed too and realised that it was the first time she had seen Emma apparently happy since they had left the hospital, including in the last few nights when they had stayed up late and spoken about everything. It had been hard for Kate to take it all in: she had no idea about what Emma had been through. Kate had been angry at first when Emma had first told her about sleeping with Jay behind her back, but Kate realised now that Jay was persuasive, and it had all been part of his plan. Emma had just been sucked into it all. Kate had found it hard to listen to some of Emma's painful experiences, such as the time when Emma had been tied up and beaten by some psycho, and was even more freaked out when Emma told her that Jay had known about it, he had been, by all accounts, completely responsible for it. It sickened her to her stomach. Emma had also been beside herself with grief when Kate told her about losing the baby, but Kate had said as scary and devastating as it was maybe it was one of God's small mercies, as she had been spared from being tied to Jay forever. The fact that she could no longer have kids she kept to herself; Emma had too much of her own stuff to deal with right now without Kate adding her own problems to the list. Besides, Kate had been trying to block it out of her mind, saying it out loud would mean she would have to deal with it, and she wasn't ready for that yet. Kate could see that Emma was struggling without the drugs, but she was determined to stay clean. The doctor at the hospital who had treated her said he had rarely seen anyone who had become so dependent on drugs leave without medication to help them through the cold turkey process, but then he also added he had never seen anyone as adamant as Emma about staying clean.

"You know," smiled Kate, "I think having someone like Paul watching out for me is not such a bad thing."

"Oh?" Emma raised her eyebrows.

"Yeah, I know I have Billy looking out for me, but sometimes I have to be so careful about what I say around him, you know how over-protective he can be."

Emma nodded. Anyone who knew them knew that Billy guarded Kate with his life; she had to admit though from what Kate had told her that Billy seemed to be easing off on her lately. He had given them this place, for starters, and he had given them space, just a few text messages every now and again just to check that they were both alright.

"Well, Paul is just so easy to talk to; he doesn't judge me or quiz me about stuff, he just says his piece and that's that; he's been a really good friend."

Emma couldn't help but think that if Kate actually filmed herself when she spoke about this guy she would realise how her eyes lit up, that she was smiling and glowing. There were definitely some feelings there, but knowing Kate, it was far too soon to push it, especially after everything that had happened with Jay. As much of a shit that man was, Kate had loved him, although now Kate questioned how she ever had, now realising that she knew nothing about the real Jay Shaw. Kate needed time to get over that relationship.

Hearing the doorbell ring, Kate jumped off the sofa, placing her hand on her friend's shoulder as she went to open the door, she whispered,

"Just be honest with them: remember they love you and they are here to help."

Kate opened the door to Emma's parents. She had rung them earlier and told them that Emma needed to see them urgently; she had warned them that what they would hear would not be easy to take in and they had sounded worried, although thankfully they had not questioned her any further. Emma sat nervously in the lounge, bracing herself for a very long, painful evening.

36

"What the fuck do you mean: you're over?"

Tanya rubbed her temples; she felt her headache returning. She had had the most heavenly massage and had finally started to feel more chilled; at least her shoulders were no longer up round her ears with the stress of everything: and now this. If only she hadn't been so quick to come back to her room, if she had gone for a nice drink at the bar, she could have given herself an extra half an hour of feeling like a normal person. But here she was, back in the room, looking at Jay's swollen and bloodied face, as he sat slumped on the bed like a wounded soldier.

"Just like I said, Tan, I'm fucked, good and proper. Billy has seen to it that I can't get back into my house, I can't do business with most of my fucking contacts, and I no longer fucking work for him: but that goes without fucking saying, obviously."

Throwing his keys onto the table, Jay groaned at the sudden movement, feeling pain shooting through his chest, he'd probably had a couple of his ribs done in.

Tanya paced the room, her relaxing massage now feeling like a distant memory, like she'd never had it. She knew how Billy worked, he would close down all of the options for them both, and no one would look at Jay after this, let alone do business with him. He would have to start at the bottom, like a fucking loser, dealing outside schools or in grotty little parks for pocket money. Tanya was too old for that shit, and she wanted more than pennies in her purse. Walking over to the mini-bar, she poured them both drinks: she really needed one, anyway.

"We need to put our thinking caps on Jay, and fast. If we let Billy do this to us, let him treat us like fucking mugs, we're not coming back up from it. People will think they can treat us like fucking cunts, Jay, and I'm not having it."

Taking the drink she offered him, Jay swallowed it down in one, enjoying the burn at the back of his throat and the warmness that seeped through him, slightly numbing his pain. He looked over at Tanya, now deep in thought; he had noticed how she hadn't once asked him if he was okay, hadn't once shown any compassion at all. Alright, it was only a kicking, he had been dealt worse in his time, he had a feeling that Ryan could and would have wiped the pavement with him had he wanted to, so he must have been under strict orders from Billy boy. Tanya was merciless, though, she was like a bloke in that respect; she knew what she wanted and she wouldn't stop until she had it. Even though a kind word wouldn't have gone a miss, he respected her for it; she was shrewd in that she was already thinking of ways out of this situation for them both. He had never had that before from someone; he had had to fend for himself. Even his dad had used him, they had never worked as a team; his dad had made money out of him and used his innocence for his own gains, playing the father-and-son card whenever possible to get Jay to do whatever he asked. Tanya didn't look like she had taken any shit from anyone. Pouring them both another drink, Tanya looked at him impatiently.

211

"Do you need to go to hospital, or what?"

Rolling his eyes, he started laughing, really laughing; his ribs were so sore it made tears spring to his eyes, which made him laugh more.

"What? What's so bloody funny?" Tanya demanded.

Jay was laughing so hard he couldn't speak; good old Tanya; right on cue, just about as caring and sympathetic as she was going to get.

"Nothing, babe, just glad you're on my side, because you're fucking scary right now."

She laughed, finally understanding his joke, and passed him his glass.

"A couple of them and you'll feel a whole lot better, Jay, trust me."

They sat in the bedroom for the rest of the afternoon, draining the mini-bar. As they drank, Jay told Tanya that he had the best part of fifty thousand pounds stashed away. She did her maths, and although she was very happy that she had been right all along and Jay did have a bit of cash stashed away somewhere, she also knew that it was peanuts in the grand scheme of things. They needed real money. If they were going to fuck off into the sunset, they needed a hell of a lot more than fifty grand.

Tanya sent down for a couple of bottles of champagne; she always managed to think better after a few drinks inside her, besides what she had on her mind was worth celebrating. Jay was gobsmacked at her little plan; he couldn't believe Tanya could even think about something so... well, fucking brilliant. She knew better than anyone else how to hit Billy O'Conner where it fucking hurt.

37

The music was thumping; once again the DJ was playing the top tunes and had nearly every person in the place going mental for them. The dance floor was packed, as it was most nights. Kate couldn't believe the length of the guest list: it was almost as long as her arm. Looking at the main bar, she saw Emma and was again astounded. In the three weeks that Emma had been out of hospital, Kate had witnessed such a change in her. It was amazing; like she had her old friend back. Emma had her moments, of course, but Kate would have been more worried if she hadn't have had them. Emma occasionally got tearful or would want to talk things through, but Kate was there for her. She had even got her a job behind the bar, so they worked together too.

Emma had had a real heart-to-heart with her parents and it had been very emotional for them all, she was stunned when her parents had admitted that they had always thought something wasn't quite right, but they just couldn't put their finger on what. Emma hadn't blamed them, as she had done her upmost to keep her dirty lifestyle a secret. They had promised to keep more of an eye on her in the future and told her they didn't judge or blame her, that they loved her. They were such old-fashioned parents that she had been surprised when they hadn't judged her. They had given her all the support she needed. She had sobbed when she heard that, imagining that they would both have been completely disgraced by her. Emma had had to try really hard to stop craving the drugs, but every time she needed something, to take the edge off, she pictured Jay Shaw's disgusting face and to spite him, to beat him and his hold over her, she took deep breaths and got through it. She would show him, alright. However, no one had seen Jay for weeks, and Kate had told Emma that he had done a runner with Tanya. Emma didn't care who he had buggered off with, as long as she didn't have to set eyes on him again.

Catching Kate's eye, Emma smiled. She loved working at Goldie's, and now she had met Paul, she could see why Kate talked about him every five minutes: he was hot. Not that she would even be looking at a guy in that way for a very long time. But she was grateful to Kate for everything she was doing and she was determined to see if she could work her magic and get the pair together. Paul had it bad for Kate: that much was obvious. Kate wouldn't admit it, but Emma was sure that even she had noticed how he always watched her; he was always laughing and joking with her. Kate, being Kate, swore he was just a friend and that they didn't feel that way about each other. Smiling, Emma gave Kate a little wave before turning back to the ever-growing queue of thirsty clubbers.

Kate could see that Emma being here was doing her the world of good, she would have her confidence back in no time. Kate hadn't heard a thing from Jay, but to be honest she didn't really have much of a feeling about that. She felt numb about the whole Jay situation. You can't really love someone when everything they do is behind your back and everything they stand for hurts you. He was a stranger, he felt like a figment of her imagination, because their relationship had never been real: everything about him had been fake. He was a coward of the worst kind; he couldn't even stand by his actions, everything he did was in secret behind her back; as far as she was concerned, he was a poor excuse for a man. The Jay she thought she had loved was all in her head. He wasn't the animal that she had found him out to be. She had changed her number, and Billy and Paul were watching out for her. She had called in to Sonia a few times, and promised that she would stay in touch.

"Of course I will, silly; you're like a mum to me, Sonia," she had said.

Sonia had let tears slide down her cheeks at the kind words; Kate knew she loved the bones of her. She was a decent honest girl, way too good for Jay. Sonia had cut Jay from her life like dead wood. He was nothing to her now. Sonia had felt stupid: she had constantly tried to gain his approval and love. He was bad through and through, just like his father; rotten to the core.

Kate just wanted life to get back to normal; surely it wasn't too naïve to think that now that everything was out in the open they could all start again.

Turning back to her bar, Kate smiled at the local hot-shot sitting in front of her, lining up drinks like there was no tomorrow. She loved her job with a passion, and as she poured the next round of shots, she thought how intrigued she was to know what Paul wanted to talk to her about tomorrow. He had said earlier that he wanted to have a chat and asked if she could come in an hour or so before her shift. She wondered what it was about. Things at the club were going well; they were a fantastic team. Kate knew that he appreciated and used most of her ideas, and she had seen first-hand how busy the place had become. Goldie's had made a real name for itself; this was the place everyone wanted to be and Kate was thrilled to be part of it. It helped keep her mind off everything that was going on, and that was a godsend.

"There you go darling, have one for yourself." The man winked as he placed a fifty pound note in her hand, and then, just for good measure, looked her straight in the eye and licked his lips. Smiling out of politeness, while thinking what a transparent prat the bloke was, Kate thanked the guy for the very generous tip and popped it into her overflowing tip jar under the counter. She smiled even more at the thought of the gorgeous designer handbag she had spotted in a boutique on Oxford Road, the perfect present to help cheer up Emma, and the rate her tips were coming in lately she would be treating herself to one too. Upstairs in the gentlemen's club, Billy was also smiling, while enjoying a few drinks with the lads. Ditching Tanya had been one of the best things he had done. He hadn't realised how much of a drain she had been, and after her trying to make a mug out of him with Jay he was well out of it. Candice had done her best to help him take his mind off the whole thing; it was just business to her, but that was cool with him. He had his needs, and she filled them nicely. He was quite liking being single. The house was quiet without Kate, but he was pleased that she had accepted the flat and thought that living with Emma would be great for them both. Kate was safe and that was the main thing, at the end of the day. He had also made a conscious decision to stop being so overbearing when it came to her, he had been so close to losing her because of that and he wouldn't be putting himself in that situation again. Thanks to his mate Ryan, Jay was officially off the radar and had taken Tanya with him, no doubt, so Billy could finally relax. Laughing at Jonny taking the piss out of his brother Lee and telling all their funny stories of the latest little business trip, Billy picked up his pint. He was glad to have these guys around him; they had his back. Life was good.

38

His palms were sweating. Paul took a deep breath, trying to control his nerves. He wasn't sure whether letting his feelings be known to Kate was the right thing to do, but to be honest he wasn't sure if he could keep them to himself for much longer. He had to fight the urge he had to hold her when he saw her looking upset, although she did a good job of trying to hide it. At times he could see that she looked lost, and it took every ounce of his willpower to stop himself from wrapping his arms around her and telling her she would be alright. Yesterday, he had felt sure that now was the right to time to tell her, but today he wasn't feeling confident. He was losing his bottle. What if she didn't find him attractive, or simply didn't look at him that way? Kate was nice and kind, she would never set out to lead someone on: she was just so sweet to everyone, what if the vibes he had picked up from her were just her being nice and nothing else? Paul was going to tell her how he felt and tell her about Sophia, his beautiful little daughter. He knew that he wanted Kate, but she would have to accept that he had a child. They were a package, but after everything that Kate had gone through losing her baby, Paul was not sure how Sophia would be received by Kate.

Pacing the room, he looked at the clock in his office, it was quarter to eight; even if he did call her to say not to bother coming in, he would probably be too late, she would probably have left by now. He quickly poured himself a shot of whiskey from the bottle he kept in the top drawer and gulped it down in one then made a note to calm it down on the drinking front at work, it was slowly becoming a habit and not one he intended on keeping. He liked to stay in control; after tonight, he was going to try and curb it at work. Drinking the whiskey, he was surprised that it did nothing to stop his nerves; he felt like a fifteen-year-old schoolboy going on his first date. Strumming his fingers on the desk, he glanced around as he waited for her. The place was immaculate, he had never seen it so organised. Normally there were piles of paper stacked up all over the place and falling on the floor, bills scattered amongst junk mail, scrap paper and e-mails. Kate had devised a great filing system, so everything from wages, stock takes and invoices all had their place and the whole club was running more smoothly. They made a great team, she was so good at the things he wasn't. Paul had the contacts, the funds and the vision, but he had realised that he had needed someone to work alongside him, doing the organisation, event planning and PR; he was crap at that. He just hoped that by telling her how he felt, he wouldn't make her run a million miles from him; the last thing he would want to do was scare her off; even if she didn't want him, he hoped she would want to be part of the club.

Across town, Emma was winding Kate up as she was getting ready to leave. She had done her hair and makeup and was wearing a new white blouse that wasn't too revealing but flattered her figure and looked very stylish.

"Ooh, going in early for a bit of one-on-one?" Emma giggled. Kate rolled her eyes but then grinned.

"I told you, it's not like that; I think Paul just wants to run something by me."

"Yeah, I bet he does," said Emma sarcastically, winking. Secretly hoping that the two would get it on, they were clearly besotted with each other, she hoped that all her hinting and teasing would push the idea along a bit in Kate's head. Paul Goldie would be perfect for Kate, Emma just knew it; he was a real man, a gentleman. Someone like Paul could show Kate that not all men were cheating shits; some of them were decent, with a backbone. Keeping her fingers crossed, Emma added,

"Perhaps he has an indecent proposal for you?"

"Well, I'll find out soon enough, don't you worry, and when you get in to work later, I promise you'll be the first person I tell." Smiling as confidently as she could, Kate opened the front door but then glanced back at her friend.

"Don't get too excited though, hun, it's probably just some event he's planning, probably wants my opinion on it, something like that. See you in a bit." Once the front door had closed, Emma grinned and shook her head.

Boy oh boy, they both had it bad.

Kate made her way to the club. It was only a ten-minute walk and the evening was gorgeous, the sun shining as it set and everyone Kate passed looking happy, it was funny how a bit of sunshine did that. Kate didn't feel particularly happy, though, she felt anxious. She wasn't sure what Paul wanted to see her about, and she had definitely felt that he had been acting very strangely towards her over the past few days, almost as if he was trying to avoid her, as if he felt a bit uncomfortable around her. Kate hadn't wanted to worry Emma by saying anything, not now they had moved in and had the flat together, but she had an awful feeling that he was going to let her go, that he didn't need her to work for him. She knew she had done a fantastic job, and she was almost sure that she hadn't done anything wrong, but she just couldn't be certain. She didn't know what else could it be, and he had looked serious when he had asked her to come in before her shift. She also had heard him talking about a Sophia on the phone, and Kate had felt a knot of jealousy in her stomach at his tone. He hadn't mentioned a girlfriend, and Kate had never seen him with anyone, but whoever this Sophia was she meant something to him, as he spoke her name in a tone that made Kate realise that no matter how she might be feeling, he liked someone else. There had been moments when she had wondered at Paul's thoughts towards her, but she had believed that he was too much of a gentleman to mix business with pleasure, so she had not pursued the matter. Clearly he was a decent guy who looked out for her: nothing more and nothing less.

Glancing at her watch, she saw that it was just gone eight; she picked up her pace: she wanted to get this over with, whatever it was about.

39

Arriving at the club, Emma was dying to find out how the little meeting had gone. She had her money on Paul declaring his undying love and sweeping Kate into his muscly arms, with them both running off into the sunset and living happily ever after: well, something like that. Kate had been supposed to text the minute the meeting was over, so that Emma could find out what had been said, but maybe it was a more serious matter than she had thought, or maybe it hadn't gone well, as Emma had not heard anything. She wandered around a bit but didn't spot Kate, maybe Romeo and Juliet were in a cupboard somewhere, having a bit of time out. Emma was early for her shift, so she decided she would grab a quick drink before she started. Plopping herself up on a stool, she asked Jake, the barman she had been working alongside for the past few weeks, who was a seriously funny guy, for an orange juice with lots of ice and gratefully sipped it while she caught up on the gossip of the evening so far. Then she spotted Paul coming towards her with the mother of all frowns etched on his forehead: it was not the look of a happy man. She felt a bit guilty that she was sitting on her butt, even though technically she wouldn't be paid for her shift for another fifteen minutes. She wondered if he had assumed she was drinking alcohol while she was supposed to be working, and maybe that was why he seemed so hacked off. But as he approached her, she could see that he didn't even seem to have noticed what she was doing.

"Hey Paul, you okay?" Emma was a little concerned, as she could see Paul was very pissed off, and it was the last thing she had expected. She had thought after seeing Kate, he would be floating around the place, smitten.

"I will be." Leaning down to her ear, he continued, "Can you let Kate know: next time she decides not to bother turning up for work, a phone call wouldn't go amiss. I wouldn't mind, only we're short staffed as it is, and I've been running round like a blue-arsed fly for the last hour." Paul was hurt, but he didn't want to show it, he was trying to play it down, despite his anger bubbling away. He was gutted that Kate hadn't shown up, and thought that she had guessed what he was going to say to her and had tried to save them both from what would have been an awkward knockback. He was crushed, but he guessed he had his answer. The only time Kate had not turned up for work was when she had been in hospital; she never threw sickies, so he deduced that she wasn't interested in him.

Emma shifted uncomfortably on her bar stool.

"I don't understand, Paul," she said quietly, feeling worried. "She did leave for work. She said that you had asked her to come in a bit earlier, and she left about eight: almost two hours ago."

Reaching into her pocket, she dialled Kate's new mobile. Almost whispering now, she looked at him, as she said:

"It's switched off; she never switches it off."

All of a sudden, Emma was seriously worried; she had a very bad feeling; something was not right. Kate had left the house hours ago; she wouldn't disappear like that.

Paul had known Kate long enough to know that it wasn't in her nature to just let people down; if she said she would be somewhere then she would be, or she would have at least called. He realised that he shouldn't have been so quick to think that she had stood him up, and maybe he should have called her earlier. Feeling concerned, he decided to phone Billy. Trying to remain calm, he turned back to Emma and said:

"Why don't you go and see if you can get Jimmy or Eve in, see if they're both up for an extra shift tonight, their numbers are in the book in my office, it's double bubble." Heading outside to have a cigarette, Paul called Billy's number. Maybe something had happened and Billy was with Kate right now. Hoping that he was right, he waited for Billy to pick up his phone.

Billy was in The Dog, having a few pints to start his night off in the right direction; it was becoming a nightly routine to be out drinking with the lads. The pub was packed, the darts team were all out on the lash after winning a big tournament, and he was hardly able to hear Paul's voice when he called. Instantly, Billy knew something had happened, he had a sixth sense when it came to Kate, she wasn't the type to let people down by not turning up for work; besides, she loved it at the club, he didn't even think that she looked at it as "work"; she enjoyed it so much you would have to drag her away from the place. Feeling sick, he asked everyone he came across if they had seen her but to no avail. He made his way to Goldie's hoping that she would turn up there, that maybe, just maybe, she had been side-tracked into talking to someone, or knowing her she had helped someone out and been delayed that way. In his heart of hearts, though, as he made his way down the high street to the club, he knew something bad had happened. All this shit with Jay suddenly seemed a bit too clear-cut now.

40

Tanya had organised a cottage for them about a mile out of London, in the middle of nowhere. It was the perfect location. She had booked it over the Internet using false names so that there would be no way of tracing it to them, and they had paid the owners cash. The house was on a couple of acres of land, very conveniently tucked away behind overgrown hedgerows at the top of an old, beaten track. Jay found it hard to believe that the "real world" was going on just an hour or so away, he felt as if he was on the set for Little House on the fucking Prairie or something. All they were missing were chickens.

The cottage was tiny, and cluttered, there were frilly doyleys under most ornaments. He had been amazed that there was a TV set in the lounge; the place looked so old-fashioned he was even more amazed the owners knew televisions had been invented. With just two small bedrooms, a small lounge and kitchenette and a dingy basement, it would serve its purpose. The plan had gone well; very well, in fact, it had been almost too easy. Jay had been more than a little uncertain about the whole thing, but Tanya was adamant that this was the way forward for them both. She was determined to get back at Billy; hell hath no fury, and all that.

Jay had been surprised at Tanya's level of malice: surprised but definitely impressed. She was a cold-hearted bitch when she wanted to be. The more Jay had thought about it, the more he realised that she was right, though; maybe doing this was the only way to hit Billy-Boy straight in the bollocks.

The plan was simple. They had decided to kidnap Kate, rough her up, frighten the shit out of Billy and bleed cash out of him. Tanya said Billy was good for at least a hundred grand, he wouldn't gamble with his sister's life. Besides, he owed Tanya.

Getting Kate to the cottage hadn't been too much of a problem, much to Jay's relief. The stupid cow had believed him when he pulled over next to the side of the road where she was walking to work that evening and begged her to listen to him. He had told her that he had problems: real problems. He had put on his best "feel sorry for me" face, and faked tears, swearing that he was getting counselling to sort himself out. He had pleaded with her to spare him a few minutes and told her that he would completely understand her walking away and never seeing him again, but he insisted that she hear him out for one last time first: just a few minutes and he would be gone forever. He had said that he owed it to her after all he had done, he owed her an explanation.

Looking nervously around the now not-so-busy street, hoping there was no one around to see her as she knew they would think she was a complete mug for even contemplating listening to Jay, Kate felt hesitant: should she or not? Seeing that the coast was clear, and thinking it would do no harm other than take up a few moments of her time, she got into the passenger seat. Jay did owe her an explanation, she figured, she had all sorts of questions running about her head and to be honest, some answers would be good: she needed closure, once and for all.

Jay had driven for five minutes down the road to a quiet lay-by so that they could "talk". Before she had known what was going on, he had locked the doors and placed a cloth over her nose and mouth. She had struggled for about thirty seconds, regretting dearly that she had been once again sucked in by this animal, before giving in. He had soaked the cloth in chloroform, as Tanya had instructed, and after Kate had inhaled enough of it, he was home and dry. It was just as easy as Tanya had said it would be.

Now, sitting on the cold stone floor of the dark grimy basement was a very scared and very groggy Kate. Her head was pounding, as she had recently come round. She couldn't believe she had been so stupid, how she could have been so trusting, after all Jay had done? She was embarrassed that she had fallen for his lies once more.

Kate had no memory of how she had got there; she didn't even know where she was. Her hands, feet and mouth were bound with tape; the more she tried to wriggle herself free the more her limbs hurt. Sinking back onto the mattress beneath her, she closed her eyes in despair and prayed that she would be okay. Who knew what was going through Jay's mind; he was clearly not right in the head. She wondered if anyone had noticed she was missing, and if they were worried about her. It wouldn't take Billy long to work out who was behind this, Kate just had to be strong and wait it out, and hopefully he would find her soon; hopefully she wouldn't be here long. Jay's biggest downfall was that he wasn't very smart; he was evil, selfish and greedy, yes, but not smart. It would be no time before her brother put the pieces together and found her, she was sure.

Her few minutes of hope were shattered when the door of the basement opened and a very glossy, smug-looking Tanya tottered down the stairs. Kate hadn't given Tanya a second thought, hadn't considered that she would be involved, she felt physically sick realising how she had seriously misjudged the situation.

"Well, well: Look what we have here" She grinned at Kate, amused by her own words. Looking at Kate hunched up on the floor, all nervous and panic-stricken, Tanya felt like the cat that had got the cream, and she wasn't going to waste a single drop.

41

Billy was frantic; in the last three days that Kate had been missing he had been on the brink of losing it. They had searched everywhere for her, he and Paul had been out all night the first night, knocking on nearly every door between the flat and the club, asking if anyone had seen her. They had rung everyone who knew her, but they had not seen nor heard from her. All the local hospitals had been contacted, all the side-roads checked in case something had happened. She had seemed to have vanished into thin air. He hadn't been able to sleep and sitting across the kitchen table from him, Emma noticed that the dark circles under his eyes and his unshaven face made him look even more scary than normal.

Billy had insisted that he stay with Emma, not only because he felt that if there were any news, it would be the best place to be, but also because he knew Kate would want to make sure Emma was alright. She looked like death warmed up, and he noticed that she was chain-smoking, but apart from waiting to hear something, what else was she supposed to do? Paul had told her to stay at home, sit by the phone and call him if she heard anything. He had then proceeded to call her every hour or so to see if anything had come up. Emma was still was clueless to where her friend might be.

Billy had put the word out that if anyone saw Jay or Tanya, that person was to come straight to him, he was positive they had something to do with it. It was the only possibility. This was Jay's style: cowardly, picking on someone weaker than himself. Emma had insisted on contacting the police, too, and reluctantly Billy had agreed. However, although the police did put her on the missing persons' database that was just about the level of helpfulness they could muster. The police knew exactly who Jay was, and assumed that any girl associated with him was just as low down the food chain, so they hadn't seemed that concerned all in all. They figured that the poor girl had probably done a bunk with him; they could see Billy was really over-protective and maybe she had just wanted to get away. They were also very familiar with Billy, information on him and his dodgy dealings had come to light over the years, suspected money laundering mainly, so they had used this opportunity to take a closer look at him, they had a keen interest in his warehouse, and his "career", but Billy always covered his tracks and until they had solid proof, they could only sniff around.

Emma put out her fourth cigarette of the morning, and lit up another. Billy could see that she was genuinely worried sick about her friend. "We are going to find her, you know; make no odds on that, she'll be back here in no time," but as he spoke the words, even he didn't believe them.

"I'm just so worried, Billy, Jay is an animal, he knows some real dodgy people, I hate to think what she might be going through," her eyes watered as she spoke, and she inhaled a long lug of her fag.
Tapping his fingers agitatedly on the table top, Billy didn't even want to think of any of that right now. He knew, in great detail, what had

happened to Emma, and if that bloke had even harmed a hair on his sister's head, he was a fucking dead man, in fact, fuck that, he was a dead man anyway. Billy should have done what he had wanted to do in the first place and got rid of the scummy piece of shit ages ago.

Jay Shaw was over.

Across town, Paul Goldie was lying awake, staring at the ceiling, trying to muster the energy to get out of bed. He too had had a crap night's sleep, tossing and turning, imagining all sorts of awful things that Kate could be going through. He felt helpless; until they heard something, they were playing a waiting game. He knew as well as Billy did that this was one hundred percent down to Jay, and there was no way he was going to get away with it. Getting out of bed, Paul padded down to the kitchen to make a pot of strong coffee, to wake him up.

The house was gorgeous, a modern three-storey townhouse. He had every gadget and gizmo possible: it was a typical bachelor pad. His TV was huge, a giant plasma with a state-of-the-art speaker system. There were big leather sofas and oak floors throughout. Large bi-fold doors led out onto the patio, with a large seating area that lit up with the most amazing lighting effects. It was a dream pad for a guy like him, and it was just ten minutes away from the club. Except he wasn't your typical bachelor, was he: he had responsibilities. Sophia. Her sweet face stared at him from the photos dotted around the house; with her beautiful blonde curls, she was like an angel. He smiled at the thought of her piercing blue eyes. She was so innocent. He felt lonely at times, but thoughts of his baby girl kept him sane and helped him to remember that he wasn't really alone: he would always have her.

Shaking off his thoughts, he finished his coffee, and then decided to get showered and go over and see Billy. Maybe he would have heard something, although surely they would have called him. But he had to get out, had to do something, staying here was driving him crazy.

42

Kate was freezing; she couldn't remember a time when she had felt so cold. She tried to keep warm under the blanket, but not being able to move her hands or feet properly because of the tape meant that she could only cover some of her body up, and so she had spent the night shivering violently.

She was slowly losing patience now; she had lost track of time but guessed by the light in gap of the curtains that she had been here for about three days, and she had seen the sun come up about an hour ago, so she figured it was probably around five in the morning. She had expected that either she would have been rescued by now or that Jay and Tanya would have let her go. What were they playing at? She couldn't believe that they were getting away with it.

There were moments of sheer panic that swept over her, when Kate thought about what might happen if they kept her there, what if no-one came looking? She had no idea where she was, and wondered what if she was never found. She kept telling herself that she would be rescued; she knew she wasn't being left for dead as Tanya and Jay were still in the house, she had heard them talking just outside of the door at the top of the stairs, saying that Billy would be just about ready to call, that they had made him sweat it out for a few days and now he would be willing to pay, whatever the cost. She had been shocked at Tanya's voice, talking as if she hated Billy now; she was clearly out for everything she could get.

235

This was all for money, Kate thought disgustedly: the pair of them deserved each other.

"That will teach him and that tarty little bitch he's shagging," Tanya had said nastily, obviously still seething at the fact that he had replaced her so quickly and in such a humiliating way, she would be a laughing stock now. Well, she would show him; he would be very sorry he had treated her like a piece of rubbish he could just throw away at a moment's notice. Kate had been surprised to see that Jay had been behaving like a pathetic little puppy when he was around Tanya, it was clear he didn't know how to play this situation out, and Tanya seemed to be the one barking out all the orders. Jay was just going along with it all like her little puppet; it was truly pathetic to witness. He hadn't even had the bottle to look Kate in the eye on the few occasions he had brought her down food; mind you, if it had been left to Tanya she would have probably been left to starve, as she had seemed to take great pleasure in Kate's predicament and made Kate feel as degraded and helpless as possible. Tanya had taken her to the toilet and watched as Kate struggled for privacy and didn't give her the chance to clean herself up afterwards. She called her names and told her how much she hated her, how she had always hated her. That she blamed Kate for ruining her and Billy's relationship and it was all her fault that she had started things up with Jay. She had muttered the same things over and over, appearing to make herself more and more irate each time. Kate wondered if Tanya was mentally unstable, she seemed to be losing the plot and acting irrationally, getting in more and more of a state about Billy as time went on.

Kate looked around for ways to get out should the opportunity arise, hoping that there might be a way for her to escape but from what she could see, other than the tiny window constantly covered by the dark curtain, there was only a door at the top of the stairs that led to the main house.

Tugging once again at her taped wrists, she knew there was little point even trying to think of an escape plan; there was no way she was getting out of the bloody tape, let alone the grimy basement. Wanting to cry with despair, she rocked herself to sleep; she was like a caged animal: hungry, cold and scared. All she could do was pray: surely, it would not much longer now... but where was her brother, and where was Paul? Thinking of Paul she realised that she did have feelings for him. Emma had been right. She had done nothing but think of him since she had been here. She missed him so much and would have done anything to feel his arms around her right now. She had not made it to the meeting with him, she had been on her way there when she had been lured into the car by Jay, and she was still wondering what that was all about. Sometimes she let herself believe that he felt the same as her, and that he had been about to tell her. She knew she was being stupid and it was probably just something to do with the club but the warm, comforting thoughts kept her going as she closed her tear-stricken eyes and gave in to sleep.

Upstairs, Jay was struggling to get his head around what Tanya was saying.

"You've got to be fucking kidding me, Tan: what's the point? He's going to know it's us, he's not fucking stupid."

"Of course he's going to know it's us, Jay, from the minute he hears our voices on the phone he'll know it's us; that's exactly why we need to do this, it's the only way he's going to take us seriously. Jay, he thinks you're a fucking mug, trust me on this one. I've heard just about every opinion that bloke has on you a hundred fucking times; he has no respect for you whatsoever. We need to show him that we mean fucking business, or he's going to think you're just fucking with him."

Tanya lit up her first joint of the day: six o'clock in the morning was too early for a glass of wine, even by her standards.

Pacing the floor, Jay didn't know what to do; in a way, Tanya was right, Billy had no respect for him, and Billy hated him with a passion and had treated him like a cunt. Billy had publicly made it known to everyone and anyone that no-one was to do any kind of business with him, and that was what pissed Jay off the most. He had worked hard to gain clout, and now he was going to have to go back to square one, dealing pathetic wraps to school kids. He needed this money as much as Tanya; and he needed to show Billy that he wouldn't be mugged off by him... but this? This, he wasn't sure he could do.

"I've done a lot worse, Tan, you and I both know that, but I don't think I can do it. I guess I've been too close to her. Isn't there some other way we can make him see we're serious?"

"No, Jay, there isn't. I want Billy to be sitting in his kitchen, my fucking kitchen, eating his poxy cornflakes, with that little slag, and I want him to get the shock of his life when he opens his mail and gets a couple of his sister's fingers staring up at him. I hope he fucking chokes on his own vomit."

"There must be some other way, surely—?"

Cutting him off, Tanya shouted, "There is no other way, Jay, this is it. Grow some fucking balls, or I'll go down there and chop her bloody fingers off myself."

Jay felt sick. Kate irritated the life out of him, but she was a good person at heart, a bit prim and proper but decent all the same. He knew he had treated her like a piece of crap on his shoe, she had been nothing more than a toy of which that he had quickly become bored and had then tossed aside. He had put her through more than one person deserved in a lifetime, yet she had not retaliated. She had simply picked up her bags and left, with not a word to him, and every ounce of dignity she had in her. He respected that.

Jay couldn't even look Kate in the eyes when he had gone downstairs to give her food and water. Every time he had gone down to the basement he could feel her glaring at him, he could feel the hate radiating from her; he couldn't bear it, he wanted to be a heartless bastard to her and take his anger out on her, but he felt none, in fact all he felt was guilt. There was no way he could do what Tanya wanted, and he knew he had to find a way of delaying her impulsiveness.

"Tan, babe, you've been watching too many gangster movies, we do mean business and we don't need to start cutting people's body parts off and sending them via Royal Mail to prove it love, trust me. We need to make the call: today. We tell him what we want, and we tell him that unless we get it then, and only then, Tan, will we take more extreme measures to show him we're serious."

Tanya finished her joint; she stubbed it out in a little floral ashtray and sank down onto the sofa. She knew it made sense; she just really wanted to wipe that fucking grin off Billy's smug bloody face. Tanya was starting to get pissed off with Jay, though; she could see that over the last few days he seemed to have a real problem doing anything that involved sorting out that sad cow, Kate. He didn't even want to take food down to her, they had almost had a barney over it, and he had backed down. Tanya couldn't stand the bitch, and the less she did for her the better. Tanya couldn't understand what Jay's problem was; he swore he didn't have feelings for Kate, so why couldn't he do what they had talked about? Why was he leaving it all to her, it was like he had no balls all of a sudden.

"Fine, we'll do it your way, we'll call him soon, but you tell him if he wants to see his perfect little sister again, we want two hundred and fifty thousand pounds. I'm not going through all this shit for loose change,

Jay, I think a quarter of a mill should see us right for a bit; get us started, you know."

Relieved that he had managed to delay her, if only for a little while, Jay knelt over her and started kissing her softly, smelling the sweet scent of her perfume, pound signs swimming around in his head.

43

The warehouse's office, normally buzzing with noise and banter, was eerily quiet. The four men seated around the table were not only deep in thought but also silent from the shock of what they had been told. Nobody could believe what they had heard.

"So, let's get this straight then." Ryan rubbed his forehead fiercely, as if the information he had received had gone inside his head and caused it to throb like it might explode at any second. "Jay Shaw has rung you and demanded you give him a quarter of a million pounds. Is he having a fucking giggle? Does he seriously think that you're going to hand it over so that he can skip off into the sunset and live happily ever fucking after? What is he, a fucking comedian? I can tell you this now, if he thinks he's getting a penny from you he's a real fucking joker."

Ryan looked at each of the men around the table; the tension had created an atmosphere that was intense, to say the least. Billy had just turned up with a face like thunder: they knew it was bad from the look in his eyes. He had called them into the office with an urgency that made them all worry.

The call that Billy had been waiting for had come in at nine o'clock that morning, it had confirmed what he had known all along, Jay was behind Kate's disappearance, and so Billy hadn't been shocked when he heard the familiar, malicious voice. What he had been surprised at was Jay's demands.

Jay had spoken quietly and calmly, informing Billy that his sister was alive and well and would be returned safe and sound once he had paid the cash that Jay asked for. Billy had started to lose it: what a fucking cheek, how fucking dared he, who did he think he was messing with? He would not get away with this. Taking his sister was crossing the line big time. Billy would break every bone in that imbecile's body once he got his hands on him. Jay interrupted the name-calling and threats with a warning of his own.

"You have twenty-four hours to get the money together, Billy boy, if you fuck this up or try anything stupid, I can't make any promises. Kate will be returned in one piece if you do what I say: do I make myself clear?"

Billy was silenced at the thought of his sister being in danger and the loaded threat reminded him that he was dealing with a sick, twisted bastard. He reluctantly agreed to Jay's ultimatum of paying a ransom for Kate's safe return. Billy was told to sit by the phone at nine the following morning to wait for further instructions.

The room was silent; so far, Jonny hadn't said a word, although he and Lee had exchanged numerous looks between themselves. They were all just sitting there, waiting for Billy to say something: anything. They could see that he was not up to dealing with this; he was finding it hard to keep it together. Breaking the silence, Lee said,

"When he calls you, we need to tell him that we agree to whatever he asks."

Ryan laughed out loud in complete disbelief; if it was up to him he would be out hunting this fucker down and when he found him, he would treat him to the slowest and most painful death possible, he wouldn't be complying with his brainless demands.

"Let me finish." Lee held one hand up, to stop Ryan from interrupting, and continued: "We need to play the game. Go along with what he says, and make him think that he has us by the short and curlies. If he thinks that he is the one giving out the orders and making all the demands, then we can catch him off guard. We will be ready when he picks up the money, we will be three steps ahead of the cunt."

As always with the Ellis brothers, Jonny finished off his brother's sentence:

"We cannot risk Kate's life in the smarmy fucker's hands Billy; this is not a time for games. Pay Jay whatever he asks, we will get Kate back, and we will personally serve Jay up on a plate for you, he'll be like a lamb to the fucking slaughter."

Billy nodded at the men, his friends, whom he trusted with his life. This was exactly what he needed to hear, he was so emotionally fucked up about the situation that he couldn't think straight, and he needed their support; only with their help could he possibly get through this, it was Kate's only real chance. Jonny and Lee were the brains of the group, and he hoped that between them they would sort out a plan that would leave no room for fuck ups, and by the time they had executed it, Ryan, the muscle of the group, would have great pleasure in carrying out Jay's reprisal. Billy, however, was going to make sure that he was there at the end, he would be the one to finally turn the lights out in Jay's little fucked-up world.

44

Paul had spoken to his security team; every single one of his guys had been called in to work. It was being treated like a military operation; these were his best men, they knew what was expected of them, and Paul was confident that they would do as they were asked. He had briefed them about what was going on, and everybody was on red alert. They were expected to watch everything that happened in the club tonight, not even so much as a bag of speed was to pass through the doors. No fights; no scumbags; no trouble. Paul needed them to focus their attention on Jay Shaw.

Every man who came in this place tonight was to be searched, and Jay Shaw was no exception, if he thought that he could just walk in tooled up, demands or no demands, he had another think coming. Paul knew that they had the upper hand, really, as everybody who worked at the club knew what Jay looked like: the door men, the security, even most of the bar workers. He was a good looking fucker, one of the only things he actually had going for him, and a bloke like him stood out from the average crowd. Most of his security team had worked alongside him at some stage, so Paul had been surprised that this was how Jay wanted to play it. It seemed strange that he would want to make the exchange somewhere as public and personal as the club.

Paul was aware that there may be more than met the eye going on, particularly as Jay had been outed by him and by Goldie's in general: he

246

wasn't taking any chances that Jay might be using this as a chance to get a piece of revenge.

Yesterday had been the longest twenty-four hours in Paul's life, there were moments when it had felt like time had actually stopped ticking. He and Billy had sat for most of the afternoon together, talking about Kate and how they thought she would be coping and what they would both like to do to Jay when they got their hands on him, as well as going over the plan for this evening. They had talked it all through so many times that there was nothing left to say and then they had mostly just sat there in silence, both worrying at the worst-case scenario that this all could possibly bring them. Neither of the two men wanted to voice their fears about what this could be.

Paul had been gobsmacked when Billy had called and told him that Jay's second call had come this morning demanding that the money be left by the DJ booth at midnight that night. Jay had said once he had picked the money up and got out of the club safely without anyone interfering or trying to do him any harm, then and only then would he text Billy to tell him Kate's whereabouts: he said that he was the only one who knew this. He had stating categorically that if anything happened to him while he was picking the money up, Kate would be left where she was, in a remote location where she wouldn't be found for weeks, by which time it would be too late for her.

Billy had asked what if he was being set up, what if he paid up and Jay didn't stick to his end of the deal? Jay had just replied that he had no other choice but to trust him.

"Pay up, don't fuck it up and you'll get your sister back. Any trouble and I promise you this, Billy, you will never see her again." Jay must have fucking lost the plot, picking Goldie's was the stupidest location anyone could have thought of. The door was being manned, there were cameras everywhere, and Jay must have known that. He must have known that both Paul and Billy would be watching for him like hawks, not to mention Billy's guys, who would be all over the place. Jay must be mental if he thought that he would be walking out of there with his legs intact, let alone a bag full of cash, was safe. Maybe he thought that there was safety in numbers or something and that he would be able to just sneak in undetected, but there was no way that was going to happen.

Billy was getting the cash, a cool half a million; it would be there any minute. Paul knew that Billy had no intention of letting Jay get away with it, though. He had been sorting out the plan of action with Jonny and Lee all day, and they had decided that they would have two cars ready, one at the front entrance and one at the back; they would let Jay walk in and out without any interference from anyone and when Jay tried to get away they would tail him from a distance; once they knew where he was hiding out, they would wait it out for a bit, hopefully getting Kate back. They would give it a bit of time, just enough to lull Jay into a false sense of security, let him believe that maybe he had actually got away with it, then they would make their move with Billy and Ryan's help: they would ransack the place and, more importantly, ransack Jay Shaw.

It was only nine o'clock now; the clubbers normally didn't start arriving until after ten, the night was still young. Hoping that he had enough men in place and praying that the night wouldn't throw any nasty surprises, Paul wandered up to the gentlemen's club; he had decided he would stay up there and man the security cameras with Joe, his security manager. He had a great team on, and even though everyone was on strict orders not to approach Jay or get in his way whilst he collected the cash, Paul wanted all eyes on him. They needed to keep him in their sights long enough to establish where he was going to, otherwise the money would be long gone and Kate's fate would be left in his slimy and untrustworthy hands.

45

Emma had almost bitten her nails down to nothing; her nerves had got the better of her. She had smoked more cigarettes in the last few days than she probably had in her entire life, so many that she felt like throwing up; she thought it was the fags making her nauseous but she was worried for her friend too. Every time she thought of poor Kate and what she might be going through, she felt as if she would throw up. Emma knew that the chances of what had happened to her repeating themselves and happening to Kate were slim, but that didn't stop her mind going into overdrive and making her fear the worst. After all, she knew Jay better than all of them; she had been the one to witness first-hand what an evil bastard he could be. She knew Jay would want the cash badly, but even he wouldn't be stupid enough not to go through with the deal: surely?

Emma was behind the main bar, just like any other Friday night, except this wasn't like any other Friday night. The time had passed so slowly, and every time Emma had had a chance to glance at the clock between serving people, it seemed like the clock's hands had barely moved. The atmosphere was so charged it was like electricity thrashing through the club, everyone was on tenterhooks, just waiting.

Billy had looked a state when he had turned up, he hadn't shaved and his clothes looked like they had been slept in; judging by his grey, shadowed eyes he had had very little sleep, Emma thought. She had been having trouble sleeping, too, and had been grateful that Billy had stayed in the flat with her; she didn't think her nerves would have been up to staying there on her own, not with this crap going on. Her nerves were already shot to pieces, and knowing that Billy had been lying on the sofa downstairs had been a huge relief to her.

Billy was upstairs with Paul at the moment, in the gentlemen's lounge and as she looked around at the amount of shaven-headed beefcakes dotted around the place she hoped with everything she had, that one of them came through tonight for Kate's sake. He couldn't get away with this. So many things could go wrong tonight. Emma hadn't wanted to work, but Paul had insisted that everyone carry on as normal: they should keep their heads down and get on with their jobs no matter what the night brought. It was finally a quarter to twelve; there had been no sign of Jay. Emma's mind was whirling and she had been mucking up orders all night. To make up for it, she had been dishing out free shots to keep people happy and was now surrounded by a pissed crowd who was laughing and dancing without a care in the world. She was trying hard to concentrate but she kept looking around, scanning the club to see if she could spot his face like everyone else working tonight seemed to be doing: just looking and waiting.

Paul was doing his best to keep Billy cool upstairs, they had been glued to the monitors for over an hour and so far no one had seen Jay enter the club. Paul was worried that if Billy saw Jay, he would lose all sense of reason and want to annihilate the fucker, and Paul didn't want to risk anything fucking up getting Kate back in one piece. He had told Billy that the best place for them to be was upstairs, and it was true. The cameras were on every entrance, including every fire door, all the stairs were covered and, most importantly, so was the DJ booth. It was ten minutes to midnight now, and as they had discussed Paul was going to take the bag of cash and place it next to the DJ booth. In ten minutes, they would finally have a lead as to where Kate was: they all needed to stay on the ball.

46

The dance floor was heaving; sweaty bodies grinding to the music while drunken people chatted, laughed and sang along to the songs pumping out of the speakers. There must have been three hundred people bopping away on it and hundreds more standing at the sides or lounging on the huge comfy sofas or in the secluded booths.

It certainly was the place to be usually, but maybe not tonight. She was sipping from a bottle of something fruity and alcoholic, which was too sweet and too cheap, not her usual tipple, but then nothing about her was usual tonight. She felt she had surpassed herself, and was feeling very smug once again, lapping up every second of it. Earlier that day she had gone to a salon and had her long hair chopped off and had it styled into a shaggy bob with a fringe that hung into her eyes; she had then asked them to dye it black. The hairdresser had tried to persuade her to keep her lovely golden locks, but Tanya insisted that she wanted a complete re-style. The hairdresser had reluctantly done the cut, and actually said in the end that it quite suited Tanya. Some women were lucky that way and could do pretty much anything to their hair so that it looked great no matter what, she had admitted. With her new hairstyle and racy clubbing clobber, she looked like a completely different girl: unrecognisable. Tanya had hooked up with a bunch of lads when she had first come in to the club: it had been too easy. They looked as if they couldn't believe their luck, drooling at the sight of her dancing up against them and acting like she was right up for it. She had no time for any of them, of course, they looked like a bunch of complete and utter losers but she needed to mingle and not stand out by being alone, which would draw attention to her. That was what she didn't need tonight. Most of the time she had been there they had been plying her with drinks and compliments so it wasn't that hard a task, she figured, to make a tiny effort with them.

She looked at her watch; she had been here for almost half an hour and Jay would be about to kick off the first part of their plan by making an anonymous call to the police. It was a fool-proof plan, Tanya's handiwork. Jay would say that there was an armed gunman in the club and that he was about to open fire; any minute now, the club would be in complete and utter mayhem. Perfect.

Looking around, Tanya could see the security guys, all eyeing the bag that Paul Goldie had placed down carefully by the DJ booth as instructed. Glugging down the last mouthful of her drink for Dutch courage, she whispered to herself that it was now or never. Reaching under her very short skirt, she pulled out two very well-concealed smoke bombs that Jay had managed to get hold of from some dodgy ex-soldier he knew. Pulling off the tops, she threw them onto the floor in front of the stage. The smoke poured out within seconds and people started swinging their arms and coughing. A few of Paul's security men looked at each other in alarm before making their way over amongst the coughing people and the now giant smoke cloud that had formed around them all. Tanya quickly threw herself down and crouched on the floor; crawling on her hands and knees to get a better view of the bag, she grabbed it with both hands then quickly made her move to the ladies' toilets before the smoke started to clear. Taking her opportunity as she ran through the cloud Tanya screamed, as loudly as she possibly could,

"Oh my God, he's got a gun, he's going to fucking shoot us all". It had the desired effect, people too pissed to think straight started panicking all around her, screaming and pushing to get away from the smoky dance floor in terror at the thought of a gunman amongst them. Everyone started running in all directions; there was chaos everywhere. Hearing the commotion and seeing the smoke and panicked faces, the security moved in and was making their way through the haze to the booth. They thought that Jay might be there; maybe he was the one with the gun. They knew their orders: they had to get a visual and keep him in sight, but they couldn't see anyone matching Jay's description.
People were fleeting in utter panic, as they rushed about trying to get away. Paul and Billy had seen the commotion on the screens and had made it down there in seconds, desperately trying to see Jay. How had he got in without them seeing him, and armed too: it just didn't make sense. Shouting to try and calm everybody down, Paul took charge of the situation.

"It's okay, people, it's a false alarm, there's no need to panic: everyone is perfectly safe." He hoped what he was saying was true, he hadn't seen anyone with a gun, and as far as he knew none of his security men had either.

Just when Paul thought he was starting to gain control again, the front doors swung open and dozens of armed police officers stormed the club, charging in fully kitted out in riot armour.

"Everybody stay where you are; get down on the floor with your hands on your heads." Bodies dived to the floor, the music had stopped playing and the harsh main lights had been turned on, most people were starting to sober up.

Billy and Paul were side by side on the floor; Paul put his arm up and shouted to the officer who had commanded them to get down that he was the club's owner, and the officer let him get to his feet but told everyone else to stay where they were. Looking around the officer could see that there was no trouble here. When they had first arrived to all the running screaming people they had thought they were going to enter a massacre scene from a horror movie, but it turned out no one was hurt. Nobody knew who had initially seen the gunman either. After checking the club and making sure that no one had been hurt or threatened they decided that it had probably been a hoax call.

People started getting up, dusting themselves off and slowly filtering out of the club. The drama had ended what had been a good night out for most. The officers started filing out too. There was no sign of Jay, and as he looked towards the DJ booth Billy shook with anger when he saw there was no sign of the bag of cash anymore either.

47

"We are laughing all the way to the bank, babes." Jay picked Tanya up and swung her around in the tiny cottage lounge, which in itself was a hard task as you couldn't so much as swing a kitten. Tanya lapped up his praise and tilted her head back playfully.

"I can't believe you did it, you're fucking amazing, Tan... did I ever tell you that?"

Kissing her hard on the lips, he put her down, feeling dizzy with excitement. They had done it: they had really done it. Oh, the look on Billy's face right now would be priceless: they had just taken a quarter of a million pounds from the bloke, he must be sick as a fucking parrot. Jay's adrenaline had been pumping all night long, he had been so worried that someone might have recognised Tanya and fucked the whole thing up for them. This was the biggest job he had ever pulled off, and with the enemies he had now made it had been the riskiest, but even he wouldn't admit out loud how he had been shitting himself tonight. Tanya, once again, had come up trumps. Jay had led them to believe that this was his plan; that it was all his doing, and that they were dealing with him alone. He shook his head in wonderment, Billy had taken it as read and not realised that Tanya was involved at all: let alone the main instigator.

"I know, I know; I'm a fucking genius!" Tanya was also pleased as punch with herself. She couldn't keep the grin from her face. She had walked into the club and swanned around amongst them all, in disguise, and fleeced them for everything they had: well, everything Billy had. Men were pitiful. They had been so busy looking for Jay and searching all the men who went into the club, they hadn't considered that they should have been looking out for a woman. Billy wouldn't have thought for a minute that it would have been her coming for the money, but then he probably hadn't given her a moment's thought since he had thrown her out. It proved what a stupid little man he was. He didn't have high expectations of her. She was unwilling to let that thought get to her, however; he had underestimated her and that would be to his own cost; nothing was spoiling this high for her tonight.

"How the hell did you manage to get out of the club in one piece with that bag in tow?" Jay nodded at the holdall Tanya had smuggled out of the club, which was now sitting in the middle of the coffee table, full of fifty pound notes. Tanya explained while she poured them both nice big glasses of cold Sauvignon, that she had lowered the bag out of the toilet window into the little passageway at the side of the club and then she had made a dash for the main door, along with the hundreds of other screaming people who were trying to get out of the club. There were people everywhere, running about trying to get to the main doors, in fear of an imaginary gunman; she had slipped out unnoticed. Just as she had got out and reached the passageway, the police had turned up with sirens blaring and all lights blazing. Unbeknown to Tanya, Billy's lookout, Jonny, had been so consumed with the drama of the clubbers running out looking terrified and the police turning up he hadn't spotted Tanya running with the bag of cash and getting into the Golf that was sitting a little further down the street. She had got away with it: easy money. Downstairs Kate could hear the commotion, she had been drifting in and out of sleep all day; dreaming was the only thing that had broken up her time whilst she had been here, it was the only thing that took her away from this waking nightmare. Tanya's car pulling up had woken her and Kate could hear the sound of her and Jay laughing loudly now upstairs, obviously both very pleased that they had pulled their plan off. Her brother had paid up, it seemed. Kate could imagine that he would be going through hell, not only because she was missing but also that he had just been fleeced out of a quarter of a million pounds. As long as her brother had breath in his body, Kate knew that he wouldn't rest until he had it back: every single penny. Tanya and Jay were as good as dead now after pulling this little stunt.

Trying to sit up, she swung her legs round and moved so that her back was against the wall. The whole time she had been here, her hands and feet had been tied; they treated her worse than a dog. She felt filthy: and she was filthy. She wondered when they would let her go; she had heard them say that they would as soon as they had the money, so she hoped that it wouldn't be long. Wriggling her toes, trying to relieve the cramp in her legs, Kate stretched out and tried to think positively. Soon she would be out of there; soon she would be at home.

"We can dump her in some lay-by, or leave her in a motorway cafe toilet; give Billy a call with the details and then just keep on driving." Jay was excited about starting their new life; a new start was what he needed. He would always be able to start from the bottom and work his way up, he had done so many a time. With Tanya at his side, the world was his proverbial oyster; he knew they could make it. He loved her so much, he really loved her. It was something he had never felt for anyone else. There was a fuzzy feeling in his stomach when he thought about her, as if he craved her: like a drug, he had to have her. Jay had decided it was a good thing, this love business, that he would finally give in to it and see where it took them. Tanya seemed happy, looking at her tapping her feet to the music playing in the background and sipping her drink, apparently deep in thought, he had never seen her look more beautiful. As if his look had interrupted her thoughts, she glanced up.

"Drive where though, Jay? Where are we going to go? Do you think that Billy is seriously going to let us get away with this? That we can start again anywhere? It doesn't matter where we go, because he'll find us. Two wronguns like us, we'd have to change our names, keep ourselves to ourselves, which in our way of life would be hard to do. Reputation's everything, and if we lay low, what sort of money will we ever be able to make? It'll only be a matter of time before he catches up with us. We'll be forever watching our backs."

"Nah, Tan, he'll never find us; give it a few months and it will all be forgotten; he'll be so happy to have his sister back in one piece and me gone for good, he won't give a shit anymore, he'll probably think that it was money well spent," he reassured her.

"You don't know him like I do, Jay. He will never, ever, let this go; this will eat away at him, he will be looking for us, mark my words, we'll constantly be playing a waiting game, it'll only be a matter of time. We've just fucked him over with two of his prized possessions, his precious little sister and a massive chunk of his money." Tanya stared into space, deep in thought now as she downed the rest of her glass. The mood in the room had suddenly changed. She had not stopped to think about what was going to happen afterwards, it had only just dawned on her that there was no way that they could just up sticks and start afresh elsewhere. She had only got as far as her little revenge plan; she had not thought past the provoking Billy bit. The sort of circles that Tanya and Jay mixed in, the sort of dealings they would be doing to make some cash: someone, somewhere, would leak it back to Billy and they would never be free, not really. She had to think of another way forward, something that would guarantee them a way out, she was starting to realise that Jay was a liability, and he really wasn't seeing the bigger picture at all. Tanya needed to think about the situation before they made their next move; she had an idea, but she decided that this was best not shared with Jay.

"We need to keep her for another night," Tanya nodded in the direction of the basement door. "Let Billy sweat it out while we sleep on it and tomorrow we'll decide what our next step should be. I'm going to bed; it's been a long night."

She bundled up the cash and took the holdall upstairs with her, leaving Jay sitting in the chair racking his brain for some idea as to what they could do. The mood was bleak; he had thought they would be celebrating, but Tanya was stressed and uptight. Maybe she was right, though, they did have to think about their next move; he would be stupid to take Billy letting this one go for granted.

48

Billy couldn't believe it: he had been fucking done over by Jay Shaw. That fucking sponger had walked into the club and taken a quarter of a million pounds from him without being clocked; no-one had caught a glimpse of the bloke.

Neither the smoke thing nor the hoax call to the police were rocket science, he supposed, but clever enough. He had wondered how Jay would do it. Billy and Paul had gone over and over the tapes for hours and there had been security everywhere; how the fuck Jay had got in unnoticed, neither could say. Billy should have known that Jay would play silly buggers.

Billy gulped down a shot of whiskey; he was fuming. The only way he would have been able to track the bastard down was to have caught him in the act and followed him, he had got away unseen and now Billy was again at Jay's mercy, and he fucking hated every second of it. Tomorrow, his sister would have been gone for six days, and he was worried sick about her. If that bloke had done anything to her, he would fucking slaughter him.

He had been at home for a couple of hours now, sitting at the kitchen table, staring at the phone. Like a fucking mug. Jay would be laughing his smug fucking head off at him.

He couldn't even think about the dilemma of Jay calling his bluff and demanding more money. Billy had made a small fortune from his dealings over the years, and he had wisely tied it up in property all over London. Getting his hands on quarter of a million pounds in just less than twenty-four hours had been a challenge, and one he begrudged to say the least. He had worked hard for that money, made a promise that he would never struggle for anything. He had vowed years ago never to be at the mercy of anyone, like his mum had been.

He realised that he had been quite tight with his cash up until now; he didn't spend on anything much in particular. He always had cash in his pocket, enough to buy anyone he was with a few rounds in the pub, and okay he had invested wisely, but he could have done more with it. He could have taken Kate on holiday, treated her to nice clothes; they could both have lived life a bit. He smiled at the thought, Kate was almost as stubborn as him in some ways, and her pride would have told him not to waste his money on her, but he should have done so anyway. As soon as she got back, he was going to take her to Westfield on a shopping spree, treat her to a slap-up meal and then maybe ask her about going away somewhere, God knows she would need to go on holiday somewhere after this ordeal; he had no idea what state she would be in.

Emma could come too, of course, and he may even ask Paul. Paul had been a rock over the last few days, Billy was thankful of the support. Paul was the strong silent type but he had a big presence, and he was not a man to be shafted by anyone. Paul had confided that he really cared for Kate, and Billy could tell that he had been genuinely upset when he spoke of Kate, and how he hoped she was okay. Yeah, Billy had a good feeling about Paul. His sister could do with a decent man: one who would look after her; respect her; give her the life she deserved. Maybe, this time round, for once Billy really would step back and let her get on with it. Billy took his phone to bed. He would probably toss and turn all night, waiting for the call, but he needed to rest, and he had no idea what else he could do. It had been another long day. Jay assured him that he would let Kate go when he had the money, but it was gone five in the morning, over five hours had passed since Jay had taken the money, and there had been no call.

Tanya looked at the clock on the bedside cabinet: it was almost five thirty. Jay hadn't come to bed, and she guessed that he had fallen asleep on the sofa. She had been lying in bed for hours, unable to sleep, wondering what to do. She knew their plan wasn't going to work. Tanya knew that with Jay, she would be in for a life of dodgy dealings, and as much as she thought she could cope with that if she had to, she knew deep down that she didn't want that for herself. She wanted more: more than Jay was able to offer. It was fair to say that she had had more than her share of fun with him, and using him to help settle the score with Billy had made her very happy. At the end of the day though, Jay was a man, so he couldn't be trusted. It would only be a matter of time before he fucked everything up or pissed even more people off. It seemed to be a habit of his. Trouble turned up wherever he went, he was a magnet for it, and getting into more trouble was not a risk she wanted to take. Sure, he was all over her like a rash at the moment, but give him time and his wandering eye would return.

She had loved Billy, and look where that had got her. He had replaced her in a heartbeat, and actually while she was with him she hadn't been anywhere near as close to him as she would have liked to be, with the 'lovely' Kate about, there were always three people in her relationship. No, this time, she decided, she would to do it alone. A quarter of a million pounds was more than enough compensation for putting up with Billy bringing that slag into her home, humiliating her. As far as she was concerned, she was owed every single penny. The only place where it was possible to hit Billy where it hurt, other than his perfect Kate, was his wallet: Tanya hoped that she had fucking wounded him.

Tanya had made up her mind; she would take the money and run. On her own, she could make it, she trusted herself not to slip up nor let her guard down; besides, Billy wouldn't be interested in her, he was after Jay, who was behind this as far as Billy was concerned.

Realising that she may have a Get out of Jail Free card, Tanya thought about calling Billy, saying that if he promised to forget about the money she would tell him where Kate and Jay were but on the condition that she could keep the money. Knowing Billy, it would be an offer that he couldn't refuse. The more she thought about it, the more she decided against it, though; if she did that then she would still be lowering herself to asking his permission, and she would be making a deal with him. She wasn't prepared to do that. Besides, how could she know that he would stand by his word and let her just walk away with his money. No, she wouldn't ask him, she had set this up, this was all her work, she had earned this and she was keeping the cash. After much debating, she decided she would text him the address of where to find Kate, and maybe that way he would come to his own decision once he realised she was involved. She would offer Jay up to Billy; it was the only chance she had that she might be able to keep the money.

Tanya had the "pay as you go" phone they had bought for contact with Billy, she figured that if she texted Billy the cottage address she would have about forty five minutes to get as far away as possible before he turned up. All Billy wanted was his sister and having Jay handed to him on a plate meant that Tanya would possibly have a chance of not being tracked down if she tried to vanish. Kate could fucking rot, for all she cared, but this way it may seem that Tanya gave a shit. It was her only chance of taking the money and getting home and dry.

Carefully packing a few belongings into the holdall and zipping it up tightly, she sent a text message to Billy saying simply

"Pines Cottage, Eastwick Lane, Surrey - Kate!"

Tiptoeing down the stairs, she stopped on each creaking floorboard, and prayed that she didn't wake Jay.

Jay was stretched out on the sofa, snoring, his mouth wide open and one arm hanging off the edge. He was out for the count.

Tanya picked up the car keys from the table, being careful to grip them firmly so that they didn't jingle, and made for the door. Looking back, just for an instant, confirmed to her that she was doing the right thing, Billy would have caught up with Jay eventually, and by then she would be far away. As she slipped out of the back door into the cold night, the only person Tanya was thinking about was herself.

49

Paul was pulling on his clothes as fast as he could. He had only been in bed a little while and he must have been exhausted, as he had actually drifted off. Billy had just called to say he was on his way over with Ryan. Billy said he had an address: he knew where Kate was. Paul's head was spinning, if Billy really did have the information about where Kate was, he would be seeing her shortly, and he couldn't quite get his head around that. He prayed to God that she was okay. He hoped they would get to her in time. Who knew what she had been through over the past week?

Billy was driving like a lunatic. He had picked up Ryan as soon as he had received the text and he called Paul. He guessed that Jay wouldn't be stupid enough to text him Kate's whereabouts and then hang around, but he wanted back-up just in case. He had no idea what he might walk into, and he felt nauseous; he didn't know how Kate would be or if anything bad had happened to her. If anything at all had, he knew he would lose it; his sister was everything to him.

Billy kept his eye on the road as he swerved around bends at eighty miles an hour, sending Ryan flying in the passenger seat. Outside his house, Paul ran to the car and got in the back seat.

"What's happened; where is she?" he demanded.

"Jay did the big manly thing again, for a change, he texted me the address of some cottage in Surrey. He'll be long gone, I bet, the fucking chicken shit." Billy put his foot down; every minute felt like ten; he needed to get to her.

"Jonny and Lee are meeting us there," Ryan informed them after his phone flashed up a message. "Jonny said to wait for them; he said it could be a trap you're walking into."

The thought had crossed Billy's mind, too. Jay could be up to anything. At least if Billy turned up mob-handed, then he would have more of a chance if it were a trap. He seriously doubted Jay would have the bollocks to try anything, he would have legged it with the wedge as soon as possible. Mind you a few weeks ago Billy would never have believed Jay would have kidnapped Kate and had Billy over for two hundred and fifty K, so who knew what the guy was capable of?

"Fucking hell, mate, you'd give Lewis Hamilton a run for his money, that's for sure," Paul joked, as he swung around in the back seat, as Billy rounded another bend. Paul knew how Billy felt, though, all this time of hoping and praying that she was okay, and now they were on their way to her. They couldn't get there fast enough, as far as he was concerned.

Billy had arrived at the quiet country lane in just over half the time it should have taken, thanks partly to the fact that there was little traffic on the roads at this time of the morning, and partly to the fact he drove the whole way like a fucking maniac. The cottage was down a long, winding track; Billy could see some lights up ahead, behind hedges. He parked the car at a distance from the cottage and killed the lights.

Ryan opened the boot and got out a sawn-off shotgun, for Billy, and a bag of tools. Paul went empty-handed, and on Billy's instructions stayed back a bit, letting Ryan and Billy approach the cottage first. The sun had come up, it was almost six thirty. Looking around, Billy could see that the next house was a few hundred meters away, down the lane; checking there was no one else around, they made their way down the track towards the cottage.

Ryan put his hand on the back door handle and was surprised to find it opened; he wasn't sure what the fuck was going on but this seemed a little too easy. He didn't want to call Kate's name in case it was a trap, he wanted to give the place a once-over first. Signalling to Billy and Paul to follow him, they tiptoed through the kitchen. Looking around, it looked like any normal person's kitchen, there was nothing unusual and there was no sign of Kate.

Glancing into the next room, Ryan did a double take; he could hardly fucking believe it. Jay Shaw was sleeping like a fucking baby on the sofa in front of him. Nodding at Billy to grab his attention, he gestured him over with his hand and pointed over to where Jay was lying. Billy was gobsmacked; it didn't make sense; why would Jay send that text and then go to sleep? The realisation hit him like a brick. Tanya. He should have known, of course she was involved; she was probably the mastermind. This was her style. Fucking hell what had he ever seen in her? That piece of shit, Jay, had been well and truly set up and was now lying there snoring, probably dreaming of spending Billy's money; that mug had not an inkling of what was going on.

As the three men tiptoed into the room and crowded around Jay, he had no idea that his sweet dreams were just about to turn into his worst fucking nightmare. Rubbing the end of the sawn-off shot gun against the tip of his nose, Jay brushed it away, and carried on sleeping. Feeling something rub his nose, Jay put a hand up to itch it and opened his eyes. Billy, Ryan and Paul stared down at him.

"What the fuck?" His whole body jumped so high it nearly hit the ceiling, and he looked like he was actually going to shit himself.

"This is your early morning wakeup call," snarled Billy as he brought the barrel of the gun down hard on his head. Panicked, Paul looked at Billy's angry face, the veins were popping out on the side of his head, and he was probably using just about every ounce of willpower he possessed not to shoot the man who was now lying sparked out.

"Do you think that was wise? We don't even know where Kate is," Paul said.

"Wise….? I could have blown the cunt's fucking face off. It was only a tap on the head, he'll come round in no time, and he looked like he could do with a few extra minutes of shut eye. Shame to disturb his beauty sleep," Billy said.

He told Ryan to stay with Jay, he would look upstairs and Paul would go to the cellar. The cottage was the size of a shoebox so he figured it would take them all of five seconds to see if she was here.

Paul tiptoed down a flight of stairs that seemed to lead to a cellar. He opened the door, terrified that he might find something that he didn't want to see. It was cold and damp and the room was dim. In the corner was a mattress, and as he walked towards it, he saw a figure on it, looking as if they were asleep. Kate. Bending down, he could see that her hands and feet were bound with tape. She looked like a mistreated animal on an RSPCA advert. He felt relief as he saw her stir, she looked gaunt and dirty but she was still his beautiful Kate.

"Kate," he whispered, as he stroked her fringe out of her eyes. Slowly waking up and hoping that she wasn't still dreaming, she looked straight into his concerned face.

"Paul, oh my God it's really you, thank God you're here, where's my brother? Where are Jay and Tanya?" She had a million questions to ask. Because she was weak and her mouth was dry, she sounded quiet and raspy. He picked up a bottle of water that had been left just out her reach, opened it and poured it into her mouth. She gulped it down as if her life depended on it.

"Billy's here, he's just upstairs, you're okay, Kate, you're going to be okay." He was undoing the tape around her feet; they had been bound so tightly that the skin was red and puffy where the tape had cut into her. As Paul was undoing her hands, Kate's brother rushed towards her.

"Billy, I knew you would find me." Tears were rolling down her cheeks, throughout her whole time here she had never once been in doubt that he would come, and he hadn't let her down. He never had, and he never would.

Hugging her to him now, he asked her:

"Are you okay, he didn't do anything to you, did he?" She shook her head, and the two men in front of her sighed with relief. She was really okay. Paul and Billy helped her to her feet, she was weak and exhausted.

First things first, Billy wanted to get her home and looked after her; she needed a nice hot bath, decent grub and a warm bed. Then, he was going to come back and deal with Jay for the very last time.

50

Sonia was in her element: she had just made the biggest cooked breakfast known to mankind, and there had been more than enough food to feed an entire army had she needed to. It had gone down very well, judging by the content faces that were sitting around the small kitchen table. She had been over the moon when Emma had called early this morning to say that Kate had been found and Billy and Paul were on their way to the house; Sonia had quickly stuffed her bag with everything she could find in her fridge so she could make Kate and the lads something decent to eat. Always the mother hen was Sonia, she had quickly made her way over to the flat so that she could be there when Kate arrived back.

Sonia had been worried sick about the poor girl, and of course she had the whole guilt thing going on, too: Jay was her son, after all, her blood, and she felt responsible for him in some way. The manner in which he had turned out sickened her; she regretted, deeply, leaving him in Den's hands all those years ago. The damage that man had caused, God only knew. Jay was like his father in every single way: selfish, cruel and motivated by money. He, like his father, would step over anyone who got in his way, no matter what the cost. She would never, as long as she lived, speak to him again. He was dead to her. As far as she was concerned, she didn't have a son, but she did have a beautiful daughter now: Kate, who she loved like her own. She had practically run around here, and she had smiled when Emma had opened the door and quipped,

"Fuck me, what did you do, Son, get Richard Branson to fly you around?" She had been driving Emma mad these last few days, constantly texting to see if any of them had news. Emma knew the woman was as worried sick as the rest of them, and now they had the best news: Kate was safe and sound and, more importantly, she was coming home.

It had been an emotional reunion, to say the least; Paul had walked in with Kate leaning against him, steadying her while she walked; she had looked as if the life had been sucked out of her. She had lost weight and she had hardly any energy left in her at all. Her hair was a tangled mess, and her skin was grey, no doubt from not having fresh air or proper food all week. There had been tears cried by them all. Mostly now, though, they were tears of joy and relief at her safe return.

Kate was so glad to be back: the last few days had been a living hell, and she wasn't sure in the end what Jay and Tanya would have been capable of, especially Tanya, that woman was mad. Kate had seen genuine hate radiate from her, and she could admit now that she had been very frightened. Jay was a weak and pathetic man, she could see that now; she had known from the start that it was Tanya who was the one to worry about, Jay was just her little puppet, Kate hadn't been worried about him at all. Tanya had really lost it, though, she had appeared unhinged with had a few screws loose, and that had scared Kate, Tanya was capable of just about anything.

"Oh, that was fucking lush, Sonia, just what we all needed." Finishing his last mouthful of bacon and eggs, Billy stretched his arms up, realising that was the first proper bit of food he had eaten all week; he hadn't really felt any hunger, he guessed worry did that to you. It was probably the same for all of them. They had all survived on a diet of fags, tea and extreme stress for the best part of the week.

Emma had been on cloud nine after Billy called to say they were on their way back, and that Kate was with them. After calling Sonia, she had done a quick tidy up of the place. Everything had been neglected this week, as she had been so preoccupied with what was going on with Kate. She didn't want her to come home to a pigsty, so she spruced the place up a bit, and then got cups of tea ready for them all.

"Yeah, that was a mean fry up, Son," Paul thanked her, "I don't think I'll need to eat again all day."

"All week more like." Emma winked at Kate. "I saw you shovelling in those extra sausages, Paul."

"They are big strong men, Emma, they need their fill of good grub," Sonia smiled, pleased as punch that she had been of some use to them all this morning.

"Yeah, come on, Em; get the kettle on again, will you? Us 'big strong men' need another cuppa." Lifting his cup and waving it in Emma's direction, Billy smiled. Emma had grown on him, she was a good friend to

Kate; he was glad that she was around for her. Shaking her head, but smiling back at him, Emma put the kettle on.

The smell of bacon, combined with a diet of what might as well of been dog food all week had been a lethal combination, and Kate had eaten like she had never seen a plate of food before; she had scoffed it down so quickly, her stomach ached afterwards. As she sat there, and looked down at her clothes, she realised that she probably stank to the high heavens. She hadn't had a bath in seven days, and her hygiene hadn't been under her own control either. Kate decided that she would bin everything she had on, even her shoes; she wanted no reminders of what she had been through. The hardest thing she had ever had to deal with was losing her baby; this would be nothing in comparison. She was determined she would get through this; she wouldn't let them beat her. Kate had told Billy everything on the drive from Surrey: how Jay had lured her into the car, and how he and Tanya had plotted what they would do to her if Billy hadn't paid. She told him how Tanya wanted to make her suffer. She had wanted to get revenge on Billy and knew hurting Kate would have been the ultimate means to do this. They both thought that it was Tanya who had been the brains behind the whole sorry episode, after all, as Jay was too dim to come up with any kind of plan worth worrying about.

Tanya, on the other hand, had been another story. She had legged it with Billy's money, leaving the man that had risked it all for her to take the rap: what a catch she had turned out to be. As per usual, Billy thought, she had been out for herself. Well, Billy would be having the last laugh with that one. The poor bitch had no idea what was coming.

No one had mentioned Jay or Tanya, or anything to do with Kate's ordeal since she had arrived home, though, it was as if they were all trying really hard to act normal for her sake and make her feel at home again, and for that Kate was thankful. That was how she dealt with things: not bottling them up as such but not going over stuff that had happened, it would only torment her. She couldn't change it and nor make what had happened go away, she just had to keep moving forward.

Looking around the table at them drinking tea and ribbing each other, Kate realised that these were the people that she cared about most in the world, the ones who were always there for her no matter what: when the shit hit the fan, they came up trumps. It was good to be home.

51

Billy had thought long and hard about what he was going to do to Jay when he got back to the cottage. He had played out countless clips a suitable punishment in his mind. What he had done to Jay's father a few years back had been very apt and seemed to fit the crime, and that's what he needed to think of now: a truly fitting punishment for Jay's crimes. Going in and blowing the cunt's head off was just a bit quick and easy for Billy's liking, Jay wouldn't really be aware of what was going on, and he would be out of his misery the second the bullet tore through his brain. Sticking a knife in him would be pretty much the same, far too quick and easy, and after the initial deed was done not very satisfying. After everything that piece of shit had put Kate through he was going to really make him pay, with the only thing he had left, his worthless scummy life.

Torture definitely seemed the best option; a slow painful death would be right up Billy's street, but Ryan would probably have started dishing that out already. Never one to sit about, Ryan got bored easily; he had probably had hours of fun with Jay today already. Ryan was an evil bastard when you were on the wrong side of him, he had dished out punishments to many people over the years, and his reputation preceded him. He didn't tolerate violence to women or children, and as friends go you couldn't ask for better. Billy had known him since they were kids and trusted him implicitly; Ryan had never let him down.

Billy had left Kate to rest at the flat; they had all spent a few hours having breakfast and all got through enough tea to fill a large swimming pool. She had seemed a bit better by the time he left her; more like herself. He had left her soaking in a nice hot bath, and she had said that after that she just wanted to go to bed. Billy was so grateful that nothing serious had happened to her; he was so happy that she was home safe and sound.

Billy had dropped Paul off at his gaff before driving back to the cottage. Paul had wanted to go with Billy to sort Jay out, but Billy insisted that he wanted to do it himself, once and for all, and besides the less people involved the better; he didn't want this coming back on any of them, especially not Paul: the guy was a diamond.

Paul hadn't said much to Kate while he had been at her house, not in front of Billy, but his presence spoke volumes, as it must have done to Kate. He cared about her. Billy had seen the way the bloke looked at her: Billy had never seen anything more obvious. Kate had been through a shitload this year and probably needed time on her own, but a good friend in Paul would not go amiss, Billy was sure.

Pulling up outside the cottage, Billy gave a deep sigh: what was coming had to be done, but it never got easier. But sometimes you started things and just had to see them through, he muttered to himself.

Looking out through the curtains, Ryan smiled.

"My, my, what a popular boy you are, Jay, looks like you've got yourself another visitor."

Jay, tied to a chair, tried to lift his head up to see. He could feel blood trickling down one side of his face, and he could taste it in his mouth. He couldn't believe that Tanya had handed him over to these fucking animals after everything he had done for her. He realised that she had well and truly used him, it was hilarious when you thought about it, he had gone through life using women like toys, as and when he had wanted, and the one time that he had let his guard down and trusted a woman, the devious bitch had all but fucking crucified him.

Ryan had pushed Jay to his limits with the pain, any more burns or cuts and he would pass out again, his heart was pounding so loudly he wondered if Ryan could hear it, so it was perfect timing to see Billy walking to the door. Even though there may be worst to come, he prayed for a break for just a few minutes from the pain inflicted on him.

Pulling out a cigarette, Ryan sat opposite Jay; inflicting pain was a tiring job.

Billy didn't even look in Jay's direction when he came in, he saw the state of the kitchen, and could smell that Jay had crapped himself. Ryan, as always, had taken it slowly and caused maximum injury without killing the bastard.

"I need you to help me get him in the boot," Billy said to Ryan. He nodded towards Jay, but still didn't fully look at him: he couldn't, he was feeling so much rage at being in the same room as the horrible fucker.

"No worries, mate, how are we going to get rid of him?" Ryan was up for whatever Billy suggested; he enjoyed this part of it: he had a taste for blood today, especially that of someone as despicable as Jay.

"We're not," Billy answered bluntly.

"What do you mean, we're not; he fucking deserves this, Billy, he has it fucking coming, you can't be thinking seriously of letting him go?" Ryan couldn't believe it; Billy must be going fucking soft.

"No, Ryan, you heard me wrong: we're not getting rid of him, I am. I just need you to help get him into the boot of my car." Ryan understood; Billy needed to do this himself, it was his fight and he needed to finish it.

After they had placed a bound Jay in the boot of Billy's motor, Billy told Ryan to get all his shit out of the cottage: the Ellis's were on their way over. Unfortunately, the cottage was about to have a bit of its own misfortune; Jonny and Lee were going to start a fire and stick around to make sure the whole place went up, just so that nothing that had gone on here in the last week came back to haunt any of them. Billy thought that although the place probably wouldn't have been booked out in Tanya and Jay's real names, but he didn't want to take any chances on anyone looking for either of them, or him. Anyway, Billy figured a nice little insurance pay-out would much more to the owners liking than to come back to find Jay's shit and blood over the walls of their precious little cottage.

Getting into the motor, Billy wound the window down so he could feel the breeze as he drove. He turned up the stereo and started to feel upbeat, he was back in control. No-one would make a fool out of him: especially not Jay.

He drove for miles, into the middle of nowhere; it was funny because the little place he was heading for he had stumbled across by accident a few years ago. He had done a bit of business for someone and had been ripped off; he and Ryan had taken care of them, in exactly the same place. At the time, he had made a comment to Ryan about the place being fucking creepy. It was an old industrial farmhouse that had been abandoned many moons ago, judging by the state of it; it had been so eerie that the whole place had spooked him out. It had felt as though they were the only people for miles, well, they actually had been, no one came out to those parts. Pulling up next to the old deserted building now, he switched the engine off.

The place hadn't changed one bit, even at this time of the morning it was scarily isolated.

Lifting up the lid of the boot, Billy looked in at the bloodied mess that was Jay, and smiled at the fear in the eyes that stared back. Billy lent down past the flinching Jay and picked up the shovel that was also in the car.

"People are going to be talking about this for years, you know, Jay."

Jay didn't have the energy to lift his head; he hoped whatever Billy had planned would be over as quickly as possible, but he had a feeling that he was doing a bit of wishful thinking.

"People are going to be talking, Jay, about you, the little prick who tried to do one over on me and take my hard-earned cash." Billy poked Jay hard in the ribs with the end of the shovel.

"They're going to be talking about you, the guy who shagged my missus behind my back." Billy brought the shovel down on Jay's stomach.

"About you, the little cunt who thought he could kidnap my sister, and do you know what they will be saying about me? Do you?" He bellowed the words, furious at the audacity of the scumbag in front of him.

"They'll be saying when they hear about your rotting stinking corpse that no-one, but no-one, should fuck with Billy: he won't fucking stand for it. They'll be talking about your death for years, mate. Which is just as well, you'd be forgotten in an instant otherwise, a sorry fucker like yourself. No-one cares if you live or die."

He brought the shovel down with more force, hitting Jay on the head. There was an almighty thump, which sounded worse than it was. Jay was out cold, and Billy set to work again; the next time Jay woke up, Billy wouldn't be there, it would just be Jay and his demons.

52

Kate's stomach was full and she felt clean after her long soak. She had closed her eyes the second she laid her head on her pillow and had no trouble falling asleep.

When she awoke she felt safe, and that was a good feeling, one that a few days ago she hadn't been sure she would have again. She knew Billy had gone to sort out Jay; she was scared about what might be happening, but she didn't want to know the details, she was just relieved that he wouldn't be harming her again.

Emma and Sonia's voices floated up to Kate from downstairs, just the normalness of the moment made her feel happy, she had been so terrified that she wouldn't see her friends and family again when she had been trapped in that dingy basement.

The phone rang on her dresser and, as she pulled herself up and wrapped the duvet snugly around her, she got that fluttery feeling in her stomach as she looked at the caller ID: Paul.

"Hey, Kate, I just wanted to see how you are?" Paul asked. "We didn't really get much of chance to talk earlier with everyone around." Kate smiled. They had been surrounded by people, yet she had felt that she and Paul were the only two in the room. Had he felt that too?

"Thanks, Paul; I'm feeling a lot better now I've had a sleep."

"Well, in that case, how would you fancy dinner at my place? I can pick you up in a few hours. There's someone here I'd like you to meet, if you're up to it."

"Okay." Kate felt wary; dinner with just Paul would have been heaven, she just knew he felt the same way she did, surely she hadn't got that wrong. He wouldn't want her to go to his house for dinner to meet a girlfriend, would he? Whoever it was must be important to him. Not wanting to sound stupid over the phone or question him further in case she heard something that she didn't want to, she agreed. He then said he would pick her up in two hours.

Putting the phone down, Paul called for Sophia. Running into the lounge, wearing a bright pink Disney princess dress that she had insisted on wearing every day since he had bought her the movie, Sophia threw herself onto her daddy's lap. He hugged her; it was hard to imagine that this child hadn't been in his life forever, it had only been four short years, yet he couldn't remember life before she had come along. She was his world.

"I have a friend coming over to meet you later." Sophia fiddled with her princess ballet pumps, he could see that she felt shy at the mere thought of someone else coming over. It was his own fault, he knew, Sophia was forever at home with the nanny while he worked. Apart from nursery in the morning, they rarely had visitors. Deciding to play it from a different angle, he whispered:

"My friend is very special, Sophia, I think that you are really going to like her." Looking up at him not quite sure what to make of what he was saying, he continued:

"Her name's Kate; she is a real princess, just like you."

"Wow, will she be wearing a princess dress like me?" Sophia seemed to be excited now; she had always wanted to meet a real princess.

"She hasn't got a lovely princess dress like you but she is very, very pretty, and she is very kind. Maybe we can have a look in your bedroom and see if she can borrow something of yours to wear, I bet she will love your dress."

Bouncing off of her daddy's lap, Sophia ran to her bedroom as if her life depended on it, desperate to find something for her daddy's princess friend to wear.

Smiling at her innocence, Paul couldn't shake an anxious feeling. This was a big step. He had decided, years ago, that he would never let anyone close again, but then that was before he had met someone as special as Kate. He had never felt like this, not even about his ex, Caroline. Caroline hadn't batted an eyelid when they had separated; she continued to go out partying and coming home at all hours of the morning. She had treated Sophia like she were a big inconvenience and it had broken Paul's heart to see his baby left to cry in her cot, ignored by her own mother. When he left, she had told him to take Sophia with him; she had dismissed Sophia as if she were nothing, as if Caroline had not a single maternal bone in her body. Paul had done that. He had never heard from Caroline again and knew in his heart of hearts that he never would. He had got over her, that was for sure, but it hurt that his little girl was growing up without a mummy. Since Sophia was nine months old he had brought her up, with the help of the nanny. Sophia was the love of his life; his sole reason for living. Building up a reputation and a business in the clubbing world was hardly a place for a small, beautiful baby; he had always kept them separate. He never spoke of his personal life; the less people knew about him, the less chance they would be able to hurt him. But he had fallen for Kate, and he wanted her, and he knew that it was time to let someone in. Tonight, the two most important girls in his life would meet. And he just prayed that after tonight, Kate would feel the same as he did.

53

There were moments when Tanya thought about her disloyalty to Jay, but they were so fleeting that they passed almost as quickly as they came; she certainly didn't lose a moment's sleep over it: far from it, as a matter of fact. Tanya had been living the high life. The life she was convinced she was born for. To some people, a quarter of a million pounds would be a lot of cash, the sort of money that would allow them to put a nice-sized down payment on a little house where they could settle down, maybe buy a flash car and new clothes, and generally be quite content with their new-found fortune. It was a decent start. But Tanya wasn't "some people". She wanted five-star luxuries all the way: a penthouse in London, somewhere upmarket like Mayfair, a Bentley with a personalised number plate, and designer clothes. A quarter of a mill was just a taste of what she thought she needed in order to get by. It wouldn't last five minutes with the plans she had, she needed to use it wisely. Tanya had always believed that money came to money, and now she had a little it was her chance to get more. So she had come up with quite a plan. In order to find a nice rich man, she would have to go to where the rich men were and to appear as if she had come from money. Tanya, never short of male attention, expected to catch the attention of a rich guy looking for a woman on whom he could spend his fortune. Tanya had checked into the Dorchester, a hotel she had always wanted to stay at, in the hub of London and she actually felt quite at home there, she drank endless amounts of champagne and indulged in treatments at their top-class spa, figuring that she wasn't frittering away the money, it was an investment. These rich men could be quite clued up on gold-diggers, there were plenty of them about, even she knew that, and although a young girl may think she was in with a chance with a man, often they would be on to them in a heartbeat, and they would get what they want from the girl, with no real intention of losing a single penny of their cash to her.

Tanya was acting as if she was loaded; spending her money as if it were limitless. That way, when she fluttered her eyes and flashed her cleavage at some unsuspecting old bore at the bar, they might actually believe that she was interested in them and not just after their hard-earned cash; her motive would be concealed, as she so obviously had enough of her own wealth.

So far, she had gained admiring glances from most of the guys staying there, single and attached, much to her amusement. Men were so fickle, she thought. Normally she played it cool, letting men come to her; that way she wouldn't come across as if she had initiated anything or seemed desperate. There had been a few men who had approached her, but they had turned out to be dirty old men with a wife in tow somewhere else in the hotel, trying their luck while they thought they might have a chance. One even hinted that he knew she was a call girl: top class, of course; it took a lot of effort not to get out of her chair and lump him one. She had decided to be very bold this afternoon and had taken it upon herself to send a glass of champagne over to a very good-looking guy at the other side of the terrace bar who had kept catching her eye. She figured he must be shy as every time she had caught him staring, he had looked away, so she decided to take the initiative. Waiting for a rich, eligible bachelor wasn't working out quite the way she had anticipated and Tanya decided that she would have to do a bit of catching and reeling in herself. She could see that the guy had been very surprised by the drink and had looked uncomfortable accepting it, but Tanya was sure that she was in for a chance with him, he had been watching her from the minute she came into the bar. Raising her own glass to him and smiling, she took a long sip of her drink and enjoyed the bubbles fizzing on her tongue whilst she thought about what a catch she had stumbled upon, he was much younger and much better-looking than the old farts around here that had been on her 'hit-list' so far.

Interrupting her thoughts, the hotel's duty manager approached her and asked if he could have a word with her, she felt that it was most inconvenient right at this moment in time and asked if she could pop to reception and see him a little later on, but he insisted it was urgent. Reluctantly following him to the desk, she felt like a naughty schoolgirl; picking up on the attitude of the manager, it was as if she had done something wrong. She assumed it was to do with her payment, as she had no card to put down as a deposit when she had checked in she had told them she would be settling up in cash. There must be a lack of communication or something going on as she had already paid for the room up-front for a week, just to keep them sweet, and she had only been here two days. So she couldn't imagine why he seemed so grumpy with her.

As she reached reception she could see several of the staff looking at her as if she had two heads growing out of her neck; she was starting to get a little pissed off now.

"Do you mind telling me exactly what is going on here? I was in the middle of a drink." She gestured to the bar.

"Perhaps you wouldn't mind stepping into my office." The manager nodded towards the door next to the main desk, and Tanya went in, eager to get whatever issue the guy wanted to discuss over and done with so she could get back to her drink and, more importantly, back to that dishy bloke.

"Miss Wright… it is Miss Wright, isn't it?"

Tanya, sitting in the chair opposite his desk, picked up on his tone which implied that he was in fact questioning if her name was actually what she had booked herself in as and was not a friendly question that he wanted an answer to confirm.

"Look, if this is about my bill, then there's been some sort of mistake; I paid it two days ago when I arrived; in cash; in full." How dare he drag her in here like this and talk to her in this manner?

"Well, you see, 'Miss Wright', that is exactly why you are here." He coughed and looked uncomfortable.

"Your bill so far has been paid for just the room, it does not include your spa treatments, and all the bottles of wine and champagne," he emphasised the word 'all', much to her annoyance. He coughed again, and she could sense that he was having a bit of a dig at her. It was her choice how much she bloody drank: the cheek of him.

"Your suite is three and a half thousand for the week and so far all the extras bring your entire bill to five thousand one hundred pounds," he continued, ignoring her look of disbelief that he was speaking to her in such a way. Tapping her foot impatiently, she wanted him to stop dragging whatever he had to say out and get to the bloody point.

"Yes, and I paid the receptionist three thousand and five hundred pounds when I arrived; if I need to pay more than I will, but as I keep telling you the room is all paid for."

"Well, you see, that's our problem, actually; unfortunately it was Sally, our new girl, who checked you in on Monday night, and she is not really very well trained when it comes to these matters."

"Matters? What matters do you mean exactly?" Tanya was starting to get really fed up with this guy, he was wasting her time, and his attitude towards her stank; making a note of the name on his badge, she decided to make a formal complaint. What an arrogant little prick: clearly having a little bit of power round here had gone right to his thick little head.

The phone on the manager's desk rang and, turning his back on Tanya, he answered it and spoke in a hushed tone. How fucking rude, thought Tanya, as she heard him tell the person on the end of the phone to 'send them in': what the hell was going on?

"I'm afraid, Miss Wright, that the money that you paid us with is counterfeit."

Tanya stared at him in complete disbelief; he may as well have been talking in another language, because she didn't understand what he was talking about. Her ears had heard the words, but there was definitely some kind of a mistake going on.

"And unfortunately it was undetected by Sally when she checked you in two days ago; otherwise, we would never have let you book in. I'm sure that you can appreciate our concerns about your now unpaid bill."

Tanya's mouth was on the floor: she was speechless.

"And I'm afraid, Miss Wright, that it is also my duty to inform the police, not only because of the outstanding balance but because you have committed a criminal offence."

As if on cue, there was a knock at the door and in came the young, good-looking man who Tanya had been giving the eye to at the bar for most of the afternoon. Clearly he had been interested in her for reasons other than the obvious. He was followed closely by a similarly dressed in smart dark suits, older man. Realising now that they both had that familiar cop look about them, Tanya wanted the ground to swallow her up. Feeling all her hopes crash down around her, she fought to stop herself from smashing up the fucking room in anger. Fucking Billy O'Connell, she should have known that he would never have let her walk away with all that cash; trying to gather her thoughts she went to start on a long elaborate story of how she had obviously been conned herself, maybe she could say that she had sold something and the guy who had bought it had clearly ripped her off, but she stopped as she saw the older officer placing her holdall, with all the money in, down in front of her, her room had obviously already been searched.

"Would you care to explain how you came into possession of this bag and its contents, Miss Wright?"
How the hell was she going to talk her way out of this one? A few dodgy notes were one thing, but a quarter of a million pounds in a holdall was not a very good look. She could hardly say that she had been ripped off by some bloke after she had kidnapped his sister. She hung her head in defeat.

"I want a solicitor, and in the meantime no comment."

54

Kate felt like a little kid, she was so excited she thought she would burst. Looking out of the passenger window of Paul's car, she saw the sign for the Gatwick Airport turnoff ahead, a few hours from now they would be sitting on a plane on their way to the Caribbean.

Paul had booked it as a surprise and she had been really grateful to him, she really needed a break. She had been at home for two days, and she still felt shaken up, more by her constant thoughts of what could have been than anything else. Tanya and Jay were scum, she knew that now: she was sorry that she had been so trusting and had let herself get into that situation. She felt stupid about that.

It had been good to be home, but everyone had been fussing; bless them, even though she knew they meant well, she was sick of constantly having to say that she was okay. Sonia had made her many cups of tea and homemade cakes, the cakes to "put some meat back on your bones", and promised her that she had disowned Jay; she had told Kate that she wished she could make it up to her, which meant everything that her son, now 'that boy', had done. Kate had reassured her that there was no need, Sonia had done more than enough for her: she had taken her in when she had been pregnant, she had helped her and her brother sort out their differences and been like a mum to her, what more could she possibly do for her. She told her that she adored her, and Sonia had been extremely grateful to hear it.

They had all vowed to never speak Jay's name again. All they knew was that he was gone, and Billy guaranteed that he would never be troubling them again. Kate had tried not to dwell on the ins and outs of Billy's promise too much: what she didn't know couldn't hurt her. She knew not to ask any questions on the matter, she was sure she would not want to hear the answers. Any ounce of guilt or worry in that respect, and she just reminded herself of what he had done to her and, more importantly, to her friend, and left the rest to karma. Whatever he got, it would have been deserved.

Emma and Billy had been constantly watching her every move, and of course they were just worried about her, but every time she looked up she had caught at least one of them keeping an eye on her, checking that she was okay and not about to fall to pieces at any moment like a fragile doll. They had become really good friends, which pleased Kate.

Kate had gone to dinner at Paul's house two nights ago too, when she had certainly discovered more than she bargained for. She had almost geared herself up whilst she had got herself ready to meet his new glamour-puss girlfriend, had visualised that she would have to sit there pretending to be happy for him and smiling sweetly. So when she was greeted by an adorable little girl, who was as shy as she was beautiful, Kate hadn't known whether to laugh or cry. She had an amazing evening with Paul and fell in love with Sophia in a heartbeat. Paul had cooked a lovely meal and the three had had a really good time, sitting together and enjoying the food. Kate had worn a sparkly pink tiara throughout the meal, at Sophia's insistence, and had laughed heartily when Sophia had whispered that her daddy had told her the secret about Kate being a real princess, but that Sophia wouldn't tell anyone.

Kate helped Paul put a very tired little Sophia to bed an hour or so later. If Paul had been in any doubt of how Kate had felt about meeting his daughter, he needn't have worried. Kate had soon had him laughing with her when she had explained what she had first thought she may have been walking into at the beginning of the evening. Admitting that she had felt jealous before she had arrived, she had been relieved to see that the special person had in fact turned out to be a beautiful little girl.

They had spoken for hours about everything: Kate's kidnap, her mother's death, Paul's ex-wife, everything had tumbled out. They laughed, shed tears, and finally in the early hours they had fallen into bed, where they had spent the night completely wrapped up in each other.

Now, she could hardly believe that she was sitting in Paul's car on her way to the airport, it was all a whirlwind. A two-week, all-inclusive holiday in the Caribbean. He had insisted that a holiday was just what she needed. He had mentioned it to Kate, and by nine o'clock last night it was all booked online and paid for; it was exactly what she needed, the thought of getting away for a while to somewhere hot and sunny was just what the doctor ordered. Paul had arranged for the three of them to go, including Sophia, and Kate was very happy.

Sophia had taken to her straight away and vice versa, but this would be the perfect opportunity for them all to get to know one another properly.

Kate had barely had time to pack, but she had thought she could buy more bikinis at the airport.

Emma and Billy had waved her off this morning and told her to enjoy herself. Billy had told Paul that he would keep an eye on the club, and Kate had a feeling that Billy would be keeping more than an eye on Emma, too, while they were away. She had seen a few glances between them; they seemed to be good mates, and there was definitely the potential for more, she had a strong suspicion that maybe something had already begun between them: because if it hadn't already, it was just a matter of time. Billy was really making a real effort with Emma, Kate had noticed. Billy had never really taken to Emma before, he had always thought that she was a bad influence on Kate, but ever since he had found her at the flat, he was much more patient and caring towards her. Kate had seen them joking together over the last couple of days, and they seemed at ease in each other's company. Hopefully they would both put the past behind them, and it pleased Kate that some good had come out of the whole thing. Kate was pleased at how well everyone seemed to be getting on; it was amazing how a crisis brought people together. Her brother and Paul got on famously; it was almost like they were best mates and it made her happy that there was genuine respect and friendship between them.

Paul pulled up into a space at the airport's long stay car park, looking at his watch he smiled at Kate.

"We're almost four hours early; is that enough time for you to squeeze in a bit of retail therapy, missy?"

She smiled back; she had nagged him to pick her up as early as possible this morning, she was so excited, she would have gone to the airport last night if she could have got away with it.

"Yes, four hours should be just enough time, and who knows we may even have a spare two minutes at the end of my little shopping spree for a quick coffee." They made their way into the terminal to check in their bags, Kate holding Sophia's hand while Paul got a trolley for their luggage. Kate couldn't stop smiling; how life had changed in just the space of a few days. It was like everything, for the first time in her life, had fallen into place. This holiday was what she needed: sun, sea and Paul to herself. Then, looking down at the gorgeous girl holding her hand and smiling up at her, she thought 'almost' to herself, if she had to share him with anyone it would be with this adorable little girl. As if he could read her mind, a habit of his, Paul took Kate's hand.

"Come on Kate, let's get rid of these bags then go and do some serious damage to my credit card. Four hours isn't very long for a woman to shop and, knowing you, that will be barely enough time to do just one store." He laughed, as they made their way to the check-in desk.

55

Jay slowly shook his throbbing head. It was pitch-black; he couldn't see anything. He had no idea how long he had been unconscious and no idea where he was. Pain seared through him, making him feel weak and sick. He felt as if his body were covered in bruises: which, after what he had endured from Ryan, it probably was.

Trying to sit, he whacked his head on something hard and fell straight back down into a lying position. Reaching to feel where he was, he seemed to be inside a box: a small, solid, wooden box. Pushing the sides, he began to panic, he wasn't good at being closed in at the best of times and the feeling of claustrophobia was making him feel physically sick with fear.

Shouting for help, he wondered where the hell Billy had put him; he prayed that someone, somewhere, would hear his cries. Clawing his fingers across the top of the box, splinters from the wood piercing his skin, he tried to see if he could climb out; he tried to use his whole body by turning onto his stomach and putting his back behind the top of the box as he tried to force his way out, but he could barely get off the floor, it was stuck solid.

He figured that he had been in there for a long time, as he now noticed the lack of oxygen he had, and was sure that he would run out quite soon. Fear and panic made his breathing erratic, and the air was gradually dwindling.

Frantically, he kicked and hit the walls but nothing gave. He was trapped. He started to cry. It was a sign of weakness, he knew, but there was no-one to see his tears or witness how low he had sunk. There was no-one to help him, this was it for him. Billy had caught up with him, and he was going to end his days buried alive.

Jay thought about all the people he had done wrong to and all the shit he had gone through in his life. He had wanted so much more than this for he had had. He had always said that he would do better than his old man, and for a while he thought that he had. But he was no better; in fact, he was worse. Billy had been right, nobody would give a shit if he was dead or alive. Stupidly, he had let Tanya get one over on him. He was sure that he would have got away with it if it hadn't been for her damn greed. He had had no idea how callous she was. She was a cold-hearted bitch that one. It was ironic though, he thought, that he had used woman all his life and the first woman he had ever loved, the first women he had ever trusted, had done nothing but use him back: although none of that mattered now.

It's funny the thoughts that pop into your head as you die; he remembered hearing about how a person's life flashes before their eyes when they're dying: a slideshow of photos and video clips kept in the subconscious. Memories you shared, the faces of people you loved and that loved you. He waited for the slideshow, but all he saw was darkness. He could taste the salt of his tears, and he could smell that he had soiled himself. It wasn't the exit that he had imagined he would have from this life. He had often wondered if he would have died from a beating or a stab wound. The kind of dealings he had been involved in, knives and guns were never far away. A bit more fitting for him, he felt, would have been to go out in a blaze of glory. This was something else altogether. He was alone, crying like a baby and scared, and as he struggled to gulp his last few mouthfuls of air, he could almost feel his lungs explode with the struggle.

The face that flashed before Jay Shaw's eyes as he slipped out of this life minutes later was that of a smug-looking Billy O'Connell.

Printed in Great Britain
by Amazon.co.uk, Ltd.,
Marston Gate.